Samantha Harvey

All is Song

JONATHAN CAPE
LONDON

Published by Jonathan Cape 2012

2 4 6 8 10 9 7 5 3 1

Copyright © Samantha Harvey 2012

Samantha Harvey has asserted her right under the Copyright, Designs
and Patents Act 1988 to be identified as the author of this work

First published in Great Britain in 2012 by
Jonathan Cape
Random House, 20 Vauxhall Bridge Road,
London SW1V 2SA

www.vintage-books.co.uk

Addresses for companies within The Random House Group Limited
can be found at:
www.randomhouse.co.uk/offices.htm

The Random House Group Limited Reg. No. 954009

A CIP catalogue record for this book
is available from the British Library

ISBN 9780224096324 (Hardback edition)
ISBN 9780224096331 (Trade paperback edition)

The Random House Group Limited supports The Forest
Stewardship Council (FSC®), the leading international forest
certification organisation. Our books carrying the FSC label are printed on
FSC® certified paper. FSC is the only forest certification scheme endorsed by
the leading environmental organisations, including Greenpeace.
Our paper procurement policy can be found at
www.randomhouse.co.uk/environment

Typeset by Palimpsest Book Production Limited, Falkirk, Stirlingshire
Printed and bound by CPI Group (UK)
Ltd, Croydon, CRO 4YY

ALL IS SONG

BY THE SAME AUTHOR

The Wilderness

For my family

They've come, they've come, he was thinking, and there they were all around him spinning through the darkness, and lighting the darkness. It was all just an illusion, they said. You weren't ever alone. How happy he was to hear it. He opened his eyes to their bright limbs and was repeating to himself that saying, Nothing happens until something moves. And thinking, therefore, I must move. Lovely formless limbs wrapping around him, or were they just drifts of light? Extraordinary beauty anyhow, extraordinary. Behind him a sound drew on his mind and stole his rest away, a semicircular sound that scooped anxious shapes into his thoughts, and began, though reluctantly, to make sense to him. I know this sound, I must move.

Then he opened his eyes and sat up. These were the first bruised moments of waking, the moments when the sleep-softened brain was so susceptible to fear and the world was at its least consoling; he spent these few moments thinking hell had come. Ah, Leo, how ridiculous you are, he thought. Hell and all; you only ever think like that when your back foot is still in a dream. There was the ululating of the sirens that had woken him up. The room is on fire, he told himself, but it was a lazy warning; there was no heat and there were no flames. He got up and went to the open window.

The view showed smoke not more than half a mile away to the east. It was pushing the night apart with a strange, muscular solidity. It could have been any number of buildings – the residential streets between there and Shoreditch would pass fire freely between their terraces. There was the school and the shopping streets, and the hospital, though he had to hope not the hospital. The idea alone could make one shudder. And yet, no, thankfully the hospital wasn't quite there, it was much further south towards St Paul's. He opened the window wider and the air was warm and smelt burnt, and the sirens pitched deep along streets. He closed it entirely.

He went back to the sofa where he'd been sleeping. But for his underwear he was naked by the necessity of the heat, and still he was too hot – such a queerly warm July they had just had, and too hot to have the window closed. He lay down and tried to sleep again with his palms facing upwards in relinquishment. Be gone, he thought, and then said, Be gone. It might have been that he meant the heat, or the noise, or in truth any number of things that drove vaguely at the mind and kept it littered and clumsy.

When he closed his eyes there was only the feeling that flames were creeping around his feet, and four times he opened them against all reason in order to check, and then to sigh, and then to close them again, and then to curl his toes up against an imagination that wouldn't let him rest. He saw flecks of light that ordered and disordered themselves in and out of human shapes and he remembered that was what he'd been dreaming just before, but he couldn't think where the dream had been going or what he should make of it, except that it had for a moment given him happiness.

Finally he settled for looking up at the chandelier in the centre of the room, and at the outside lights that travelled palely across it. The Bellevue displayed an unusual vulnerability, or so it seemed to him, in the occasional hot and tired creak somewhere deep within the floorboards. Maybe it was just that he was so unused to sleeping there, and that the room always felt that way at night, but he became convinced that it was flinching from that fire, having known a fire of its own. The creaks in the floorboards were empathetic little recollectings, the way a healed bone would always recall being broken.

He got up and poured himself a glass of wine from the open bottle on the table in the hope it would help him sleep, and after ten minutes he did feel sleepy, and lay down again. It was after three a.m. and his journey and the trauma of the day before had made him tired. He went into chattery and circular pre-sleep thoughts about the time he and William had redecorated the Bellevue, after the fire, and of how they'd spent those long hours playing games. It was word games sometimes, or riddles and logic problems, all while they swept up cinders and the deformed stalks of wood that had once been table legs, or chair legs. That was when they'd invented the shape whistling game; one would whistle, one would guess. Four equal whistles was a square, three an equilateral triangle, and it went on in that way – but inevitably it got more complex. Tetrahedrons, dodecahedrons, parallelograms, spirals. William had perfect pitch and could take a spiral from its central inception out through sound into the last expansion, the last curve, and end promptly with air still in his lungs. The first time the spiral had been sounded Leonard had guessed it right away, because it could have been nothing else; it had been drawn with air, onto air, and was almost traceable with the finger. But he'd let the shape complete its beautiful audible form all the same, just for the pleasure of hearing it, and for the pleasure of feeling so close to his brother. Only then had he inhaled on his cigarette, exhaled, pointed the cigarette's tip diagnostically at the space the shape had occupied, and said with confidence, A spiral, William. Precisely, William had answered. A spiral.

Outside the sirens had stopped, and maybe they'd stopped some time ago, Leonard couldn't be sure. He took a last sip of wine, pulled the blanket over him for comfort and not for warmth, and pressed his cheek into the cushion, which smelt of tobacco and all the years of something unwashed.

In the morning William came. Leonard watched from above, leaning slightly over the rail of the spiral staircase as he emerged. The body angled sideways to account for the narrow space, and corkscrewed slowly upwards. It was never easy to climb that staircase, the feet had to pick at the treads, which tapered to an inch width at the centre of the spiral, and the right hand was always feeling ahead of itself for support. Even so, the awkward climb held a small spiritual consolation. Hadn't their father breathed repeatedly just before he died: Up I go. Their father, who claimed to know all about the glorious things that happened after death. Leonard could be forgiven if, for a moment, he fell upon the idea that revolving upwards around a central column might get you to heaven, or if he held an inbuilt bias for the vertical in general, or if he felt in some way that his position at the top of the stairs asserted his benevolence and his welcome.

Halfway up, William's dipped head entered the sunlight. Apparently he'd still not noticed Leonard standing there. Some fortunate gene in the Deppling line had granted them both hair for life – in William's case a thick mess of it, now greying and wiry, curling protectively against his skull. The morning sunlight spilling from the high, rear window in the Bellevue Room made the last black strands glow blue. William's head was notably large, a feature which made him look comical. There were, surely, sound physiological reasons as to why a human head should be the size it is, and why its furniture – nose, mouth, eyes, ears – should be in proportion to it. William seemed to prove that the slightest variation from this design stole an ounce of the human and replaced it with an ounce of the animal, so that all his life he'd been likened to some creature or another. A bull, a seal, a St Bernard, a bear. Now that head, that face, found the light falling from above and basked momentarily in it, upturned, eyes squinting, and Leonard took the moment to make his presence known.

'William. It's me.'

William peered into the blanched space, and then he must have made out Leonard's figure. He smiled warmly, without excitement. 'So it is, at last.' Then he dipped his attention back to the act of climbing.

It had been more than a year since they'd seen each other, which, in a sibling relationship of such consolation and deep, quiet dependence, was considerable. So Leonard opened his arms to William's ascent.

'There,' he said, as if a long choreography were drawing to a pleasing end. He hugged his brother, closing him reverently in.

In that second in which the light spilt down on William's face, Leonard's heart quickened for a beat. He felt like a point of salvation, and he felt the responsibility he'd used to bear towards William when they were children. The younger child wasn't supposed to bear such responsibility for the older; their parents had worried that this would affect them both in all sorts of staggered and difficult to measure ways. But what else could be done? William had never been a proper child. How seriously he used to sit with his toys and stare at them quizzically, how joyless he was about other children; he would make them cry with his staring and questioning. Leonard in turn had been gregarious and bouncy, a proper ray of light. Socially, he'd been his brother's saviour, and in that brief lit moment it was as if he were his brother's saviour again.

'I'm glad to see you. I'm glad to be back,' Leonard said, withdrawing from the hug.

'You haven't changed. Have I changed?'

'You haven't changed.'

Well, it had only been a year. But they would always check, to be sure. For fifty years they'd run this test, briefly looking behind ears, peering into eyes, stepping back to appraise. The consensus was always that no change of any sort could be registered; the stacking up of years was so seamless, so delicately done and relentless, that in generous moods at least they could both say honestly that it hadn't happened.

'There's a bike protest outside,' William said. 'They're about to come down this way, in a couple of minutes. I think they're passing through into town, maybe to Westminster.'

'I can hear it, the horns. I did get wind of it anyway, that it would be coming past here.'

The two of them stood somewhat adrift in the morning light of the room. William went to the window, opened it and looked out. The noise amplified, voices and the bleat of car horns, and as background some distant, unrelated sirens that were as indigenous to London as the song of finches.

William was in silhouette against the large rectangular window; in a way they were alike, both in their fifties – Leonard the earlier part, William the later – with their hair an inch or two longer than was common for men of their age, and their ill-fitting clothes, so generic as to be, in essence, invisible. That was to say, if they robbed a bank in their everyday clothes, witnesses would struggle to remember anything useful or exceptional. Their only defining traits, Leonard thought, were bare feet in William's case, and in his own, really spectacular eyes. When they talked about their tendency for the mundane they concluded happily enough that they were to humankind what pigeons were to birdkind – work-aday, diurnal, indiscernible.

Beyond these generalities they weren't equivalent. Leonard was taller, which gave him an advantage, and he was gentler in the face; his expressions were diplomatic and couldn't always be read. William's expressions, in contrast, were knotted, and belonged to clear brain states: surprise, happiness, sadness, amusement. He went from one to another as an engine slides between gears. But it was of no real use. Leonard thought this even now as he looked at his brother in silhouette, unable to see his face clearly, but knowing it well. Readable William's expressions might be, but not necessarily believable. Even Leonard couldn't always tell whether William was being ironic. It was the eyes that caused the problem, because they gave nothing away and thus left nothing to be trusted quite. They were inscrutably blue and deep-set, always lit from beneath, always moist.

'There were well over a hundred when I saw them,' William said, motioning to the cyclists who weren't yet outside the window.

'No doubt it will grow to a thousand. A nice Saturday morning will always bring people out to fight a cause, I suppose.'

'As we know, principles are solar-powered.'

'You're right, of course.'

Leonard went to the long oak table in the centre of the room and uncorked a new bottle of wine. The remains from the night before was not enough to share. He poured a glass for each of them. William was indifferent to drink, but Leonard was the reverse – he never felt better than when he had a glass of wine travelling his blood, and he was conformist enough to find sedition in it, which in turn glorified the conformity. When drunk he loved the little things and the simple things. Being human seemed really quite agreeable, quite unarguable.

'Will you have some, William?' He gestured for him to come and sit at the table.

'It's barely eleven o'clock.'

'Well, these are hard times.'

William came, and sat opposite. Leonard pushed a glass of wine towards him.

'Scotland was difficult,' Leonard said, in answer to the unasked questions. *How was your trip? How have you been?* He knew William would never ask. 'I wish you'd been there, William, at least for a visit.'

No response, but then it hadn't been a question, so he continued as if unperturbed. 'Mind you, if you had come what would you have found? Me drinking wine too early in the day and watching films and scratting through boxes of things in the attic, like a weird animal. I can't say I've really been in possession of myself.'

'I don't know what that would mean anyway. To be in possession of oneself.'

William smiled with intrigue as he said it. No comment on the events and outcome of that prolonged stay in Edinburgh, no query or evident grief over the loss of a second parent within a year. Leonard realised he would have to go through the usual process of assimilation that always followed any absence from William, in which he let drop his expectations about the norms of brotherhood, and calibrated, realigned, and finally – and with hope, efficiently – came to the island of understanding they had together managed to occupy for so long.

'I think I've found some peace,' he said.

'At last, that's good.'

'I think Dad had to die before I could find it. I don't feel regret that I could have done more, should have done more.'

William sat equably in the sunlight, his shoulders falling to a relaxed hunch as they did when he was composing a question.

'What use would regret be, Leonard? The dead are in a good place, I do believe that.'

William reached his hand across the table and Leonard extended his in response, meeting for a moment, a firm squeeze, and that was the extent of it. Yes, Leonard thought: What use would regret be to a man who's passed into eternity, as their father believed he would? Indeed, what use.

'Do you know how wealthy we are now, William?' It was pointless to evade the question any longer. 'We inherited everything.'

William offered an expression of plain happiness – a smile, the eyebrows rising to meet the new altitude of his assumed mood. The tone, however, was neutral, and his shoulders didn't lift. 'Well, parents have to have some use, I suppose.' And then, 'I'm joking.'

'Do you want to know how much we inherited?'

'Only if it would help you to tell me.'

'Help me? No, it wouldn't help me especially. I just thought you might be interested.'

His brother looked more distracted than interested, in truth; he appeared to have no concern for money, an unlikely trait that had nonetheless been tried and tested against circumstance and prevailed as seemingly sincere.

'We'll have to arrange the ins and outs of the finances at some point,' he persisted. 'I need to talk to you about it. Not now, but soon.'

'Of course,' William said. 'Whatever I can do to be least trouble.'

'It isn't about you being trouble.'

William flashed a grin. 'Oh, but I *am*. Always. You've said it yourself.'

'I didn't say you weren't, I just said it isn't about that.'

The grin ebbed to a kind, focused smile. 'Whatever's mine, you can have, Leo,' he returned. 'I trust you to do the right thing with it.'

'William, don't be ridiculous, I don't want your inheritance.'

'Then we have something in common.'

'You have a wife and children.'

'So I do.'

Leonard tossed the cork in William's direction and it bounced off the chair and coiled across the floor. William smiled at him as though to say, Let's talk about something better than this. Leonard was prepared to do so. Born into wealth, every family loss the two men had ever suffered had made them richer. Surely in the furthest reaches of their psyches they were always waiting for the next person to expire? Well, it was a dire thought, low and bad. To talk about inheritance felt in some respects unclean, and William's indifference only added to this; Leonard was happy to let it rest for the time being. The death of their father two months ago had left them in a state of indisputable prosperity, and William must have known it, but was incurious. It was the kind of prosperity that could change one's stature and outlook. It delivered the weight of total freedom, a difficult weight overall and one which could, with the wrong handling, become a burden.

Leonard leaned back and put his thumbs in his trouser pockets. He found his brother's eyes. 'People were angry that you didn't come to the funeral.'

'People are always angry, Leonard. I wish it wasn't so, I wish it as much as you do.'

'And they were sad, too.'

William gave an understanding shrug. 'It was a funeral, after all.'

Leonard exhaled and extended his arms outwards along the

table, hot, frustrated. The two men had always slipped into these starched dialogues when the topic became personal. For all their closeness over the years they still didn't know how to negotiate the extremes of one another, and as soon as the *I think* became *I feel*, they faltered, as if they were constrained by the awkward fact that they were human.

It wasn't just a funeral, William, Leonard wanted to say. It was *our father's* funeral. He took his wine and trod the length of the room with it. The Bellevue Café itself, on whose first floor they now stood, was the fruit of family loss. Leonard had bought it almost twenty years before with money they both inherited from their grandparents; William had handed over his share without a blink or tremble. They'd cashed in their rustic, blowsy, big-hearted grandparents for a fire-blackened building in the city, which, as it turned out, they'd never even used as a café. Downsairs the chairs and tables, the empty shelves, the boxes of crockery never unpacked – a whole life they hadn't got round to living.

Leonard felt the whole truth of that, sitting there orphaned with his brother. They didn't speak for two or three minutes. Was it an easy silence? He must assume so, otherwise he could count himself as a man who had no true friend in the world. He thought of what he could say, and wondered if he should share those things he'd been thinking about regret, or maybe he could mention the chickens he'd heard about on the local news earlier that morning, who'd had their necks stamped on. Such things wouldn't normally bother him – the welfare of a chicken; there were enough other things to worry about. But in the vision of its feathery head bulging wide-eyed from a flattened neck he seemed to see all the futility of loss, and of anger at loss, and some flood rose in him without his willing it. Why? he'd thought in repertory with a mash of other journeying thoughts. Why the stamping, *stamping* of all things, why?

Outside, beyond the two large sash windows at the front of the room, the mass of cyclists was passing. William stood to resume his vigil of them, and slid off his sandals. A few car horns sounded on the street, and some muffled shouts. Leonard went to the other window, the one on the right, opened it, leaned out for a moment, and gave a quiet impressed whistle.

'There are well over a hundred of them,' William repeated, as if this fact had a particular currency for him. He smiled at Leonard and turned back to the view, with his hands to the windowpanes. 'Maybe two hundred. I'm not good at judging numbers.'

Leonard thought maybe more than that, but it was hard to tell. Pressed closely, the bikes made their own chaotic geometry; behind them a bottleneck of cars crawled in vexation. Leaning out briefly he could see the cyclists' progress down towards Finsbury Mosque; there was excitement in the air, once again the sound of horns, intended to be aggressive but hitting the streets as nothing more than a wail of plight, ineffectual for all its urgent pitch.

The light slanted long into the Bellevue Room. The large table was piled with dry reams of paper, and the wood of the tabletop was also dry where years of dust had settled in the grain. Above it the sun fell a thousand-fold on the crystal chandelier, and bounced back off as multiplied light. The clutter proliferated in the late-morning light, giving the room the busy luminousness of an eye close up. Leonard found the bag he had brought the day before, stowed under the sideboard out of the sun, and took from it some cheese, bread and figs, which he put next to the wine. He was struck by the unintentionally biblical array.

'Will you eat, William?'

William took his hands from the glass and turned to the room. 'You always phrase your questions this way. *Will you?* As if you're asking a favour.'

'I was just asking if you wanted to eat. I don't care if you eat, it was just a figure of speech. Honestly, you can be so difficult.'

William smiled and glanced up. They ate together quietly. In the warmth the bread had hardened, and the cheese, once firm, had a rubbery bounce that Leonard found unappetising, but he was hungry; he craved a succulent little fillet of beef to put between the bread, yes, or salami – why hadn't he bought some salami to layer on the cheese, or some of that honey-glazed ham? Surely William's lifelong vegetarianism struggled to sustain his large frame. For those short weeks that Leonard had tried it himself he'd felt in constant arrears with his appetite; but he'd seen pictures of particular dinosaurs, those great herbivorous leviathans, and, he'd thought, if the dinosaurs could live without meat, he could too. As it turned out, he couldn't, and in fact if the dinosaurs' eradication was anything to judge by, neither could they. He ate the figs, and then the majority of the cheese, and all this while William picked. When the noises outside had passed and faded, Leonard decided to embark on a discussion he hadn't planned for and had wanted to hold back on, but which pressed at him suddenly.

'I do have a favour to ask, in fact.'

'Tell it.'

'Before I left Scotland I wrote to Tela to say I'd be coming home soon, I sent the letter with a bunch of flowers, the great romantic that I am. And by return of post I had a letter back from her to say that she couldn't really see the point of us going on. It was a very detailed letter, she must have been up all night writing it. It said that she'd be going away for a month and it said when she'd be back, and it was very specific about how she needed all my things to be gone from her house by that date. Which is next week. It is her house, I suppose. I always knew I was on borrowed time.'

William's expression became gentle, if not a little forlorn. 'What's the favour? Would you like me to change her mind?'

'If only you could.'

When nothing more came, Leonard elaborated. 'I need somewhere to stay.'

William pushed his fingers through his beard and mouthed, Oh. And the dawning had no authenticity to it – of course he knew that this was the favour, he knew it from the moment Leonard had mentioned Tela's name. He probably knew it, Leonard calculated, from the moment Tela appeared seven years ago. He'd probably been waiting for this conversation with his usual patient sense of irony. But William was literal to a fault, which meant that he would only answer a question that had been asked, and thus a look of poised curiosity appeared on his face, as if to say, *And the favour is?* Leonard laughed at that – at that fastidiousness about exchange and punctuation which meant that his brother couldn't rush to his rescue until an official cry had been put out.

The laughter freed him from an impending sense of loss, one in which the image of the stamped-on necks of those chickens swam with that of Tela's pale face underwater. This was how he kept imagining her, with her eyes closed and her hands pushing the shampoo from her hair, or rising with a full crooked smile through the river's surface, and it did no good, those images, it did no good to replay them.

'Can I stay with you for a while?'

'My house is your house, Leo, you can stay as long as you like.'

'Thank you. I'll return the favour, I promise – I won't forget it.'

'Leonard, all I ask is that you do forget it, please. I'd hate to have any sense of debt between us.'

'Well, thank you.' Leonard took a mouthful of wine. 'Won't you have to ask Kathy?'

'Kathy's amenable. I will ask her, but you don't need to worry, everybody will be happy to have you. The boys will like you being there.'

Leonard both hoped and doubted it, but was silent while his brother wiped some dust from the table with his thumb. William had a way of saying his wife's name with such unfettered love, softly but strenuously also, as if the very concept of her distilled down for him all the deep and wonderful things of life. It was testament not to the fitness of their marriage, which Leonard had always thought was rather cold, but to William's insistence on loving, and to the odd massiveness of his heart. They'd mockingly used to call him the great erotic, the great romantic, William of the imperturbable belief in human nature, William who could fall in love with a bridge, a leaf.

Leonard withdrew from those thoughts to once again occupy his own. 'It was a shock to get that letter from Tela, you know,' he said. 'You'd have thought I might have seen it coming – if you leave your girlfriend for a year what can you really expect? It's just that, on the few times she came up to Edinburgh to visit, it was dreamlike. We got on better than ever. I thought, I don't know, maybe marriage could be on the cards. And now I'm single again.'

William poured a little more wine into Leonard's glass, which, for him, was a sign of utmost sympathy. He never did things like this, he never noticed or catered to other people's needs. To have the sympathy was enough to stop Leonard needing it, and he straightened. 'But look,' he said, 'I wailed and kicked out for a week or two, and now, gradually, I think I can see my way through. Conceptually, at least, it makes more sense to me to be single.' He went motionless for a moment and gazed at a vacancy a foot in front of him. 'Maybe.'

'Conceptually?'

'Yes. Just seems to me that maybe that's how my life will be. It never used to, but it does now.'

William nodded. 'Ah well, there you go.'

Of course, this meant nothing, and Leonard had half a mind to challenge it. Sitting back to drink some wine, he asked, 'How are the boys?'

'Oh, they're fine,' William said.

'They're doing okay at school?'

'They're doing well at school. They're quite bright apparently.'

William had such a light in his eye when he said this, and a mocking smile.

'Well, you've never thought much of education, William.'

'On the contrary. I think everything of education, which is why I'm sad that they go to school every day and never get any. Still, I trust they'll pull through in spite of it.'

Leonard couldn't be bothered to assess that view. 'I'm not a parent,' he said. 'I suppose I can't judge.'

'But you're a teacher, Leo, I sometimes forget that. I know I'm prone to a bit of lambasting of your profession and I shouldn't, it's probably very worthy. I'm sorry.'

'It's fine.' And it was; those lambastings were so long-standing that they'd become more a comfort than an insult and he never took them to heart. 'Oli was always very good at drawing, wasn't he? Does he do that still? He always seemed so talented.'

William shrugged slowly. 'Is he talented? I don't know, I've never really thought it matters.'

'Of course it matters, they're your sons.'

'Well, if they do wrong, does being talented make any difference? If they're miserable, does it make any difference? I'd rather they lived well and were happy.'

'All the same, Oli's good at drawing.'

'If he is it isn't my doing. I just made the necessary biological provisions.'

Leonard watched his brother for a moment. 'You always say those things,' he observed, and it was by way of saying, *therefore they aren't true.* He paused. 'I meant to tell you, it was something beautiful. At the funeral one of Dad's friends, James – you remember him – read a poem about parenthood that Dad had written when you were born. *I love this child, who is my faith made truth.* That was one of the lines – *my faith made truth* – it was really quite beautiful, not just that part. I wish you'd been there. He said that about you, William. His faith made truth.'

William considered that with brows that dropped a little, and as he nodded he ran the back of his hand slowly across his chin.

'Like I said, I wish you'd been there and heard it for yourself.'

'And that's your wish, Leo, and I suppose one of the skills we should try to perfect in life is not confusing our own wishes with another's. I wish that it were fine for a son not to go to his father's funeral, and that all sorts of inferences about love, or lack of love, weren't drawn from that. But I know they are, because other people wish very strongly for the opposite. So I try not to get confused between whose wishes are whose.'

In spite of himself Leonard smiled; a typically mechanical diagnosis of things from his brother, one that was almost a relief in its sieving through of emotions, in the rinsing of some of those things that had been clogging his heart. 'Then I apologise, for not trying to do that myself.'

'If you're apologising to me, forget it. I love you, whatever you do or don't do is neither here nor there. It couldn't put the slightest dent in that love.'

This was said with no irony or facetiousness, and it struck Leonard anew, this capacity his brother had for such frank, unmitigated declarations, and how they didn't ask or hope for anything in return. 'And also – Leo,' he said, 'believe me, I actually *am* just a provider for my children. The three times we slept together to conceive – Kathy and I – Kathy turned the other way and counted to eighty.'

Leonard drank through light laughter. 'I think Tela occasionally did that too.'

'So, we are not good lovers. Men are not good lovers any more, at least I've heard women say so, and women aren't given to idle talk. Really, men are the modern tragedy.'

They smiled at one another. Leonard was surprised by the amount of happiness he managed to feel in the midst of his abandonment; first his mother, then his father, then his partner. If he'd been told that this would be the run of things, and that in particular he would come back from one borrowed bed in Edinburgh to find himself searching out another in London, his fifty-one years clanking heavily against the massive fact of his aloneness, he might have defied himself and prayed. But reality was seldom as bad as projected reality, and he didn't know what he would pray for if he put his hands together now.

William inhaled in readiness to speak. Then silence, then he did finally speak.

'When will you be coming to stay?' he asked, and Leonard cleared his throat.

'I'd rather be out well before Tela gets back, I think if I saw her I would start begging. I'm not going to beg.'

'I am sorry about Tela, Leo. She was rare.'

'We're all rare,' Leonard offered, surprised again by that glimmer of sympathy.

'No, not all of us. Some of us are common. Some of us are out-and-out rife.'

'That can't be true.'

'It must be true. There would be nothing worse than a world full of equally special people. Tomorrow then? You'll come tomorrow?'

William stood so that he could stretch his arms above his head. He really could be bear-like in his movements, Leonard thought. All slow manoeuvrings and deliberateness.

'Yes, tomorrow.'

Leonard put his hands to his lower back and looked towards the window. The early August sun rose up above the top of the window and the light in the room fell. The table still bore minutes from distant meetings. When he looked up to William it seemed that he had slipped deep into thought, as he sometimes did, or even into a trance of sorts, in which he was nowhere to be found in this world. Alone, Leonard walked to the window and observed the small Edwardian brickwork, the white-framed sash windows of the buildings opposite, and up along the terrace to where the houses grew gradually in stature until they became the four-storey tenements that marked the wealthier end of Bellevue Street. There were times already when he wished to be back in the spaciousness of Scotland within sight of mountains, where even the cities were generous with their passing round of light and air. He turned back into the room.

'William,' he said.

William roused easily to the sound of his name and, with a smile, lifted one inquisitive brow. 'You called?'

'Have more food.'

He went to William and took his wide, short hand, squeezed it hard, opened it, put a fig in it, pushed wine towards it.

'Eat, drink.'

Without any trace of ingratitude or impatience, William put the fig back in the bag; he did take a mouthful of wine, more as a gesture of goodwill than through need or desire, Leonard thought, but still. Leonard topped up both their glasses and stood to close the windows, to bar the noise from the street. The wake of the bike ride at the far end of the street – a couple of stragglers with a puncture-repair kit, and a few flyers on the road. The street was uncommonly quiet; a success, then, because the traffic had been deterred. He turned suddenly to William.

'This morning when I woke up,' he said, 'I heard something on the local news, on the radio. Some chickens that were kept at allotments in Finsbury Park, just down there, were killed; somebody had stamped on their necks.'

He took a few strides back to the table and gulped at his wine with unfeigned indignation, because all the bike protests in the world would come and go and fade to silence, and not a single person would care about the flattened neck of a chicken. Something about the idea of flat necks horrified him; the whole concept of the killings horrified him, but that specifically. The thought of boots, human feet, and those little neck bones. 'And a few weeks before, at the same allotments, other chickens were decapitated.' He paused. 'Decapitated, William.'

William gave no response. A look of untrammelled sadness seemed to pass over his face, but was that to do with the story, or just a random movement of thought, quickly to be followed by some other movement of thought? Even after five decades Leonard couldn't tell. 'I mean,' he went on, 'it isn't difficult to kill a bird. It isn't a display of great power to kill a chicken, for Christ's sake. Why do it? What pathetic deficit of manhood makes you do it?'

'I didn't do it,' William clarified.

'Not you. One. What makes one do it?'

'I don't know.' William raised his chin a fraction. 'Would you say it's a lack of morality?'

Leonard replied, 'A lack of love, more like. A lack of humanity. Somebody called in to say maybe foxes had done it. Do you know what the presenter said? He said that, with all due respect, he didn't think foxes were strong enough to stamp on a chicken's neck.' He leaned back and pressed his palms into the edge of the table, and released his incredulity with a sharp exhalation of breath. 'Well, with all due respect, I don't think it's a question of strength. It isn't that foxes aren't strong enough to stamp on a chicken's neck, it's that they aren't desperate enough, they aren't lost enough, they aren't broken-spirited enough. They don't kill for pleasure, they kill when they want to eat.'

With that William held the back of his own neck with his hand and nodded slowly. 'I see precisely what you're saying, Leo,' he said. 'Yes.'

Leonard had missed his brother; he'd missed his serious contemplation of the small and obscure things that escaped everybody else's notice. Anybody else would have laughed off this anxiety about the chickens, forced a joke from it. They wouldn't have seen the point precisely, they wouldn't have nodded in empathy. From the earliest years of remembered childhood William would credit any subject with importance, and he would never belittle Leonard's thoughts no matter how callow. In their teens William would expose him to arguments beyond his years and in doing so bolster him, make him feel less childish. William scratched his cheek with deliberate care. How could it be that a person's face – simply the way the weight and light fell around their face – could prompt indivisible love? For all that one's family could irritate and infuriate, their mirrored genes and minds of shared memories broke down every defence. There they were, and things were perfectly simple.

The room was hot with the windows shut. It occurred to Leonard that maybe he was drinking too much. He filled his glass and wanted to say any number of things about the last year in Edinburgh, and the last weeks of their father's life. William narrowed his eyes and went to speak, then he wore, suddenly, an expression of great tenderness. This turned, as though at the flick of an internal switch, to wicked amusement. 'The season starts again soon,' he said suddenly. 'You're in for another whitewash.'

'We'll have a race on.'

'Ah, be real, Leo, Saracens will be wallowing at the bottom of the table.'

'We're fighters.'

'Well, with players like that you have to be. All over the place.' William smiled again, and stood. 'I have things to do, we'll see each other soon.'

'William – another thing.' Leonard crossed his arms in front of him. 'He died with photos of each of us on his lap, the three of us. One of Mother, one of me, one of you. I just wanted you to know that.'

William nodded a slow, cautious acknowledgement of this fact, as though he were reluctant to take on the truth of it, or as if the mental image he was forming of those photographs gathered in the old man's hands was inexplicable to him. He said after a silence, 'So then, tomorrow.'

'Yes, tomorrow.'

William went to the window, retrieved his sandals which were softening in the sunlight, put them on, and then crossed to the staircase. He was famed for his bare feet; painlessly, he could extinguish cigarettes on the soles of them.

He began his descent. Leonard watched him lower step by step, his body angled just as it had been when he came up, a cough, his full head of hair disappearing. Evanescent brother, brother always slipping from reach. Leonard thought back to him as a child briefly, his presence and joy, and then his perpetual disappearances within himself, and then the sadness, almost a grief, that had passed over him with the mention of the murdered chickens. And when William was gone from sight, his absence, as always, filled and heavied the room.

*

As for those last few weeks of their father's life, well, they'd gone slowly, so slowly, and loss echoed in every expanded minute of them. What a strange time it had been, because their father didn't so much become ill as become old, which happened with great transformative stealth and rendered him finally dead – a nebulous, unspecific yet wholly foreseen death that happened in his armchair one evening, a general stopping of the heart, as if the inevitable pressure of time, forcing itself from in front, above and behind, had acted as a pair of hands that squeezed the last of the air from his lungs. Leonard had been there, and had phoned William immediately, and William had cried lightly down the line.

For the ten months previous to that, which was the time since their mother's funeral, Leonard had been with his father every day and night. The care of the large bed of dahlias at the top of the back garden was the last full task his father had taken entirely into his own hands, and then when those flowers finally buckled in the early November frosts, so did the man. The original bulbs had been a wedding present, he'd explained, and a singular joy and ritual throughout the marriage, thus they weren't to be let go. After that Leonard had taken over the running of the house, the shopping and cooking, tea-making for the parishoners who'd come to see the old vicar on his last legs, the fetching of the milk and post from the gate at the top of the sloped driveway, the stacking of the turf in the turf shed, the fixing of the car, the lawnmower, the blocked radiators, the trimming of the trees that grew ever tighter to the house, the loading and unloading of the washing machine, the fetching of eggs from the next-door neighbour's hen house, the administering of routine pills to a man who was well enough, on paper, to walk fifteen miles, but who was accumulating time in all its heaviness and wretchedness; they could both see it, father and son – they could see how the older man had stopped springing back, had lost that certain elasticity of existence, and how his chest had caved a little, which slackened his shoulders. Because they could both see the imminence of death, they never spoke about it.

All of those domestic chores seemed to Leonard ancient and sacrosanct at first – the eggs, the turf, even the ritualistic insertion and extraction of clothes into the machine, buttons clicking against the drum with a not-quite rhythm, then the trouser legs flailing crazily on the wind when he hung them out to dry. The family home was some eight miles outside of Edinburgh but they might have been two hundred miles from anywhere, the way he felt, and the way he'd become absorbed in the business of getting along. For a time he thought about asking Tela to move up there, go deeper into Scotland, get a smallholding perhaps. He really didn't expect that agrestic and devotional sense of things to wear off, he really thought it was the beginnings of a new and wholesome him.

It did wear off. The endless, endless fetching of turf, of eggs, of milk, of post, of washing! Each morning helping his father to the bathroom and running his bath, or otherwise just flannelling his face, neck and underarms, helping him down the stairs, sitting with him in the chilly garden, reading *The New Complete Joy of Home Brewing* so that together they could embark on his experiment in making ale the partial mash way, easing him up the stairs each evening back to bed, kissing his cool forehead, going back downstairs alone to his book, or the news, or a film.

In those long days they went through some of the things in the attic – the *trappings*, his father called them – because the old man wanted to acquaint himself again with his sons' childhood possessions. They found schoolbooks of Leonard's, but none of William's. They found the sheet music William had used from grade one all the way through to eight for piano and violin. Two thick pottery money boxes in the shape of old English cottages, one with a slate roof and roses growing around the door, and one with thatch and a blue climbing flower that Leonard couldn't name; neither he nor his father could remember whose money box was whose. In any case they were empty, and Leonard was fairly certain that it would have been him, not William, who'd emptied them both. Some Corgi Classics toy cars – a couple of old Chevrolet trucks, a Lyons Maid Ice Cream van – yes, and Leonard still admired their brilliant and accurate detail even after all the years. He and William had used to race them down the stairs, and the loser had to be ball boy for a day in their games of cricket. There were some boardgames and books. Of all of this, and in that slow and reminiscing search, the only item his father was interested in was a three-dimensional wooden puzzle that William had used to love, which had over fifty pieces; he took it to his armchair and toyed with it evening after evening, saying with great perplexity, frustration and admiration, William used to be able to do this in five minutes flat.

William had seemed present to them during those weeks and months. The puzzle was a reminder of him because of the constant inferences their father made from it to William's skill and quickness – so much so that Leonard fell into a tendency he had, a tendency his parents had nourished, to think of his brother quite mythically, or supernaturally. Sometimes William would phone and talk rugby, teasing Leonard about Saracens whose bad spell was so prolonged it could barely be called a spell any longer; other times he'd phone and speak about the soul, his hopes for its immutability, other times he'd phone and demand they swapped jokes, then release his glorious, delighted laughter down the line; other times, after a particularly long or difficult day, Leonard would fail to contain his resentment at his brother's lack of visits and care, and they'd get into some discussion that

Leonard had no stomach for, concerning what it meant to be dutiful and virtuous, a discussion that was more like a medical dissection than it was a sharing of emotion or opinion. Any net result was the same, whether Leonard was patient or angry; William wouldn't visit, there was no point in pressing the matter, and so he rarely did.

It was in those last few weeks that William sent up in the post a collection of videos – that he said he'd found at a car-boot sale – of the Ealing Comedies. That had touched them greatly. Those were the films they'd watched as a family back in the late fifties when they would curl together as a foursome along a middle row at the cinema for a matinee, the boys cradling in their palms their quota of bonbons, one every fifteen minutes so that they'd last. The family had even called their cat Dutch after the trickster of *The Lavender Hill Mob*, and indeed the man and the cat did share enough opportunistic traits to justify that comparison. Leonard and his father were moved, more than they could express to one another, that William should have remembered and honoured those times. One day Leonard noticed that the photograph of William in his Falkland War naval-chef uniform, which had been obscured by the curtain on the landing windowsill, had been moved to a prouder place on the obdurate old mahogany sideboard. He not only looked younger there but altogether quite different – good-looking, almost, and sharper, cannier, as though he had an insight he'd since lost, and as though over time he'd become more, and not less, innocent.

There were twelve films, which they watched over fourteen evenings. The smell of fermenting hops infiltrated the sitting room, and at times Leonard thought his father was growing heady. What has William made of himself? he'd once asked Leonard, a rousing light in his eyes. What has he *made* of himself, after all? And often he worried, worried so persistently, over William's involvement in politics, and it had mortified him that his son might be an anarchist, a radical socialist, a bomb-thrower as he called it. He'd pressed Leonard for insight. Again, Leonard responded, I don't know, I don't know.

Yet he has God, and a wife and three good children, the older man would say, and would look for comfort at William's naval photograph again. Yet he walked away from the two short jobs he ever had – one in the navy and one at the university; and there was that trouble with the riots. What has he *made* of himself? He'd shake his head. For the duration of each film Leonard saw that his father held a piece of the dismantled wooden puzzle on his lap, which seemed to say that for all the clarity he'd gained in his life, there was one enigma that persisted at the crux of it, unsolved and unsolvable.

The packing was always going to be hard, after all. As soon as Leonard got to Tela's flat that evening after seeing William he began to extract his remaining belongings and he felt as though he were trying to remove his own shadow. All that was there had been unused and forgotten for a year and was fairly peripheral to him, but as he folded up those old jumpers and sorted through the shaving foams and obsolete credit cards he felt protective towards himself – we *are* our peripheries, he thought, we are all these forgotten things. He was disappointed with himself over the sentimentality of the process; when he had to take his few clothes from their wardrobe the loss he felt was sheer-sided, and again when he tried to find anything in the kitchen that belonged truly to him, and when he sifted through the piles of paperwork that had accumulated on the bookshelves. It was finally the shoes that broke his heart. When he sorted through that not altogether pretty pile of canvas, rubber and leather, variously battered and polished, worn most where the body's weight fell, all he could see was the vulnerability of being human. Little human feet, he'd thought. Pathetic human feet. He knelt at them and found himself crying, clinging to something already lost, and crying from his eyes, his nose and his mouth; it took him time to rouse himself from the task, bring himself up to his feet via his fingertips, his head unfurling from its grief, back up to a standing position from whence he could collect himself and get on.

He'd decided that he would only take what was essential to him, and he was brutal with himself about it. There would be no deliberation over which towels belonged to whom, which mugs, who had bought what. To divide a relationship up in this way was to suggest that those things had never been truly shared, that a line had always run down the landscape of their union. Indeed in his case this was the truth, and that was precisely why he wouldn't bow to it. He left in place much of what constituted his life, and while he didn't feel exactly good about it, he did manage to feel neutral for the most part, after the difficulty with the shoes. He came to be immersed in a pain that was like cold water – not numbing, no, he was really alive, it was just that the aliveness wasn't at all pleasant. It wasn't the state of grace of the Lord, et cetera, that his family had always encouraged him to attain. He did pack in one of his two boxes a picture of himself and Tela which was rightly hers – she had enlarged and framed it – and he took it mainly because he hoped she would miss it. Otherwise the extraction of himself from their home was barely perceptible and, for his part, generous, and altogether forgiving.

It was done too quickly. He went to bed early and in the morning, when he got out of that bed, he was amazed by how inanimate it was, given that spread across it was the full living force of so many memories. In the kitchen he took from his pocket the letter Tela had written him, which he laid on the table to reread. *I don't feel that I'll go anywhere with you: we are a dead end.* Then he looked around the room as if it would offer him an idea, and it did. He took a pen and he began to correct her sentences. Tela had always prided herself on her grammar, but her punctuation displayed mental chaos. She misused and over-used colons, and he suddenly thought less of her for that. Commas! Four commas per sentence sometimes, so that he tripped like a blindfolded child through her emotions. How had he ever stood a chance of understanding her?

He left the flat just after midday, heaving his two boxes onto the backseat of a taxi with his backpack of clothes propped against them and his guitar laid across them as though they were the very structure of his life, and he took the forty-five-minute journey to Islington. Up until the last twenty-four hours he'd been one of those men who dragged a steadily expanding cargo of posses-sions along behind him, as if he were building his own empire of objects. Of course he'd learned long ago, like all people, that one's possessions take control; the revelation meant nothing however. He'd still collected them, and had still insisted the control was his. He now felt both bereft and proud at his lack of things. It was more than a feat of logistics to own so little, it was almost that a moral, or even metaphysical, victory had been finally claimed. All those excess objects had been cast out: I have two boxes, a guitar and a bag, therefore I am. Who knows what I am, but I definitely am.

Before he'd left the flat he'd put Tela's corrected letter against the toaster, knowing she would arrive back with a bag of shop-ping and toast her potato cakes there, a ritual that she applied to every homecoming. She'd find it and read it as she chewed, probably with a raised brow and nettled smile. The thing was, she'd have the potato cakes with jam, which he found somehow terrible – the clash of sweet and savoury. You wouldn't have a baked potato with jam, you wouldn't have mashed potato with jam; it was a type of madness. And so, he thought, I'm better off without her.

At William's house that afternoon, Leonard was greeted by one of his nephews. The child looked at the taxi pulling away, then at the two boxes and the guitar case, scratched his bare stomach and announced without any other try at a greeting, 'I'll get my mum.'

'It's me, Oli, your uncle.'

The boy regarded him with impatience. 'I know.' Then he ran into the hallway, which was dark to Leonard's sun-drenched vision.

While he waited Leonard looked up at the tall house. It stretched off into a low hot sky. He surveyed the front garden. All of June and July had been this way, gently and quietly hot, smelling of night rain and tired roses. The fig tree opened its great leaves to the light and within the thickness and wildness of their growth Leonard could see scores of new figs, some still tight and green, some blushing at their crowns. The windows were open to the breezeless day and the slowed birdsong. The long grasses that always dominated William's small garden in the early summer, so rainbow-coloured and weightless in June, were becoming now, in early August, grey and webbed. Soon Kathy would cut them down, and the bed of cosmos just below the window would stop budding, and that would show that autumn wasn't far distant.

'Leonard.'

'Kathy, hello.' Leonard extended his hand to her, and there

was some confusion over its destination – her hand, her forearm, a pat, a timid squeeze? Always his first thought – how can she be my sister-in-law? By which he wasn't sure whether he meant, how can she be part of my family, or how can she be William's wife? Or even, how can William have a wife?

She glanced at his boxes, and he offered quickly, 'William did tell you I would be coming to stay for a while? Or I should say, he did ask you?'

'Yes, he did. He didn't say it would be today, that's all. He isn't here yet, he's at a – meeting. But never mind, it doesn't really matter, follow me in.'

She looked as though it might matter a little, but only that much; she was a moderate woman, damp, if Leonard could bring himself to that description – damp and pale. And as she led him into the wide hall and he watched her stiff walk, he realised he'd never been able to forgive her the fact of her closed-off heart, into which his brother tried to pour so much love. Forgive me the judgements, he asked mechanically of a God he'd never been able to fully shrug off.

'You can put your boxes in William's room,' she said. 'That's where he wants you to sleep.'

'Are you sure?'

'It's what he said, and woe betide anybody who questions what William says.'

She stated it frankly but not with ill-will; how interesting it was, he thought, the way both husband and wife seemed to think equally that the other held the power. He tried not to look down at her and emphasise the discrepancy in height, but she thwarted his efforts at equality. She seemed to screw her shoulders down in timidity, which compacted her smallness and drove her away from any space that brief body might have commanded.

'Kathy, I'm really grateful to you, you and William and the boys, it hasn't been a very good time for me, and—'

'William's your brother and this is his house as much as it's mine. You wouldn't have expected us to turn you away?'

He shook his head, no, and gave a quiet cough into his hand.

'So will you be back at work in September?' she asked.

He looked out of the kitchen window at the small yard that ran down the side of the house, before opening up into the garden. 'No, I took an extra term off so I'm back in January. It looked like I might need to be in Edinburgh longer – to be honest, I thought he was going to hang on in that precarious state for another decade.'

'Your father?'

He nodded and turned back to the kitchen. 'So now I have all this spare time. Maybe I could go back if I asked, but then I thought, well, I've got the rest of my life to work, I should enjoy it while I can. Shouldn't I?'

Her one-shouldered shrug gave nothing away; it might have meant, That'll be nice, or it might have meant, Idle, aren't you? Either way it didn't ask for a response, so he leaned back against the wall and watched her scuttle about the kitchen busily, quite pointlessly, he thought.

She was merely thirty-four, thirty-five, thereabouts, two decades younger than William. That she often looked fifty, moved like someone whose youth was truly behind them, spoke like someone whose mind was made up – these things were no longer surprising to Leonard. It was that she did sometimes look her age that was surprising. For a moment she did, when she blew a strand of hair out of her eyes – in fact she was almost girlish, a nervous twitch in her cheek, an expression of brief pleasure at the company. He smiled at her. 'Hot again today,' she said, and he agreed. Yet she was so white-skinned, as if the summer's heat hadn't bothered with her, nor she it. She collected the plait of her long brown hair over her shoulder and ran her hand down it with a wringing action that he found strange. He'd often wondered what her hair would look like loose; it was one of his frustrations with her that her one abundant feature was knotted into a rope, tidied away like that.

He noticed then that she'd started making tea. Out of politeness he stayed to drink it with her, seated at the kitchen table. He tipped the narrow bench by sitting too far towards its end and spilt a little of his tea over his hand and the table. 'Not to worry,' she said, and fetched a dishcloth. 'It can be wiped up. Help yourself to sugar.' He did, and he went to sit at the stool by the sideboard in the hope of a more auspicious start.

They made conversation, about the weather, about the three children – who ran in and out of the kitchen en route to or from the back garden, roaring and heedless of their uncle sitting on a stool, his long legs draped and his heels tapping. Each time they ran through the kitchen she harped a name needlessly or asked them to slow down or settle down or let up. It was just as it always was.

'What's William's meeting?' he asked.

She regarded him blankly.

'You said he was at a meeting?'

'Oh, yes. At the youth group. He's in trouble with them again over something.'

'Again?'

She glanced up from her mug of tea. 'Well don't act surprised, he's always in trouble with them and well you know it.'

He thought, Do I know it? Surely if it were a fact he would know it. But he said nothing.

'They say he's been talking to the kids about the wrong things. Or inappropriate things, anyway.'

'Who's they?'

'The parents of some of them.'

'I thought those kids were old enough to just go to the group of their own accord, William's *followers*.'

'They do go of their own accord, but that doesn't mean their parents don't hate it – who wants their children to be exposed to all that when they should just be out finding out what job they want or what college they should go to?'

'Exposed to all what?'

She grasped her mug. 'I don't know – sex, religion? I don't know.'

'It seems to me that sex and religion are the safe, tepid subjects nowadays,' he said with a shrug. 'I can't imagine what he would have said to upset them on that score. Do you know how hard it's become to be offensive?'

'Do you often try?' She almost smiled. 'Honestly, I don't know what he's done, I refuse to be dragged into it all. I really don't understand why he finds the need to hang around in the Bellevue with a gaggle of teens anyway, or to roam around the streets pestering people, or whatever it is he does. It's not like he's paid.' She paused. 'He used to be paid. I've never understood – if he goes on teaching university students years after leaving his job there, why did he leave in the first place? I've always said this to him. Why did I have to marry the one man in the world who has an objection to making money?' A sigh, in which she seemed to withdraw her energy from the argument. 'What difference does he hope to make? He thinks he can improve humanity somehow, but the world is the same, over and over, age after age.'

'Well, we have to hope that isn't true.'

'You've been teaching for – how many years? And have you found that people are becoming more enlightened?'

'They're not less enlightened.'

'Well.' She rested her mug down and laced her fingers. 'That's not enough though, is it?'

They drank the last of their tea and he wondered, Enough for what? She was looking out of the window in pretended interest at something there in the back yard, where the fence was closest to the house. Then, to their clear mutual relief, Richard came inside bemoaning the injustice at his having to be backstop always, without any turn with the bat. Such was the consequence for being the youngest of three, Leonard supposed. The boy's breath was made ragged by the asthma he'd always suffered from, and by the sense of iniquity. Leonard left Kathy with her son and retreated to the back sitting room, the room he knew was much more his brother's than the family's.

He sat in the wealth of its early-evening sun. The room was lined with books which hadn't been read for years; his brother had a great deal of books for a man who didn't really value literature, who deemed reality strange enough without creating a set of fictions within it. The small television and video in the corner were dusty, in a house where dust wasn't usually permitted. There were William's records, a mix of plainsong, opera, rock, jazz, and all the Nigerian and Latin American music they'd both loved even as teenagers, the protest songs of the *nueva trova* – Silvio Rodríguez, Carlos Puebla – wonderful, melancholy, darkly joyous music. We are citizens of the world, William would say when he played that music, and his face would be a simple beam of light. We aren't Englishmen, we aren't us and they them, we're citizens of the world. Do you feel that? Will you remember it?

And even the opera Leonard could warm to in the context of his brother – he was always grateful that in such a cryptic personality as William's there was room for something so dramatic and barefaced as opera. Most of the operas William had – *Don*

Giovanni, Carmen, Lucia di Lammermoor, The Marriage of Figaro, Aida – Leonard had bought him for birthdays and Christmas, bought out of desperation, received with the infectious delight with which William received all gifts. Leonard closed his eyes for a moment and felt the warmth on his nose and cheeks. Then he took his John le Carré from the side pocket of his backpack. For an hour he read; at five o'clock Kathy and the boys left for the boys' weekly karate lesson, and he was alone.

It was a narrow townhouse, whose inhabitants' lives were distributed evenly and sparsely over three floors, and then at the final point of the house an attic crammed with the past and present paraphernalia of children. Like heat, the clutter had risen and become trapped under the eaves in an expansive moving mass. When the children had used to want to play, and it was too cold or wet for the garden, they would squeeze themselves into the attic, more victims of their hundreds of toys than possessors of them, and fight each other with planes, soldiers, pick-up trucks, tanks, ships, farmyard animals from earlier days. Cows flying, a piglet stuck in an ear, a horse hurled out of the skylight.

He moved up the four storeys with more interest in the act of prying than in what he actually saw. He peered into the attic – yes, it was just as it used to be. He remembered the days when the three boys were smaller, the days of the flying farmyard animals. He'd been much more of an uncle then, at least more so than now; he would play with them for hours, chasing them with roars, and holding them upside down by their ankles to swing them, tick-tock, tick-tock, a steady pendulous trail of cackling laughter. It was strange that the boys might not remember any of that when those memories were, to him, a cornerstone, a stark realisation – if not the first – that he was an adult, that there was a generation beneath him, that there was no going back.

Then he wandered downstairs again. The rest of the house – the kitchen, the living room, the utility room, the dining room, the main bedroom, the children's bedrooms, the bathroom, the hallway and landing, even the stairs, these were all Kathy's. She'd asserted versions of herself upon them all, like pins into a pin cushion – precisely and penetratingly. Aside from the bedroom, which laboured, visibly fatigued, under conflicting patterns and fabrics all vying for equal attention, she'd made the house tasteful enough, too pedantic in its choice of curtain tie or bath tap to be generic exactly, but the sort of house anybody could live in.

He lugged his two boxes and bag up to William's room. The most striking thing about that room was the wall covered in children's drawings. From a distance they had the primary-coloured chaos of tangled wool, and the nearer one came the more those tangles ordered themselves into human forms – the crooked loop of a head, the hard-pressed wax line of a leg, box bodies, smiles spilling beyond the face. Some were more advanced, and Leonard assumed they were drawn by Oli or Abe – indeed a few were signed with their names. Oli's preoccupation was with monsters, Abe's with the valiant rescuers – firemen, policemen, knights. Leonard was struck, as he always was when he looked at children's drawings, by the very miracle they flouted – from the fusion of cells in a uterus, the creation of a new imagination. Beyond belief, he thought; beyond understanding.

Other than those drawings there was little: a double bed, an armchair, an unpopulated bookshelf, the vintage Hacker Gondolier four-speed record player given to William by their parents, and the pictures of the various animal brains on the wall, along with a calendar of Finnish landscapes which was on the wrong month and from the wrong year. It was typical of William, as though he were making clear his disregard of time. In the corner of the room beneath the window there was a tall stack of *Time* and *New Scientist* magazines, some *Scientific Americans*, and a number of other journals which Leonard knew their father had passed on to William as was his way – he would read them himself and then put them in the post, wait a few days and then call to see what William thought about this discovery or that development. It had for years been one of the main bonds between the two, and Leonard had long since decided that the kind of desperate insistence their father showed in keeping up that habit was in truth an insistence on trying to anchor William to the world at large, to keep him current and aware and equipped with fact. Let the old man think he's doing so, Leonard had thought; by some process invisible to the rest of the world, William kept himself one of the most sharply aware people he knew and would have done so regardless of those magazines. Leonard didn't know if his brother actually read them, but he always held his own in a discussion, even if it was only to dismantle whatever precious theory or concept their father brought to debate.

And the two Salvadorean crosses, there they were – he hadn't spotted those before. They were propped up on the windowsill, slightly warped in the sun and faded in colour after four decades of ownership. Christ the shepherd carved into the wood and painted blue, red, yellow, and his skin black. He cradled a perfectly white lamb – a soft, gentle Negro Christ standing in the village of his people, with their full sun, their flowers, their red-roofed shacks. That William should still have those crosses, should have kept them for forty years! Leonard didn't know what had happened to his own – had he lost them, or broken them? He sat on the bed and stared at them, and they moved and troubled him as they never had before. He shifted his gaze into the room's benign emptiness.

It was a grand gesture of his brother's to loan out his bedroom, for it meant William not only surrendered his own space but encroached on Kathy's – her complex floral bedsheets and her themed colour schemes which were feminine, exclusive and defiant. Their marriage seemed to be about protected territories, which he was now muddling.

But he decided it wasn't for him to refuse. He stood at the bay window and looked out at the street and to the public garden on the other side of it – lush, overgrown, bursting from its confines just as the smiles burst from the faces in the children's drawings. The flowers grew tall and large and seemed to him, in his ignorance, tropical; a lovely willing urban garden bordering on shambolic, and though he must have seen it in the summer before, he didn't recall having done so. The abundant leaves of three weeping willows bent down to meet the upgoing flowers and grasses in a continuous cycle of greenery. He remembered William telling him that it was common enough to see parakeets there, a fact which ignited William's love of the curious and unlikely, the theatrical. Leonard turned back to face into the room. Sometimes when he was in or near the presence of his brother, he felt that being in or near the presence of his brother was the least likely thing that could ever happen to him. He couldn't explain that feeling, neither good nor bad nor sensible as it was.

All very well, all very well, but he couldn't stay in that house for long, he knew it. As he was about to leave the room he looked out again through the bay window, above the canopy of the fig tree, and he saw William standing in the public garden. He was with a young man, who had William's hand in a clasp between his own, and who then let go. Then William's arm was outstretched so that his hand lay on the man's upper arm. Leonard couldn't read that gesture, all he could say was that there was something holy in the stance, and something that made the scene incalculable.

He drew himself involuntarily closer to the window, then he drew back. Enough watching. He left his brother's bedroom hurriedly and walked back downstairs to the small living room, where he again picked up his book. In less than half a minute he heard the front door open and close.

Soon enough William came into the back room, sat down and closed his eyes.

'I welcome you to my house with all my heart,' he said. 'I'm sorry I'm too tired to show it.'

Leonard looked at his brother's face, his closed eyes, and tried to find an explanation in there for what he'd seen outside. All was calm there; the eyelids didn't twitch, the mouth curved into no emotion.

'Yes, you look tired.' Maybe this was the truth, maybe he did, and it was tiredness, not calm, that was written blank on those features. 'How was the meeting?'

A smile from William, which was rather sardonic, and the eyes opened briefly.

'Do you know when you have an itch on your back, just there, near the top of the spine? Your left hand can't get it on the way up, and your right hand can't get it on the way down. To the parents of those kids, I am that itch.'

He asked lightly, 'So what are they going to do about you then?'

'Well like I said, neither hand can get to the itch. What *can* they do with me? They can't throw me out, since their children come to me and not me to them. I solicit nothing, Leo. If they didn't come, I'd still sit there, I'd still think, I'd probably just talk to the walls instead. No, I just irritate them, and what irritates them most is that they don't know why they're irritated.'

Leonard put his book on the arm of the chair. 'I think that was how Tela felt about me.'

'Well she was wrong; you've never done an irritating thing in your life and neither have I. People would be so much better off if they could just accept our perfection and go from there.'

'I told her that.'

'And?'

'She said that one of my most irritating traits was thinking I was perfect.'

'Well, the truth is often irritating.'

With a smile, Leonard stood and began looking absent-mindedly at the several things on the mantelpiece – a block of quartz, an ammonite, a model brass cannon, a photograph of the three boys that must have been three or four years old, judging by the fact that Richard was still a toddler; a wedding photograph of William, Kathy and close family, in which Leonard appeared tall and a little tawdry. A shock, almost, for in his memory he'd been really quite dapper at that wedding, thinking himself an eligible and rather enigmatic thirty-seven year old who looked barely thirty. How wrong one can be about oneself! He looked in fact like he'd worked in artificial light too long and desperately needed exercise. And his hair – too much of it! – a stranger might have mistaken it for a toupé. The only asset he really had – and which the camera had failed to notice – was his eyes. They were amber and absolutely beautiful. Everybody would comment. Those amber eyes had travelled tenaciously and undiluted down six or seven generations of the maternal line, the family jewels as they'd become known – and the darkness of their original Greek origins had, in Leonard, been expelled by the backlight of some Nordic intervention on his father's side, with that the colour had reached its optimum intensity of honey-yellow that, in the sun, was almost musical in its pitch, or so their mother had said. Those eyes, which had eluded his brother entirely, forgave him his careless ageing and trumpeted his innate kindness; they set him apart in their way.

41

As for William, he was in the centre of the photograph sporting the beautiful suit he'd never again worn; he was mighty, like an old tree. He had stature and bearing standing there next to his tiny bride. It didn't do to look at their parents, arm-linked and hatted at the end of the row. Leonard shifted away from the photograph and sat again with the quartz in his hand, which he hadn't meant to pick up. He transferred it casually from palm to palm, which gave the impression, or so he hoped, that his next comment was incidental enough to be made in passing.

'There must be something you do in those groups, some specific thing. Something – I don't know – inappropriate. I'm not saying wrong, just inappropriate, for the circumstances.'

'My God, Leo, could you beat about that bush any harder?'

'There's no bush to beat about, I'm just posing a question.'

His brother stared at him, not a trace of the beautiful Deppling amber, just the light blue-grey of an indecisive sky. It was impossible not to think about the young man he'd seen outside, but he wouldn't ask; he wanted to see if William would mention it.

'What do you mean by "inappropriate"? I'm not sure I know.'

'*William.* Don't always pretend to be so naïve. You know how the world works, you know how people work, don't give me this fish-eyed wonder as if your mind was cobbled together five minutes ago.'

'Fish-eyed wonder! Oh to live with fish-eyed wonder instead of these tired old pieces of kit in my head.' His hands gestured towards his eyes, which were animate with humour. Then, in a lower key he said, 'I like it that you estimate me so highly, but it's too high. For what it's worth I might as well have been born this morning, for all the knowledge I have.'

A silence, that spread with the light. The room was warm. Dear William, he thought – when had he ever taken offence or borne a grudge? Leonard had never known where his brother's irrepressible goodwill came from, or whether goodwill was the right word for it – perhaps tireless love, or something else so unknown to his own temperament that he couldn't even name it.

'Kathy says you're in trouble – are you?'

'She thinks I'm always in trouble.'

'Yes, she said that too.'

'I don't believe I am, Leo, no.'

'And the students – they're from the university?'

'I think they've all been there at some point.'

'They still come, even though you left a decade ago?'

'Well they're not the same ones, Leo – and I wouldn't get carried away imagining hoards of them – there's a handful, if that. They come, they think something radical will happen, it doesn't, they either leave or stay in the hope that it will.'

William stood and opened the window behind him, then sat again. It was true that there was something about him that made one want to follow, there in the way he turned his wrist to work the latch as though he were freeing the window, not opening it for his own gain; and people had always followed him because of this capacity he had to make one feel he was granting them something they needed. How strange, for Leonard hadn't really been able to identify that before, the great feeling he always had that his brother was furnishing an unspoken need.

He said to William finally, warmly, and he hoped by way of conclusion, 'Well anyway, they can't get rid of you, let's face it. As you say, it's your group, and you give your time for nothing, which means you hold the cards.'

'So you think the person who does something for love has less to lose than the one who does it for money?'

'There are so many things you love, so many things you could do. There'll always be somebody to appreciate you, William – all

I'm saying is that you don't have to stay where you're not wanted. Shrug them off, forget about them.'

'Such hope and faith you have, Leo.'

It wasn't true, about the hopefulness or faithfulness; of the two of them the description better fit William. Besides, it almost certainly wasn't that William was unwanted. Leonard had been unfair. Probably William wasn't wasting his time with them, and probably they weren't ungrateful or uninterested in the least.

'Perhaps I'm a plague to them, Leo. Perhaps I should let those poor *youths* grow up in peace?'

And this was said ironically; the words might have been resigned but the tone wasn't, and he gazed at Leonard in anticipation of an answer.

'You probably turn a light on in their minds.'

'My,' William said. 'No wonder I'm disliked. It isn't pretty to have the contents of your mind illuminated.'

Leonard smiled, but it was shortened by his thinking once more of that boy, or man, who'd been outside. He drummed his hands against his thigh self-consciously, because William's presence tended to make him feel prudish. Really this made no sense, for if either of them was righteous or scrupulous, or virtuous in that old, robust sense of the word – where virtues were preconditions for doing good – it was surely William, and had always been. There'd been a time in their teenage years when Leonard had stolen a sum of money from his parents and William had been suspected, only because of the convincingness of Leonard's lies, and perhaps, Leonard later thought, because they knew if they blamed William he'd accept it without a fight. They did not appreciate confrontation, they were pacifists to a fault. William did accept it, and his acceptance was complete and unconditional. He believed in justice, and though he'd been done an injustice, it couldn't be remedied with the further injustice of

disloyalty towards his younger brother. There were times, probably countless times, when William's sedulous weighing up of
virtues had come to Leonard's rescue. Leonard had never quite
known how to thank him for that, or whether to thank him at
all; when he considered it now he realised he'd never so much
as acknowledged it.

He said, by way of a final comfort that was aimed perhaps at
himself as much as his brother, 'You do have to be careful with
what you say and do sometimes, William. Whatever you talk
about in those groups – or do outside of them – it doesn't really
matter, but you have to be careful. That's all.'

William's eyes fell directly on Leonard. 'You'd like me to be
careful about what I say and what I do?'

'Yes.'

William paused to close his eyes, as though something pained
him. 'You ask me that as if it's a new thought, a one-off favour
– and yet what we say and do is what we are, Leo. There isn't
ever a time that we can be careless about them.'

Leonard didn't reply; the precision and depth of his brother's
tone brought home to him the utter foolishness of his attempt
to correct or advise him, and how he, not William, always came
out of that endeavour the weaker one, and the one who stood
corrected.

'"My speech shall distil as the dew". Do you remember Father
quoting that when we were children, Leo, to make us watch our
tongues? It's wonderful really. "My speech shall distil as the dew".'

Leonard flushed at that, he felt the blood rise slowly to his
ears with the recollection. '"My doctrine shall drop as the rain".'

'"The small rain upon the tender herb".'

They said it together, and then simultaneously smiled and
looked away from one another towards the floor.

'How do I remember that?' Leonard asked. 'I haven't read the

Bible in decades. I remember it like I'd remember the words of a song.'

Leonard looked up at his brother again and offered a distracted smile. He resisted going upstairs to get the bottle of wine he'd brought, which was at the top of one of his boxes. In Edinburgh he'd drunk steadily from early evening most days, which had seemed credible then in his solitude, as if he were just seeking friendship. But now it occurred to him that it might be a good habit to break, and so he didn't go. William had closed his eyes again and had retreated out of the reach of Leonard's efforts at conversation. At once Leonard thought, *We should take life lightly*, and also, *We should live life deeply*. A worldview could turn on a sixpence. If his brother cocked his brow in that baiting way, then life was lightness; if he stilled his features and his eyes clouded, life was depth and weight. If he closed his eyes, life was simply elsewhere. Leonard couldn't remember a time when he hadn't measured and judged himself against his brother; now that William's eyes were closed it was as though the world, of which he was a part, had disappeared. He closed his own in tiredness and saw red from the whorl of sun, and felt the forgotten quartz in his palm.

'You have a beautiful mind,' he said to his brother suddenly and without too much thought. 'Don't listen to my worries. Don't change how you are.'

Dinner that day was late and quiet; Kathy had made chicken for herself, Leonard and the boys, with potatoes and vegetables, and William ate just the potatoes and vegetables, though larger portions, and a little extra bread.

'Thank you,' Leonard said, and was unsure if he meant it. He took some offence on William's behalf that she didn't bother to cater better for him; one had to wonder at that marriage, and what sustenance the last thirteen years had provided for either. He felt some guilt too, when he observed the mound of white, rather silken flesh, so thing-like on his plate, more thing-like even than the broccoli next to it. Yes, the flattened neck, the kinked and wasted neck! He hoped dearly that William wasn't judging the push of his fork through its poor thin skin, then he rallied in hunger and cut neatly through its breast meat and filled his mouth with it, as though to do so were to defy all that futile loss.

'Did anybody else hear the sirens the night before last?' he asked, glancing around the table.

He thought Kathy was about to concur, by the way she lifted her face to him to speak, lifted it with a kind of hopeful interest – but she was interrupted by her middle son. Abe dug his fork into a potato and replied, with a tone of limited patience, 'Big deal, sirens. There are sirens every night in London.'

Kathy reached across and brushed some food from Abe's hair. 'No need to be rude, he was only asking a question.'

'I heard the underground trains,' Richard said. 'They stopped me going to sleep.'

To this heartfelt and wide-eyed confession, Abe was incited again to correct, with impatience, 'You always say that, but I can't hear them and nobody else can hear them, and besides there aren't any trains in the night so stop making it up.'

'I did hear them.'

'You shouldn't lie.'

'Boys,' Kathy said. 'Please not now.'

'But he shouldn't lie.'

'I said not now.'

She did look to William briefly as if for reinforcement, but she must have seen what Leonard saw, for she gave up on that hope – a man sitting quiet and thoughtful and present, a clipped version of himself. It struck Leonard that this might be the only William Kathy knew, this ineffective observer and listener who emitted passive love and wanted nothing asked of him. It wasn't the man Leonard knew as his brother at all. When Richard reiterated to his father that he could hear the trains, William only replied kindly, 'Then that's fine,' and rubbed his youngest son's back in consolation. Then he returned to eating.

Half a minute might have passed in quiet grumbling, bickering and under-table strikes to the shin from one boy to another, which Leonard could feel pass his legs. Kathy stared at her children and laid a hand palm-down on the table in warning.

Then as if in emergence from a haze, William blinked, put his fork down and said calmly, 'It's true, Abe, that nobody should lie. You're perfectly right. And it's true that Richard thought he heard the trains, which means he doesn't think he's lying. In fact he's upset that you should think he is. So in this case none of us are in disagreement. So shall we be pleased about that and eat?'

He offered his children a long, compassionate look which asked for their reason, and they seemed to give it. Oli had remained silent, but he nodded, and his expressions were much more moderate and sombre than his younger brothers'. The boys had changed so much in the year since Leonard had seen them; Richard must be seven, he guessed, and had just the same heart-shaped angel face that William had had at that age, and had lost so completely by his teens. It had only to be hoped that Richard would manage to hold on to his long into adult life, for that life would be so much easier if he did, surely. Abe and Oli were more like ten and eleven; he felt he ought to know, but he'd lost track these last couple of years.

When some quiet fell, William looked at Leonard. 'I think I did hear sirens,' he said.

Leonard nodded at his brother, and quelled an urge to thank him.

The next day Leonard woke up to the high bare walls of William's room and wondered why and how. He sat on the edge of his bed and took his guitar, propped by the wall at the headboard, and plucked idly at the strings. He couldn't decide if the Hacker record player dominated the room because of its great archaic boxiness, or because of the significance attached to it in his mind. His parents would be pleased to know that among William's few possessions was a gift they'd bought him. William would have been about nineteen then; first it was the piano, then the violin, at which he excelled particularly, and then when William failed to follow up on his extreme talent in these areas, they bought the record player as a last attempt to maintain William's grasp on the musical. He might never have played a record on it – certainly Leonard couldn't remember a time. The absence of records in the room and on the turntable gave the impression that the machine created and sung its own tune. It was well kept and dusted; on closer inspection he saw it had a Goldring Sapphire stylus, probably the very stylus that the player had come with.

Oh, there was never any doubt that William could have seen his whole career through as a musician – the way he could play Paganini, and then with equal skill Bach or Mendelssohn, and draw the pieces from his bow with complete understanding. Leonard played too but never so well, and perhaps that was one of the quirks that maintained life's equity, that with the odd exception it was the less good who continued and the gifted who gave up. Otherwise every field of expertise would be practised only by the gifted, and the hobbyists and enthusiasts would lose hope and motive. It was important – or so their parents had stressed – that one does a thing out of enjoyment as much as skill. With this, Leonard had come to understand, they could reconcile themselves to the under-used talent of one son and over-used talent of the other.

Leonard went back to bed for an hour and read his novel, and as he propped himself to read he thought, Here is another pastime William shuns. He wouldn't read novels and he wouldn't write anything substantial; for all those views expressed year after year, and the campaigns he made for prison reform, the rights of women, educational reform, he still never committed a single word of ideology to paper. More perplexingly still, Leonard thought, there'd been that short year or two William had spent as a lecturer in ethics, a senior lecturer no less – simply invited to the position, or more rightly the position falling at his feet as the world always seemed to have – and even then he hadn't published any papers in his own right. He'd talk openly about any issue, and if his listeners wanted to put those spoken words on paper they could, and could take the credit if they wished – but he believed, for he'd said it to Leonard himself – that the only tool that could begin to pick apart life with any degree of accuracy was language, and the only form of language that was fit for the task was the spoken word. Where the written word lay prone and pinioned on the page, the spoken probed deeply and flexibly through the dimensions, and the sung word was acrobatic, sylphlike, vaulting. And philosophy was the pure song, the purest of songs, heard only with training, and hanging at a pitch outside of the common range. Too easily obscured by other sounds, be they traffic, be they Bach; so he said, and Leonard had thought that was noble, but had struggled with it.

But what do you *like* and *dislike?* Leonard had often wanted to ask his brother. For we're animals first and humans second

– what about your appetites and the things you just happen to want? Within William's impassioned tastes things were either hated or loved, and they were hated or loved on principle; thus he hated meat because he hated the cruelty of animal slaughter; he loved to give and receive gifts because he loved to find humanity generous and beautiful, even where it erred; he loved Carlos Puebla because he loved to hear a voice lifted in protest. But who knew if, beneath those principles, he liked the taste of meat, or liked the gifts he received, or liked the music of Carlos Puebla? Of course, where basic tastes ended and the world of complex preferences began was unclear and available for inquiry in anybody's case, but the question couldn't even present itself for William; his moral stances had consumed his basic appetites. To any outside eye at least, his appetites had stopped existing in themselves, as basic, needy things. Human first and animal second.

These weren't Leonard's own independent thoughts about William, but more or less inherited from their father. He tended to agree with them all the same. Maybe he couldn't but agree when he had his father's voice so lodged in his head, repeating on him in the urgent tone of a dying man. Why is William this way, why is he that? Why doesn't he work, he used to work, why not now? That excellent job at the university which he walked away from as if it were nothing to him, and now a family to support. Once you've dirtied your hands with politics you can never wash them clean. Why doesn't he visit? Why did he give up the violin? He is so uneasy with life! Your mother and I brought him up in the normal manner, just as we did you – we allowed him to be a child and play in mud and eat ice cream with wafers and we allowed you both to fight and run about in the old quarry, animal first and human second.

From within the urgent scrutiny of these questions Leonard

did always try to form careful answers. Sometimes they weren't so much true as palliative, for he didn't know the answers himself. He *is* normal, he's just very sincere – isn't this the way you'd have him be? So much of Leonard's last year had been spent in this kind of forced consideration of his brother that those considerations had become habitual, like his drinking.

By the time he was dressed and had gone downstairs in the hope of finding William, the house was empty. He walked into Islington and then the longer stretch up to Highbury, and looked in the windows of estate agents without any committed interest. He wondered if he could say he was looking; really he was only seeing, and largely his reflection at that. He saw himself in the glass, quite solid but with rectangular absences made by the advertisements for properties, and that did seem to settle it – that somehow those houses depleted him. Well, it was a suppositional victory but a victory anyway; there was no rush to move out of William's house, neither William nor Kathy had implied any deadline; he did wonder, when he thought about it again, if Kathy didn't seem a little relieved to have other adult company even if in the form of an ill-liked brother-in-law. When he'd said at dinner that he'd heard the sirens and she'd looked at him as though to say, I heard them too – well of course she hadn't said it in the end, because she was so used to her words being usurped by her children's – but hadn't there been something like gratitude in her face, gratitude in the corroboration of that experience, in the sharing of it, in a way that suggested its rareness?

He got some groceries – cornflakes, a loaf of rye and spelt bread which he'd always used to like, coffee, a punnet of raspberries, some Kinder chocolate for the children – and then went to sit in Barnard Park in the warmth of the sun. Children scurried, flowed like little breaking waves over the adventure playground, climbing, dropping and dispersing, and their constant movement bewitched him.

He watched for a few minutes and then took out the teaching notes he'd brought with him, which he spread in a conspicuous arc. The arc soon became a single pile anchored by the bag of groceries to defy the breeze he hadn't known was there, and over this pile he leaned with some intent. The presence of the mothers with their children obliged him to appear productive – to be working, *doing* something, doing a useful thing in the world, rather than melting there in the sun. So he tried to imagine again what it was like to be a religious studies teacher and to picture himself chalking up on the board the main concepts of Islam, or Buddhism, or Shintō. That his father asked him so much about William's joblessness and never remembered to ask about his career both offended and relieved him, for he wasn't sure his father, a vicar after all, understood about a non-religious man teaching religion, or understood wrongly, as though that were Leonard's guilty concession to a faith he'd otherwise rejected.

Every year he'd start his term by playing his students five minutes of a match between Wasps and Saracens, a fairly old match on a VHS, a tight 27–26 victory to Saracens. There it is, he'd say, and he'd recount what his brother had once commented on. There it is, you watch the men run forward towards the touchline, clutching the rugby ball as if it were a firstborn, and you have it – the basis of religiosity itself, which is the determined attempt to get from here to there. Look at the grace of the game; all acts of determination are graceful because it's determination that refines us – look at the way the players weave down the pitch with mind and body in united pursuit of one goal. Look at them, Dallaglio, Hill – there's only one thing on their minds:

to get the ball over that line. What is the line? The marker between all there is and all that's still to be achieved. Crossing that line isn't the reward, it's the point, why the game is played, why the players exist.

That was always the first lesson, the video and a discussion about it. After that he went about the teaching of religion as a doctor goes about an X-ray, with a mind for the diagnosis of a disorder. He liked to teach it as a tale that revealed cultures, psyches, a certain richness of human imagination and spirit, but also as a tale that traced the progress of man's mistake-making, so that one could attempt to say in the telling, this is where and how we went wrong, here, here and here. The Inquisition, the witch hunts, the jihads. It wasn't cynicism, he only believed himself to be rational. He wanted to reveal where imagination ceased to be rich and met and fed off its own limits. Perhaps then those young people he taught could make better choices and belief systems that weren't founded on fantasies.

The heat grew, and he moved to the shade and lay his notes on the cooler grass. At some point he fell asleep and woke to a high sun. The heat wasn't as pressing now as it had been in July, and though his face was slightly burnt he could feel some lift and travel in the air. He stood; a different set of children swung about in the playground. He collected up his notes and made his way to the Bellevue, wondering if that was where William was. He wanted to coax him outside for a long, late lunch, to bring him outside to eat on the grass and maybe have a glass of wine, or maybe just to sit in the sun without having to speak at all. So he went there, but when he climbed the stairs he saw there was no sign of William or of anyone.

*

Their father's dying wish was for Leonard to find out the truth about William. That had been his lovely Delphic phrasing, *The truth about William*, and for all its profundity it actually meant only one thing, which was whether or not William had been responsible for the violence the Bellevue Group had caused on the day of the Poll Tax Riots. Leonard had decided that one must try not to be scornful or impatient with a dying man, and must appear to be on his side, but it wasn't easy; for William hadn't even been present at the riots. At most the question their father asked was whether William had been in some respect behind the Bellevue Group's actions in the riots, which was, to Leonard's mind, a hopelessly nebulous question. And if it turned out he had, what then? Would that be the truth about him, in some supposedly spiritual sense? Would that be his soul diagnosed?

An impossible and absurd task he'd been set; there was hardly going to be a piece of paper on which was written, Indeed he was responsible, or, Indeed he wasn't. Leonard hadn't intended even to go about answering that question for his father, but he found himself rounding the table and glancing through the papers scattered across it. They were notes from whatever meeting William had last had with his group of young followers, and it seemed that the discussion had been about the chickens – there were a few cartoonish drawings of the birds, one of the bird under a boot, some scant notes too that weren't sufficient to piece together any line of argument as such, but it was clear by the annotations that there'd been some kind of debate on right and wrong. *Properties of rightness, properties of wrongness; what difference between killing animal to eat (when other food available) and killing for fun? What makes somebody do the wrong thing?*

Though it ought not to have, that really amused him – the fact that his brother had challenged his protégés with the matter of the poor birds; there was something wilfully infantile or deflationary in William making a topic of them that caused him to laugh briefly aloud. Not war or sex or anarchy or Marxism, but chickens. They weren't exactly planning a revolution here in this room, he thought, and he wondered if any of those notes were written by the hand of that man he'd seen outside the house; if so, more farcical still that his keen young head should be filled with talk of the plight of a few luckless creatures.

He began to go through some of the piles of papers on the bookcase, and those also that were buttressed up against the side of the bookcase. Much of it was notes, agendas, some newspaper clippings of demonstrations, events or concerns the Bellevue Group had been involved with all that time ago; a number of magazines issued by the Anarchist Federation. He read through the scrawl on some of the papers. *Anti power*, somebody had written, as though to remind him or herself what it was they were all meant to believe. *Whose interests are at heart?*

There were papers going back years to various campaigns the group had run, from petitioning to keep the local pre-school open to opposing the Persian Gulf War. He read a few sentences on that theme. *We didn't want troops there in the first place, why should we now support them? It's the role and obligation of the commanders to do this, not the civilians – stand up for your beliefs first, and for your country second.* In the margin of another typed set of minutes was written and underlined *Shamal? Dry and baking wind.* There was nothing to which that was in connection. And in fact it was as though such a dry and baking wind had blown through the Bellevue itself, withering its ideologies and preserving them at this lesser functionless state. Leonard let the papers drop back to the pile.

There were also some photographs of the Bellevue's early days, before the Group had formed, when the disused café and upstairs room were little more than drinking dens for the wealthy and many friends of Aleph – Aleph, whom Leonard would rather, but would never, forget. Taken largely at night, and by candlelight, the handful of pictures was dark and spectral – skilled though, taken with careful long exposures that lifted the picture's subject softly forward from the background blur – a young face with bright eyes, dusk-swaddled figures so sensuous, Leonard thought, so sensuous. William was in most of them, and was always one of the figures picked into focus, always given significance and always – though inherent to the scene – putting himself somehow at a remove, not as though to say he didn't want to be there or felt himself unwelcome, but that he necessarily stood apart in the way a white ball stands apart from the coloured in a game of pool – that was, by dint of its separate function.

Aleph must have taken those photographs, for she was in none of them but one, and that one was taken by a lesser photographer. It lacked the seductiveness and quality of the others. Leonard hadn't forgotten how beautiful she was but he'd forgotten the details of the beauty; her high, broad forehead that gave to such extremely large eyes, and the perfect paintstroke of a nose, a calligraphic briefness and sureness about it, and the classical rosebud mouth, a fine chin from which scalloped the long elegant line of her jaw up to white seashell ears; she surely had more existence in her face than Leonard had in his entire body. Cropped red hair that sprung in curls and sat so sculpturally on her head, long and loose-limbed body that had artless grace; she carried it with her as if she barely knew it was there. That purple velvet coat she often wore with its high collar and fitted waist, in the style of the romantics. In the photograph she was sitting next to William and smiling at him, with her hands wrapped almost protectively around one of his and the sleek black head of her beloved dog pressing its nose towards their conjoined fingers, for the dog went wherever she did, and loved whoever she loved.

William had done well, they'd all used to joke – if you were going to save somebody's life and consign them forever to your service, it might as well be somebody rich and beautiful.

Homer talked, didn't he, about trading bronze for gold; the young man gives the older man his beauty, and in return the older man gives the younger his wisdom. The wisdom is worth more because the beauty is fleeting, but it is given anyway as part of the wise man's verdant desire to make the world less ignorant and less dark. One could almost infer Homer's point from those photographs, albeit that times had changed and that a woman might now sit in that role too. In Leonard's heart he thought William would laugh at him for those inferences, would tell him what he thought of the Classics – the god-squabbling and the hubris and the huffing and puffing of hot air. But for all of that he thought it anyway, for he had no other way of understanding what he saw. If it wasn't anything to do with wisdom and beauty then it was to do with sex, infatuation – and it was nothing to do with those. His belief in William's integrity in that respect was absolute in a way it might not be with any other person on earth. Whatever William gained from his relationships with other people, and whatever he wanted in return for the love he gave those people, it wasn't that.

He put the photographs away, and stacked the papers back in no particular order on and against the bookcase. He realised that Aleph had become so mythical to him that to see photographs of her was peculiar and unsettling; there'd been a time when he'd dreamt of her often, rising from the water, the flames or the ashes, beauteous creature reborn! It had never been possible for him to clearly imagine the true scenario in which his brother had pulled her from their bombed ship in Falkland Sound, she a junior naval chef, he responsible for her – yes, pulled her from a burning warship in a most unmodern and classical way which predestined their whole relationship to greatness, as though divine light had issued from the fingertips of God's own hand and made them heroes.

In a small, silken drawstring bag pressed just under the rear foot of the bookcase, flattened and dust-webbed, he found a crushed pack of *Peace* cigarettes his brother had bought him some six years before. How they'd got there was anybody's guess but their appearance made him smile, because he'd forgotten about that phase. For a short time William had taken to buying him those *Peace* cigarettes from Japan and *Kool* from America and *Camels* made with real Turkish tobacco, and there'd been others besides – on a mission to kill me, Leonard had joked, and received the gifts wholeheartedly. He'd been a serious smoker in those days, so much so that he didn't merely smoke but had a smoking career, one that required experimentation, research and determination. Therefore William would scour London's tobacconists for imports and post them first class from north London to Hertfordshire in heavy cream envelopes that always had such luxurious promise – a singular act of collusion, Leonard had used to think, a great solidarity between them that defied sabotage by morality or lung cancer.

He put that mostly smoked pack of Japanese cigarettes in his pocket. Enough for today, then, quite enough. He knew his brother wouldn't be offended by the little inquest; *Investigate me*, he might say, and he might well be delighted that somebody should raise him up in that way to the light. For he'd always said that a thing was most vital and relevant when it was being examined; it responded to the touch, and came alive in the hands. It became *available* again, was how he'd exactly put it – when he'd once, as a teenager, taken some of their parents' dahlias and pulled petals from stems from stamens, and set them out to have their veins and filaments scored open with a pin, that was what he'd said in his frank defence – that far from destroying them he'd made the flowers available again, available to be observed in all their elemental floweriness, relieved of form, reborn.

A delicate rain fell that night, drop by careful drop onto the wide leaves of the fig tree. By morning the green of the world had responded in what Leonard could only see as gladness. Every colour of every plant was a better version of itself, and every stalk held its flower that little more purposefully aloft into yet another optimal day of blue warmth.

There in the public garden across the street, as though part of that new purpose, was William, sitting on the bench in the moist sunlight. It was rare to see him anywhere in the morning except for his own back garden, by the fruit trees. On spotting him from the bedroom window Leonard dressed quickly, set the coffee pot on the stove, and went out to him, patting his shoulder.

'This is not English, this weather,' he said, and sat by his side. 'There must have been a mistake.'

'Some of the best things in life have happened by mistake,' William replied, shoulders rounded and heavy, but eyes bright.

'Why are you sitting out here?'

'The back garden's in the shade now first thing in the morning. I'm exiled.'

Leonard smiled. 'Not a bad exile.' And William shook his head slowly.

The day came warm and freshly minted, miles upon miles of unused light at their fingertips. In Leonard's view cities suffered a lack of horizons that pulled tricks on the soul, led one to feel trapped, led the soul to believe in small, crushed, spent things. It was odd, given that, to feel as he did in that moment a sort of oceanic lack of limits. The summer might never end, it actually might never. He turned towards his brother and asked, 'Were you praying?'

'I prefer to call it meditating, that seems to horrify people less. Meditating is for eccentrics, praying is for lunatics. But yes, yes I was.'

'Well, sorry to disturb you.'

'Don't be sorry – what I pray for is other people, the love and companionship of other people.'

'And behold, here is another person. Until the coffee's ready anyhow.'

'Ah, yes. I forgot to ask for the *endless* companionship of other people.'

'Probably just as well – the endless bit might be seen as pushy, whereas I suppose, *just until the coffee pot's boiled* is reasonable enough.'

'Quite, any old god could see his way to that.'

William angled his face up towards the sun, plant-like in that unfurling and inevitable movement.

Leonard tucked a thumb under his belt hook and sat back; along the main road there was a gathering tension of car horns and building traffic caused by a disturbance he couldn't see, but which was prompting others to stand and observe. They both turned their heads towards it, and then back to the deep, tranquil garden and birds quivering from branch to branch. He said to William, 'What are your plans for the day?'

'Oh, just the usual I suspect.'

'Which is what?'

William shrugged, and smiled. 'I'll probably go down to Regent's Canal, with the weather the way it is.'

'Regent's Canal? Is that where you go?'

'Sometimes – there are all the narrow boats down there and

people living nose to nose, and holidaymakers, walkers. I love the life of it.'

Leonard looked down at his hands and didn't respond. It might be safe to assume that this was what Kathy referred to when she said William roamed around *pestering* people; from his father's lamentations he had a vague idea of it himself anyway, that his brother liked to insinuate himself – his father's phrase – into groups and communities, an idea the old man was utterly uncomfortable with. If one had something to say, it was right to wait for others to come willingly to hear it, to a place designated for that purpose – the lecture hall, the church, the mosque, the training ground. Never push one's views, never go out to convert. If one's message is worth hearing then others will listen of their own accord. Precisely because their father had found fault with William on this score, Leonard's instinct was to be gentle and accepting about it. It really wasn't good enough to reduce a person you love to a tight diminishment of failures. Thus he kept his tone warm and leavened. 'Have you befriended people down there by the canal then?'

His brother considered this briefly. 'I'd call them friends, yes – though I suppose they might not.'

With a short pause, Leonard asked, 'And, what – do you speak to them about religion?'

'My God, no. Who'd want to hear that? To speak to them about my faith would be like speaking to them about my washing habits – completely personal and of no interest.'

Leonard looked hard up the road once more at the unrest and spoke without shifting his gaze. 'I've noticed that you pray quite often. I hadn't realised.'

'I do.' William lowered his head again.

'Pa asked me a few times, before he died, what the nature of your faith was. That's how he put it, the *nature of your faith*. He knew the nature of mine and preferred not to mention it. But yours – I couldn't answer.'

'So what did you say?'

'I said you believed in a supreme being. It wasn't a satisfying answer, I think it was so unsatisfying he decided to give up asking, actually.'

'You're exactly right in what you told him.'

'A supreme being?'

'Yes.'

Leonard regarded his brother's face, which seemed to offer an undefended kindness and hopefulness, and yet gave no ground. If the eyes looked into the middle distance before him and saw doubt, well then no twitch betrayed it. If, behind the large, furrowed forehead, ageless and tiny godless thoughts formed, no words ventured them. For once, he didn't offer his puzzlement, he didn't hold his mouth in a small o in readiness for a question. Just that answer: Yes. A supreme being. And he ventured what appeared to be an ingenuous pleasure at the certainty of his faith.

'He brought up the time you called the Bible the work of lying poets,' Leonard said with a smile. 'I think he found that a bit galling.'

William bit at his thumbnail and then brought his hands together on his lap. 'Really? I don't see why.'

'Well, without wishing to be pernickety, William, the Bible is pretty important to a vicar.'

'So it is – the tool of his trade. He must have thought I was attacking his faith itself.'

Leonard took a lighter and the flattened cigarette pack from the front pocket of his jeans, and managed to extract with care one of the less broken cigarettes, bent though it was. 'I imagine that would've been exactly what he thought.'

'And if I told a carpenter his hammer was faulty he'd think I was dismissing carpentry itself? If I told a teacher his textbooks were unreliable he'd think I was dismissing teaching itself?'

'It's hardly the same. A hammer isn't the founding principle of carpentry, William.'

'And the Bible isn't the founding principle of Christianity. That would be Christ.'

Leonard lit his cigarette and, smiling, threw his hand up. 'Fine, I submit.'

By then the cause of the disturbance had begun to edge its way into view, a hundred or so people marching along the pavement and spilling out onto the road, a fuel protest it seemed from their majuscule slogans and chants, pitching their placards up with repeated No, No, No; eighty per cent fuel tax is too high! Seen obliquely, a strange way to spend a beautiful morning, Leonard thought, to walk a gutter and shout No into such an immaculate sky. William watched while drawing his hand across his chin in some deep curiosity, and when he finally removed his attention from that sight it was abrupt, as though a thought process had been suddenly resolved.

'Did Jesus exist?' Leonard asked, surprised by the question as soon as it left his tongue; he turned to face his brother squarely.

'Yes, without doubt.'

'And he was the son of God?'

'Only in the sense that we're all the sons and daughters of God.'

Leonard looked down at his knees and watched the filigree tip of the burning cigarette, beautiful really, for all that it was. 'You mean he was one of us?'

'Yes.'

'And so how could his death save us from our sins?'

'I don't believe he died to save us from our sins.'

'*Shock exposé*,' Leonard whispered, and his brother raised his brows and smiled. There was something about the chanting of the surrounding protest that drove their own conversation into a depth and earnestness Leonard wouldn't usually have given the subject; here in the garden, quietly speaking of Jesus. He inhaled on the stale tobacco and looked across at his brother in expectation.

'I see it this way, Leo – that Jesus was just a man – an extraordinary one, but still just a man. He was killed as the Bible said, betrayed by Judas and nailed to a cross. But this is the thing – if you want to understand the spirit of Christianity you have to forget about Jesus the man and think more abstractly. And before you sigh, Leo,' he added kindly, 'don't think this is a cheap way out. Abstraction isn't a shortcoming of religion, it's a shortcoming of our grasp on enormity. Science encounters exactly the same problems.'

Leonard shrugged and nodded, and he reached down to cast the emptied shell of a snail into the foliage behind. 'I accept that.'

'Imagine that God looked on all his people and saw that somehow, though he'd created them as one, in brotherhood with one another, they'd each started to think themselves separate and disparate and fearful of what the other might do to them. God could see their unity, but they'd lost sight of it. They'd dreamed themselves clear of Him. They'd become so preoccupied with the idea that they were each one, single, vulnerable individual that they began to believe they had to harm one another if it meant defending themselves, and they lost sight of the fact that there was nothing they needed to defend, that they were safe and without sin.'

William spoke with a slowness and quiet decisiveness, without any gesticulation, with care, as though custodian to every word he offered out; even if it transpired that what he said was wrong, it was said with a clear mind. I have never been able to speak this way, Leonard thought; I have never had the clarity when it came to it.

'God wanted to remind them,' William said. 'Jesus was His magic trick, at least this is my own way of seeing it, if you'll forgive the crudeness of it. He said to His creations, Let me show you something. I'm going to send a human being your way whom you are going to kill out of fear, and in resurrecting him I'm going to show you that neither your fear nor his death had any reality. I want you to watch this piece of magic and smile. This wasn't God's punishment, it was His reassurance. This wasn't Jesus shouldering our sins, it was God showing us that we have no sins to shoulder, except the ones we imagine for ourselves.'

Leonard sat back; in part he wanted to say something facetious about, perhaps, how Jesus himself might not have appreciated the trick, or about the amateurishness of God's magic given how badly the trick turned out to work. After all, we are still fighting, he thought, we're more afraid than ever. But that very fact was what stopped his facetious remarks, for he felt embarrassed in the face of a God in whom he didn't even believe – embarrassed that he, too, had failed to notice the trick and was still slouching and doubting, still heckling, still dreaming himself clear, as William put it.

He got to his feet and went a few steps across the path ostensibly to flatten off some disturbed gravel with his foot. He extinguished his cigarette in the dust. By now the protesters had camped themselves at the mouth of the petrol station on the far side of the main road, and there was growing unease there – cars trying to drive past them, the staff of the station trying to move them, they stamping their placards on the ground in petulance.

He said, addressing his brother, 'I like the thought that we aren't sinful at least. It seems a relief.' He added, 'I mean it. I like that thought very much.'

William nodded. 'Many don't.'

'Well, of course they don't – it's part of the religious tradition to be sinners – what role would God have if He didn't need to save us from ourselves.'

'It isn't only the religious who dislike the idea. Most people are allied to sin, because if you accept that there's no such thing you not only stop being sinful yourself, but others do too. And if others aren't sinful, how do we blame them? We hate so deeply having nobody else to blame.' William put his hands to his waist and straightened. 'At least, I so deeply hate that, even though I pretend to myself I don't. But perhaps it's just me.'

Leonard gave a short laugh and scrubbed at the gravel again with his foot, thinking at once that what his brother said was true – for blame was there in everything, and everywhere in himself – and wondering also why all this contemplation mattered. What seemed to matter was having a job and feeding one's children and the price of fuel, and if there was sin or no sin, one's children still had to be fed, one's tank filled, and eighty per cent tax was still probably too much. He went and sat, feeling the heat of the bench, the heat of the air as the sun began to upend itself once again above the city, the good generous warmth of it which felt internal to him and not from an outside source.

He said, 'Jesus as man, then, is real. Jesus as saviour is spiritual myth.'

William replied, 'Myth? It's an interesting word.' He stooped as if pushed physically by consideration of things. 'Well, it's no myth that Jesus lived truth and exposed truth. And it's no myth that the living and exposing of truth is a form of life-saving – not to be underestimated, though we do underestimate it all the time.' He paused, then said, 'But yes, Jesus as saviour has become mythical to us. All stories become mythical given time – they're myths because they've endured and not because they aren't true. And in that sense, yes, Jesus the saviour is a spiritual myth, but in my humble view the deepest, most beautiful spiritual myth we have.'

Leonard smiled his surprise. 'And yet of all the ones I teach, the Christian one has always seemed the least beautiful, the most crude and blood-drenched.'

'The most misunderstood, even by Christians.'

'Well, perhaps.'

He leaned into the bench with his elbows rested on its back and tilted his head upwards, exposing his throat to the daylight. 'I found these yesterday at the Bellevue,' he said, and pulled the cigarettes from his pocket, gave them a mild shake. 'You bought them for me when I was first with Tela – do you remember?'

William looked across serenely, smiled, and said, 'What kind of real smoker are you, having some left all these years later?'

'I found them under the bookcase at the Bellevue – I *assure* you I would have smoked them sooner if I'd known they were there.'

He knew that William wouldn't ask what he was doing looking under that bookcase, otherwise he might not have brought the topic up; he didn't want, and had never wanted, to go into the matters of the past with his brother or be seen to be one of the people who doubted him. But there, now he'd raised it and nobody could say he was avoiding speaking about it; just that there was clearly nothing to speak about, and no will for it on either side. He took one of the four remaining cigarettes, snapped it in half where it was broken, then lit it and pulled a foot up onto the bench.

A small number of the protest group, some fifteen or twenty, had broken away from the petrol station and had crossed the road towards where he and his brother sat. They began marching around the outside perimeter of the garden and posting flyers onto the windscreens of parked cars. 'They're rounding us up,'

William muttered, and folded his hands in his lap to watch them with something akin to amusement.

'"Around the sheep do the wolves gather",' Leonard replied with a smile and some jauntiness, and a lungful of smoke. He had no view on fuel prices and he wondered if he should. He looked backwards at the house, to the windows darkened against the bright day, and was taken by a strange urge to see Kathy inside there doing some unselfconscious thing – picking something up, putting something down, closing something, opening something, saying unheard words.

'You said, William, that we've forgotten about the unity between men, this brotherhood that God still knows about and is trying to remind us of. The thing is, I see nothing of it in humans. I see kindness at times, among all the bullshit, and I see love. But that doesn't amount to unity.'

William made himself intent on a small mark near the collar of his own shirt, in such a place that he could barely see it. His chin was forced into his chest, his eyes craned down and right, and he began working at it with his thumb as though it absorbed all his focus. 'Do you look?' he asked.

'For unity?'

'Yes – you say you don't see it. I wondered if you looked.'

'No, I suppose not.' He took a more shallow draught on his cigarette, because two in fifteen minutes was excessive for him these days and not the great liberation he vaguely hoped it might be. He said, 'But if there's a truth as big as that I expect it to come and find me – isn't that in its remit?'

William ceased worrying away at his shirt and he answered, 'Yes, it's well within its remit. But if a truth came and found you, without you having the slightest interest in it, would you recognise it?'

'I don't know.'

'It seems to me that seeing is nothing without looking, just as hearing is nothing without listening.'

Leonard could see that his brother's hands had contracted to fists in his pockets and that they were held tight and still with sincerity. 'And so when you pray you're looking, and listening. I take it that's what you mean.'

'All of life is recollecting the truths that have been forgotten, Leo. All true knowledge, as they say, is recollection – so I ask to remember.'

'That you're not separate from God, you mean?'

'That when I partake in the perfection of God I'm not separate from anything, that I belong, as we all do.'

'And how do you *partake in the perfection of God?*'

'By never ceasing to question what's put before me, and never assuming I know what anything means. Complacency and arrogance will be the first to undo us.'

William's smile was untroubled but vulnerable, as if he recognised fully and properly that this partaking in God wasn't a thing he knew well enough or did often enough – that he wasn't expert, just willing. He stood and wandered a few steps away. Leonard pushed his shirtsleeves further up his arms in the gathering warmth and stood also.

He said, 'Well, I've just recollected the truth that I put the coffee on twenty minutes ago.'

William turned to him. 'In my next prayer I'll ask for forgiveness for the ruination of the coffee pot.'

'Do you think it'll be granted?'

'The Lord will be relieved, Leo, that for once that's all I'm asking for.'

That remark coincided with a strengthening of the protest calls, and a car alarm sounding. What Leonard felt suddenly was an enormous unrest in the world. An irritable fidgeting of the soul rising up in dispute against every issue, rather like the kicking and keeling of a baby in an outgrown womb. Every age has its unrest, he thought then, but this one more so, or the irritation is more noxious and fevered; there is more fear. Women are out on the streets shouting about fuel tax; there is a new century, there are more of us in the world, we are more worried.

He did manage to bury the thought, but he disliked it that the small prompt of a number of people with placards and voices had darkened him when he'd always kept his chin up, always. Must get inside and hope that the coffee pot hasn't exploded, he thought. William gestured to him with comic elaborateness, in the direction of the house, *after you*, and kicked the stiffness gently from his knees.

For the next few days Leonard found that he was observing his brother's small rituals around the house. William tended to get up early and sit first in the garden and then, moving with the light, across the street. He watched the birds in the two apple trees in the centre of his lawn, and if it weren't for the fact that he flexed his toes he might have looked peacefully dead. He ate crackers and piccalilli. He seemed not to shower, at least not often. If the telephone rang, or the door, he never answered it. Unfussily he did housework – collecting in the washing, putting out the bins, refilling the shelves from the extra store of groceries in the cupboard under the stairs. He was attentive and accurate in these tasks, as if he found some reverence in their triviality.

For all the housework he did with quiet willingness, and for all that he'd used to be a naval chef by profession, still he never cooked; to Leonard, his being a naval chef deployed to cook Britain's way through the Falklands War was a fact that had reasserted itself bewilderingly. Brother of mine, fighting for Thatcher and an empire we don't believe in. Don't you remember saying, We are citizens of the world! But whether or not he understood his brother was academic, for he knew that William did nothing haphazardly even if the reasons were unclear to others. There was always a seam of logic, no matter how raggedly sewn, that joined the events of his life, and in the large view observation of him did clarify more than it obfuscated.

In any case the observations went on. William wasn't dismissive of his sons but spoke to them little, and when they brought a punctured ball for him to fix, he gave them a repair kit and told them they should learn. He told them kindly and with respect. The boys brought the ball to Leonard; Leonard mended it on the quiet.

He went out for most of the afternoon; sometimes presumably to the Bellevue for his youth group, or to the canal, and who knew where else – but he didn't offer explanations and nor had he ever. He watched cartoons with the boys in the early evening and his eyes sparkled with laughter; then he used the back room to stretch, which consisted of him circling his arms stiffly forwards and backwards, and twisting his spine to the side, and releasing several cracks softly. He was a man of routine, which Leonard kept finding himself interrupting; but even in those intimate ten minutes of stretching he didn't resent Leonard's presence – he invited Leonard to stay. No, Leonard said; it's fine, I'm just fetching my book.

He prayed, also, irregularly but often. Leonard didn't know how many times a day or week, but he walked in on him doing so the morning after their conversation in the public garden and hurried out of the room before the silence of the prayer was disturbed. He prayed standing, and not with the usual dipped head but with his chin tilted up, and his eyes closed but alert like those of the dreamer. His hands didn't supplicate, but rather hung irrelevantly at his sides, so that it might not seem that he was praying at all except for that lifted votive chin, and the movement across his eyelids that reminded Leonard of sunlight moving across the surface of water. He didn't look at all entrenched in a dead tradition when he prayed, but engaged in an act of reinvention and pioneering that altered the very dynamic of a room; you could walk in and you'd know right away: William's praying. So then you'd walk away again.

And he had no friends. That was a guess on Leonard's part, for how could he know – yet he knew. He had the youth group, of course, but aside from that, when he came back from his afternoons out he had all the shortness and distance of a man who'd been alone, even if alone amongst people. Or maybe to say he had no friends was too simplistic a way of putting something quite complex – for he'd always been a relentless socialite who was loved – not liked – and admired, and generous in his admiration and inclusion of others, so that it had seemed to Leonard that he lived in an exulted sphere of fealty and zealous affection that Leonard himself couldn't even begin to enter, and so never tried. And yet, what occurred to Leonard during those few days of observation was that William's actual attachments had probably only ever been few and that the sphere, if it existed at all, was for him a place of transit on his way to a deeper solitariness that seemed beyond love, love in all its phantasmal *fantasticalities*, love with all its comic failures. If he'd always kept for himself that aura of distant self-containment, the trait had become so much more exaggerated with age, and that was what Leonard noticed most – that even when laughing at a cartoon with his sons or declaring global brotherhood alongside that restless shiver in the strings of Puebla's guitar, still a more significant part of William was alone.

There were also the trances. Leonard had hoped those trances were something his brother would grow out of as he got older, but as he lugged the lawnmower out of the shed one afternoon he saw William come into the garden and stop as though something had grabbed his attention, then stand motionless and stare ahead for some minutes. Leonard had called to him – William, all well? – but he didn't get a response, nor truly expect one. His brother was an unhurried creature and capable of strangeness. Catalepsy, their father had worried; William suffers from a form of catalepsy, needs medication for those trances or he'll get himself knocked over by a bus one of these days. Why always a bus? Leonard had wondered in dismay, and had dismissed the worry with placating comments – just silences, Father, silences and contemplation, just ways of escaping the pace of the world for a moment, like praying.

But their father was right in a sense – the trances weren't really like praying, for the stillness of the prayers was energetic and wakeful whereas the trances were inert, they were mid-motion stoppages, Leonard had often thought, or little breakdowns. Catalepsy was possible, the doctors said, maybe that or maybe something else. They'd been linked at least to his abnormally low heartrate which sat at around forty-five at the worst of times, a languid thrub that couldn't keep up with the second hand of the clock. Once every test had been run to eliminate this ailment or that, it had been reluctantly agreed that he was just unusual, and might not live an especially long or energetic life. He'd been offered a pacemaker which he refused. He'd told nobody but Leonard about the heartrate and the refusal of a pacemaker because he didn't want others to worry or to try to change his mind. I have the heartrate of a crocodile, he'd said to Leonard quite proudly, as though that in some way safeguarded his health. More animals would come to mind. A cow chewing the cud, her heart winding slowly on with the gathering and disbanding of clouds. A fish blubbing its vacant search through water. Leonard strove not to see that animal aspect in William, but at that moment in the garden he could – he could see the heaviness of life collecting around his brother's shoulders, back and waist – the bunching together of matter, the surplus physicality for which the mind, that was travelling elsewhere, temporarily had no need.

And each morning, he plaited his wife's hair. At about eight o'clock on the morning after the conversation in the public garden, Leonard had got up to use the bathroom and seen, across the landing, that little moment of intimacy. The sun had been threading whitely into the main bedroom, whose door was fully open, and William and Kathy were up and dressed, Kathy sitting on her stool, William standing behind her. The light was falling just there onto William's hands, which wove the hair into those perfect plaits Leonard had always disliked. The next morning he got up by chance at about the same time, and there was the same scene, his brother and sister-in-law half-dissolved in the rinsing light, their heads bowed and Kathy's eyes closed. How could he dislike those plaits any more, knowing their origin? Knowing the mute and peaceful transaction that brought them about day after day.

It was Sunday morning and the house was empty. He walked up to Finsbury Park in the early heat and let himself in at the Bellevue. The truth was that he wanted to see that picture of Aleph again, or perhaps see if there were any others, and some faint dream of her that night propelled him towards his goal without much thought for what it was meant to achieve. The dream itself he couldn't grasp except for those limbs again, the bright limbs he'd dreamt of before, which were a siren and a call to beauty. The dream had left an erotic trace in his mind, but it hadn't itself been erotic – more light-filled, cool and pure.

He didn't need to be told that it was a senseless mission he was on, and if anyone were to ask where he'd been that morning he wouldn't say. It was such a doomed interest he'd always had in that girl, when she'd never so much as registered his existence – but what did it matter? He'd never hoped for anything anyway, he'd just stumbled like the rest of men towards what was most beautiful, and he did again and supposed he would always. Even with his heart worn thin by Tela he had it in him to do that.

He pushed open the Bellevue door and came into the café, or what he fondly thought of as the café despite its being so completely obsolete in that role. It was hot and airless in there where the glass frontage acted as a greenhouse, and the tables and wicker chairs looked to him not only disused, but as though they'd served their term and weren't willing to be used again. Such a theatre of broken dreams, for him at least – for when he'd first looked around the Bellevue, fire-blackened and glorious, it had summed up a reality running at a diagonal to his own. With his grandparents' inheritance to spend, he felt that he was at the single intersection of who he was and who he could be. A teacher no more; he'd run a café, have live music, put tables on the pavement. Both the winter and summer sun would stream in. In all honesty he'd used to blame William that this never came to be, that instead, by some will or another, the Bellevue had turned into a venue for William's groups and the mirrored and marbled café had devolved into nothing but their thoroughfare en route to the room upstairs. But he couldn't any longer blame his brother; he'd since learned that even if there were no such thing as fate and destiny there were traits in a human that emulated them, that made one incapable of doing a thing that his or her character wouldn't stretch to. No, it wasn't any use apportioning blame, even if it was satisfying to. He ran his fingers across the cold, oily surface of the marble table.

Upstairs there were voices – a girl's, then William's. He went to the foot of the spiral staircase and waited, supposing his entrance must have been heard. Nobody came down to see who was there, so he rested his foot on the bottom step, his hand on the swirl of iron at the rail's end.

'I try not to be selfish,' the girl said.

Then William's voice. 'Good – does that mean you sometimes do things that don't benefit yourself?'

'Sometimes, yes.'

'What things?'

'I guess—' There was a pause. 'If a friend needs me, I give up what I'm doing to see her.'

'Why do you do that?'

'Because that's the way to treat friends – that's what it means to be a person's friend.'

'And does being a true friend make you feel good or bad?'

'Good.'

'Is feeling good a beneficial feeling, or a harmful one?'

The girl paused again, briefly this time. 'I suppose beneficial,' she said and she laughed a little. To Leonard's ear there'd been nothing hostile in his brother's challenges, and nothing defensive in her replies. She said, with the laughter still present, 'So yes, maybe I do benefit from those kinds of things.'

'But that's just one example – maybe you can think of other times when you *don't* seek to benefit from what you do?'

There wasn't a reply. For the first time Leonard became aware of the presence of other people aside from the girl – a male cough, some slight movement, a general sense of combined thought, and he realised he'd intruded on one of William's groups.

'Sometimes,' she said finally, 'we do things we know are bad for us, like smoking. I know it doesn't benefit me but I don't have the willpower to stop.'

'When you light the cigarette, when you inhale, doesn't it benefit you at all?'

When no response came, William asked again, 'Isn't there any pleasure, say, in that moment? Or the expectation of pleasure at least, or the memory of it?'

'Yes, I guess there is.'

'And the same in drinking and eating too much, having sex with someone who isn't your husband or wife, speeding, gambling?'

Again there was no reply, but a sound of restlessness and some comments Leonard couldn't discern.

'What about, then,' William said, 'somebody who appears to do something senseless or evil – to another person, or an animal, say? Are they seeking some good for themselves, too? Perhaps momentary pleasure in revenge, or momentary pleasure in power, or the momentary relief of an urge, no matter how irrational?'

'Probably, yes.'

'So it's possible that in every action, we look to benefit ourselves in some way, even if what we do turns out to be wrong?'

'Yes.'

'But we've already agreed that fundamentally when we wrong others we wrong ourselves – when the chicken stamper kills the chicken he does some damage to his own self too, even if he doesn't acknowledge it. Or do we take that back now?'

'No, we can keep that.' The girl's voice was demure and sweet then, Leonard thought.

'So, if we always seek to benefit ourselves, and if in doing wrong we harm ourselves, then doesn't it seem to be that we must never seek to do wrong? We may, in fact, do wrong, but we never seek to.'

Leonard shifted and trod back on the floorboards so as to be heard, and he began to climb the stairs. When he reached the top he found himself faced by a perfect brightness, within which a number of figures – five, six – appeared in a kind of fine, unresolved form as if they were a continuous part of the room's light and air. He'd never experienced that before, and the vision didn't last. As the brightness retreated and the figures became definite, he found himself facing six people who were gathered around the table; four women, two men, none of whom were older than their mid-twenties he guessed – none of whom, either, was the man Leonard had seen outside the house. William was at the table's near end on the right. They were all turned towards him in mid-thought and movement, William's blue eyes clear and shallow, their faces inquisitive in a way Leonard couldn't say common among his own students.

He said, 'I'm sorry, I didn't realise you were in the middle of something.'

William was expansive, almost elated. 'This is my brother Leo,' he said, and he extended his arm towards the staircase. 'Come and sit with us.'

'No, thanks, I won't.'

'I'd like to show you off. I've told everyone about you.'

Leonard laughed to defy the idea that he might be worth the show. 'I only dropped in to do some quiet reading,' he said. 'I can come back, it's nothing.' When he smiled his brother's generous smile came in return. *We never seek to do wrong*, William had said with a tone that was warm even as it was unsparing. Leonard hadn't followed the reasoning of the argument at all – it really wasn't his thing, this habit of analysing. But as he set about the narrow stairs, he felt that he was turning away from a blessed light into gloom; the beauty of the young, he thought, though in truth that didn't quite explain it since he'd never found his own students very beautiful.

As for Aleph, well, the dream had deflated in his heart, for it struck him now as trivial. His brother gave the energy of his thoughts to the intricacies of human nature, while he gave his to short-lived and hapless desires which emptied him even as they overflowed in him; the serpents – as William had once said – that eat their own tails.

Ah yes, his brother was the better man – guardian of the chickens, guardian of the downtrodden, gatekeeper of justice and goodness; he who'd attracted the attentions of the likes of Aleph with his quick mind and smile. He who'd deflected them too. He who never sought to do wrong. He of good, bold heart.

He'd slept for an hour, because the prolonged heat kept forcing him into snatched rests. In his sleep he thought he heard William's voice at one point and when he woke up at about five, he did stand on the landing and call his brother's name, and wasn't answered. Then, to his own dismay, he rifled through William's things. Except that after quarter of an hour he realised there were no things of much note to rifle through.

After the failed prying he opened one of the bottles of wine in his bedside cabinet and lit a cigarette, and found himself instead going through his own unpacked boxes. How little he had that was of use. An enamel bento box that Tela had given him after a trip to Japan, with rabbits painted on the lid – a nation obsessed with rabbits, she'd lamented. He'd once tried to take his lunch to school in that box, but it wasn't made for sandwiches. He liked it though, and it struck him as something that might have a use one day. There were books, many on religion. There was a lever-arch file marked Finances which was too understocked to look like it belonged to a rich man. There was a pack of cheese straws, which he'd forgotten about. He opened and ate them, and smoked again.

Down among it all, tucked and bent, his mother's cloche hat and his father's chequered newsboy cap that they'd worn every time they went out, and had worn that way almost all their lives.

It might have started out as a joke. There was a pair of his mother's flat blue espadrilles that she wore around the house after a day of midwifery. She would always be exhausted when she put these shoes on, and would rub her feet with her thumbs first, and then ease the espadrilles on with a sigh.

By half past seven the wine bottle wasn't far from empty and any hunger had been extinguished; the household was in the grip of a strange aimlessness, with the boys on holiday from school and himself in a hiatus that drew his life continually back to the point of the present, and with the heat drawing long the hours of the day. He wasn't sure how he'd become the type of man who counted days and spent time spying on his own brother. He thought he'd like to be less solitary. He thought that he'd used to be quite gregarious, a sociable sort of man full of largesse that unravelled him world-wards so that he had no real internal shape at all.

He stood from the armchair and went to the wall to examine the diagrams of brains. The only clue about William, the only thing in the whole room that could be considered a confession or personal touch, was on that picture of the human brain where he'd written, *Here I am*, with an arrow to the narrow cavity between the brain and the skull. Leonard couldn't think if he'd seen it before. Had the writing been there all along? It was faint and in pencil, he might have easily missed it. It surprised him mostly because he couldn't remember if he'd ever seen William's adult handwriting, not in a card or a list or on a cheque, and least of all in a letter. Now these three words: *Here I am*. It reminded him of one of Galen's theories, that the fluid bathing that cavity – spilling from a well deep in the brain – was the *vital spirit*, the seat of the soul. *Here I am*. Such a slender little statement, and he found it eccentric and amusing, the idea of the great entire poundage of his brother folded like a yogi in that cleft.

As well as thinking William cataleptic, their father had said obliquely but often enough that he was something else too; he'd say just that – *something else*. Then when pressed he'd refer to articles he'd read in the *Scientific American* or some psychology journal – it was from his father that Leonard had heard of Galen – and say with awkward speculation: autism perhaps, some sort of obsessive personality disorder, very mild schizophrenia. Those maladies he plucked from the wide array as if they were all more or less the same – slightly differently hued fish from one deep pool of disorder. We must identify and accept his differences, the old man had said in a perverse attempt at compassion, we must try not to normalise them. Father, Leonard had thought – *normalise* is one of those words people use when they've lost track of what normality is and have started assuming it means *like oneself*. We must try not to make another like oneself, they say – and yet it's the very unlikeness to oneself that made one judge the other in the first place.

He went to the window, an absent-minded journey to which he had become quite habituated, and he saw William in the small front garden shearing down the threadbare long grasses. He hadn't realised he was home. He knocked on the windowpane and William looked up and waved his shears. He lifted them and scissored them at his neck, and pretended to cut his own head off. Richard appeared briefly to the scene with a squawk of laughter and William downed the shears and stroked the boy's head. Then he went back to his work. And, with a lingering smile, Leonard stepped away from the window.

The heat made the week begin slowly. On Leonard's second Tuesday at his brother's house, they set off at just after four and made the train journey to Shepperton with their swimming shorts in a bag. It was a strange heat that had become shabby and was making shabby. The heat was trapped in an airless gap between summer and autumn, and when they opened the train windows one could believe that the air that rushed in was relieved to be given respite from the outside.

He'd been thinking anyway of saying to William, Let's go for a swim. He hadn't had in mind that narrow urban cut of river at the bottom of Jonathan's garden; he'd more been thinking of Swift Ditch and he'd been preoccupied with his childhood memory of that stretch of water flowing across a Thames meadow, tree-lined and frantic with insects at the water level. But at the mention of going to see Jonathan he became enthused for he hadn't been there in a long while, and for all its lack of glamour and openness he liked the way that one had to enter the river from the garden, leaving a cup of tea on the boards in readiness for getting out, and the domesticity that added to the cold, raw swim.

By the time they arrived it wasn't hot any more, but warm and moving between rain and sun. The air had cleared and opened as it had begun to do in the evenings. Still parked in the drive, as it must have been for a decade, was the old baby-blue Austin 1800 that he and Jonathan had taught William to drive in. William had never been interested in driving and nor had he been able to take it seriously; it had been Leonard and Jonathan who'd persuaded him to learn just after he was married, but everybody's keenness for it faded when the extent of his ineptitude was made plain. William patted it meekly as they passed. 'She's still frightened of me to this day,' he said.

Jonathan unlatched his front door to them with a jolt of surprise and then a wide smile. He was wearing the familiar brown corduroy trousers and maroon jumper that he wore often, and was as tall and thin as he'd ever been. He patted Leonard's back and said, 'You're in London, I hear, and that's wonderful. I

take it you've come for a swim? Go, go, before the clouds come.'
And to William he held out his arms and hugged him long.

There wasn't any doubt that Jonathan was William's friend
first and foremost, not that William was proprietorial, but
Jonathan was. A devotional friendship, a loyal one, at least
on Jonathan's part. How wrong Leonard was whenever he tended
to think that his brother had no friends, when there in Jonathan
was the one person in the world who did appear to accept William
for who he was and without a second thought, a man Leonard
had always quite envied for his capacity to do that. He was the
only good friend Leonard had ever known his brother have – but
perhaps so stalwart and unchanging in that role that the role
itself had become background, just part of the way things fell.

In all the time Leonard had been away he'd spoken to Jonathan
once, just once, and it had been a query about partial chord
shapes; Jonathan wanted him to explain how to play F more
compactly, or maybe it had been G, but, yes, what did it matter?
Leonard went out to the living room and left them talking, and
in the last of the day's sun he changed into his shorts, hanging
his clothes over the arm of the sofa, and went out of the back
door, through the ten feet of neatly potted garden and onto the
boards. Crouching with his back to the river he leaned past his
point of balance and allowed himself to fall in. Immediately he
moved his limbs. Pressingly cold, cold tightening his stomach
towards his spine, cold becoming the sum total of all he knew,
and then suddenly warm from within, a stubborn warmth that
was the burst of argument between the body and the element.

He swam a few metres under the wooden bridge, then turned
and came back. The setting sun poured low through the trees at
the riverside and bowls of bronze wobbled on the black water. It
was the one time he still liked his body. He threw it this minor
plight and it proved itself very keen to survive, which was good

of it – decisive and generous. The water was silt and silk. The spokes of sun turned his vision a mellow gold. He swallowed gnats and midges as he breathed, and it wasn't of any concern to him what he swallowed, nor what aquatic unknowns brushed up against his leg or stomach, nor how he looked to anyone else, how white or graceless.

He swam slowly towards Jonathan, who'd come to sit on the boards with his long legs gathered up uncomfortably, one knee pulled to his chest and the other dropped, tensely, wide to the side. 'Tea here when you want it,' Jonathan said. 'William's just getting changed.'

So he propped himself up with his arms and took a mouthful from the old teacup, whose flowers had blanched to green and pink outlines, then swam away again, upstream. The Ash was a brief waterway and half-forgotten, except by those whose back gardens it passed. It flowed into the Thames rather than the sea, and Leonard was glad of it – he liked rivers that ran into rivers, not into seas; he liked the merging and joining, not the emptying and the surrendering.

When he turned and came back downstream William was climbing in. Leonard made a landmark of Jonathan's waterborne hand flowing back and forth through the water; he swam vaguely towards it and when he came close he faced upstream again and front-crawled thirty metres, and then crawled back down again. William oared towards him and they swam past one another. They smiled cold-constricted smiles, and William slapped the water with his foot as he went past, and splashed. Leonard did likewise.

'Kids!' Jonathan shouted.

'Just trying to move to stay alive,' William responded.

Leonard got out then, just as he was beginning to feel how cold his feet were. A sort of glory filled his body, one that enabled him to individuate himself against the lazy warm merging of things, bark into trunk into branch into leaf into sky into cloud into rain into river. His body was warm within and cold at the edges, and he could feel the heat of the tea moving down behind his chest.

Jonathan handed him a towel. 'You two are the only ones mad enough to swim in it.'

'You used to swim in it all the time.'

'Yes.' Jonathan gulped back a mouthful of tea. 'I don't any more.'

'Why not?'

'It seemed disloyal to Jan, you see,' he said, 'because she can't. And she loved it so much.'

'Then she might want you to carry on the tradition.'

'The tradition was for us to swim together.'

Jonathan smiled; such a serious, sincere man, Leonard thought. He'd always been. He worried over technicalities, points of definition. Maybe that was why he and William were so close, because they put their focus into those strict, logical concerns that the rest of the world missed or dismissed. Though they were very different too; Jonathan more emotional, more anxious.

As if he knew he were being thought about in this way, he offered an incongruously wide smile, and Leonard said, 'I understand.' Which he did in his own lesser way, because just as Jan haunted that water for Jonathan, Tela haunted it for him; and yes, though he'd only been there twice with her, one of those times was the first time he'd ever seen her, when she'd been swimming with Jan. She'd grinned toothily up at him and ducked under the water. And how quickly then she'd gone from being Jan's friend to his girlfriend, then briefly his fiancée, like a fish captured. Perhaps that had been the problem all along, that he considered he'd captured her and couldn't stop feeling that, and was forever checking for holes in his net. And, well, how many holes there'd turned out to be in that net.

He watched the water carefully, the way light hit it, the way it spiritualised things. His brother continued to swim. He wanted to wrap the towel around himself but decided it would be too boyish, so he dried himself with a desperate enthusiasm; the warmth was fading from his body and he could almost feel the fat around his heart cooling and solidifying.

'I see you still have the old Austin,' he said to Jonathan. 'Must be a quarter of a century old by now.'

Jonathan's smile was rueful. 'I want to be rid of the thing, to be honest. Had enough of it lurking around out there reminding me of things.'

'Maybe you'd get a good price, it must be vintage by now.'

'Come on, it was always a heap of crap, even back in its day.'

Leonard laughed; I first kissed Tela in that car, he wanted to say. In fact they'd tried much more than that, but it had worked out terribly, he being tall, the car being small, Tela being prone to an acute sense of the absurd that made her throw her head back against the seat in laughter. It was hard to feel passionate, she commented, when he looked like a cat stuck in a paint pot. He looked at Jonathan suddenly and said, 'I'd buy it off you.'

Jonathan frowned in surprise and then gathered himself to standing. 'The blood's left your brain. I wouldn't let you part with your money for that rustbucket.'

They went indoors and said nothing more about the car. Leonard wanted to, but perhaps Jonathan's dismissal of the subject was his way of saying the Austin wasn't for sale. The thought of getting a car hadn't even crossed Leonard's mind until that very moment, no, they were of little interest to him – but suddenly it had struck him that he was soon to be rich enough to buy an Aston Martin DB9, or a Cadillac Escalade, or really anything he set his heart on, and that very fact made him want the old Austin, that rustbucket, for its pricelessness and its sincerity, as if it would protect him against the material life to which he'd now be forever prone.

He stood rubbing his bloodless hands. Jonathan lit the ready-laid fire. Barely past mid-August, but the back room got no sun and he and Jan had never been prepared to be cold – it was something Leonard liked about them. Of course, it bore forward the characteristics of humanity – the need to be warm and to be comfortable. William had always been impervious to cold, heat or comfort, a fact evidenced by glancing outside where he swam methodically up and down, twenty or so metres each way, slow and sure. Leonard stood near the fire and watched the flames hunt out fuel. If heat came from that violence of flame annihilating wood, how could one generate heat from peace or mild goodwill? He pulled his gaze from it and looked instead at Jonathan, who was crouching at the grate as he coaxed flames.

'I'm still having such trouble with those partial chords,' Jonathan said. 'I've been trying to play some backbeat rhythms, Motown style – it all just goes to pot.'

'You've learned the fingering?'

'More or less – it just doesn't twang in the right way, do you know what I mean? You know that Steve Cropper or Albert King sound. That crispness, as if the sound is jumping from the strings.'

Leonard looked around the room for Jonathan's guitar and brought it to the sofa. He played a few chords, twanging, yes, as Jonathan had said, and crowding his fingers around a few short, neat notes.

He said as he played, 'It's about the strumming – you have to snatch the sound from the strings. Only play the strings you want to be heard.'

He handed Jonathan the guitar and watched him play. 'Cut out the top three strings,' he said. 'Yes, like that. You see it makes it sharper.'

He leaned forward and watched; Jonathan thought too much and that hindered him. One only had to cast their eyes over the books on the shelves behind him to see the source of his troubles – Derrida, Sartre, *Cognitive Science and Phenomenology*, Husserl, *Existentialism and Communism, The Visible and the Invisible*. He could see three books right there that Jonathan had written or co-written. If one could die of thought. Leonard watched his brother's friend and felt tenderness for this effort he made with his fingers to free himself from himself.

'Perhaps you shouldn't worry, Jonathan,' he said. 'Perhaps you should just strum like mad, make a racket.'

'The right to make a racket comes with first learning how to play properly.'

'If you say so.'

Jonathan glanced up, biting his bottom lip in concentration, and Leonard left him to his practice and went out onto the narrow pontoon, where his brother was persevering with his slow wide stroke. None of them – Jonathan, Tela, Jan – had ever heard William play music. They probably didn't know that he even could. He did present himself as a singularly limited and ungifted man, professing always to know nothing, to be able to do nothing. Why was it that when he picked up a violin and bow he could shake off the great burden of his thoughts in a way Jonathan couldn't, and why, also, did he choose not to?

'You'll die of cold,' Leonard called upstream. 'Are you coming out?'

'Unfortunately I can't get out – my body has dropped off, Leo, I'm just a head.'

Leonard said, 'A lie, I can see your shoulders.'

'You have me. All right, I'm just a head and shoulders.'

He bent to fetch the old, mould-speckled net on the boards. 'Here, then, I'll have to fish you out.'

'And then what? Will you carry me around in a bag for the rest of my life?'

'If you like.'

'I'll be heavy.'

'We can get one of those good jute bags.'

'Or a trolley. I might prefer a trolley.'

Leonard smiled and propped the net by his side.

'I'll get you tea, William. I'll leave it here.'

He went indoors to make a fresh pot. Jonathan had given up on the guitar and was in the kitchen making cheese on toast, which was traditional. They'd used to eat it with the packets of Danish fried onions that Jan's family sent over from Finland – a treat, simple and homely to Jan and exotic to them.

'He's still swimming?'

'Yes.'

'He and Jan used to be able to spend an hour in there, just floating up and down on their backs. They were like birds of a feather.' Jonathan paused and rechose his words. 'Like fish of a fin.'

'They did get on.'

'William riled her though. I never knew anybody make her as angry as he did.'

Leonard poured milk into the three cups and he hesitated with the milk in his hand. 'As he does with many people it seems.'

'Ah, but it's only light-hearted.' Jonathan turned the toast under the grill and added the cheese. There ought to be fried onions, he thought, with ill-proportioned indignation; it felt as though those rituals should go on as normal, but Jonathan slid the grill pan back under and wiped his hands on a tea towel. 'It was always light-hearted with Jan.'

Leonard thought, I remember it otherwise. But he said, 'It wasn't light-hearted when William came to blows with the university over the riots.'

So now you've thrown that deliberate ball of fire into Jonathan's hands just to get a reaction, he thought – though what he wanted or expected Jonathan to say about it wasn't clear at all. Really he hadn't meant to bring it up, for he sensed that if Jonathan wanted to talk about William at all it was only as a way of talking about Jan. More even than this, Jonathan had long avoided his potential role as informer on William, as single remaining witness to his short days at the university – he was the loyal and unjudging friend and above conjecture, gossip, hearsay, did not interpret, did not extrapolate, not interested in the slightest in helping others do so. There was only the hiss of the grill between them in the kitchen, and the licking flames which Leonard suddenly thought were crass, like himself; he clattered the spoon when stirring the tea, to trivialise the demands on the silence.

'It wasn't light-hearted, no,' Jonathan said then. 'Not at all. But then politics was involved, and nothing is easy when politics is involved.'

Leonard leaned back against the sideboard and rested the hot belly of the teaspoon against his palm. 'My father – our father – thought that William might have been responsible for the Bellevue Group's violence during the Poll Tax Riots. The policeman who was injured. It worried him right up to his death; maybe the worry's what killed him. He thought, because of that, the Bellevues were some kind of, I don't know, anarchist Trotskyites. Led by his own son.'

There was gentle amusement in Jonathan's eyes, and a quickness about his mouth. 'Those are strange words to use.'

'I told him William was no such thing.'

Jonathan's only response was a nod and a confident, quite unbalancing silence, as was characteristic of him. Leonard went on, 'Just that our father couldn't get over the fact that William left the university – he always felt he was safe all the time he was part of that great *institution*. It pained and worried him, all of it. He worried that William hadn't left but been fired.'

'What should reflect most on William isn't that he worked at the university – though that in itself was something,' Jonathan said in those same equal, kind tones, 'but that he left it – wasn't fired, but left it – because he believed there were better ways of educating people than gathering them up like sheep in a room and telling them what others thought. He wanted them to think for themselves. Unqualified, inexperienced, but brilliant, Leonard – so brilliant and passionate about the matters of the human soul. And he still is, despite not being paid or thanked for it. Your father should have died proud.'

With a pause Leonard added, 'He had a great fear of being excluded from anything, my father – be it a university, a club, heaven. That's why he was religious, I'm sure – to secure his place in this world and the next.'

'Well, that was his axe to grind.' The comment was coupled with an askance gaze across the kitchen. Then Jonathan lifted his eyes again. 'I can't think of a single other member of the department who could leave and have his students follow him the way William's did. You normally have to force those kids to listen, not sit upstairs in an old café and have them come to you. For ten years – year after year.'

'I realise that.' He truly did; his own students wouldn't, that was as certain as anything could be.

'You know, don't you,' Jonathan said, 'the gentleness of your own brother? How good he is?'

Leonard drew back slightly. 'Yes, yes I do.'

'Nobody could be less interested in rioting – I'm astounded your father could ever have questioned it.'

'I know. I do know, I agree.'

Jonathan squinted in to assess the cheese bubbling under the grill. 'There's a beautiful passage in Mill's *On Liberty*. He speaks about how powerful our opinions are – the prevailing opinions. If you swim against the stream of them you suffer. Society is a punishing judge, believe me. William swims upstream, not always, and not on purpose, but it's who he is, and there'll always be people who don't understand or accept him.'

'Even his own parents,' Leonard said quickly.

'Even that.'

'And these ones who swim upstream – what happens to them?'

Jonathan hesitated and inclined his head in the direction of the river. 'Easiest thing would be to go outside and find out.'

A flippant answer, but a distant wince across the mouth and cheeks suggested that Jonathan wished not to progress any further along that road. Leonard held out a cup of tea to him and smiled. It might have been the longest conversation they'd had and he suffered from his usual sense of inadequacy. He a teacher, Jonathan a professor – he knew, an outdated vulnerability to have, for what did these things matter? – and his anxiety that Jonathan could only ever see him as the lesser and poorer of two brothers. But inadequate or not, Leonard still had it in him to pity that poor man, stooped at the shoulders, awkward, without his wife, his beloved wife who'd come from Finland to England to find trees and had remained for the rest of her life sweetly excited by them – the oaks and the aspens and the horse chestnuts. Horse chestnuts in particular.

'I'll take this out to William then,' he said.

Jonathan twisted his head to speak. 'Have the car, by the way. Try it out for a couple of weeks at least.' The words were thrown as nonchalantly as possible over his shoulder.

'I couldn't, Jonathan—'

'Have it – I want to get the drive done anyway, I need it out

93

of the way. It'll be doing me a favour. Then if you want it after that it's yours.'

'You'll need it yourself.'

'Why? I never drive it.'

Leonard paused long and Jonathan offered, with more finality, 'If nothing else it'll save you a train ride home.'

'I don't need it,' Leonard said, and then could no longer see the point in resisting. He relaxed his shoulders and face into acquiescence. 'It's really kind of you – thank you. Just a couple of weeks while your drive's being done; a couple of weeks and then I'll bring it back.'

'Whatever works.'

He left Jonathan in the kitchen putting the cheese on toast onto plates. When he got outside he saw William was still in the river. He sat on the boards with his knees drawn up and his arms wrapped around them. The old Austin! In which he'd been with Tela, in which William had learned – or tried to learn – to drive. Just think of its cranky black engine that had outlived Jan's heart, his mother's heart, his father's. To get in it would be to get into a piece of stilled time and to drive it would be to carry that stilled time around with him – the time, for example, when William reversed it into a pond and then frowned and asked if that was the right choice of manoeuvre. And he might well have said no to Jonathan's offer except that he'd thought for a moment of the fuel protests a few days before and decided that he wanted nothing to do with that fearing and resisting and that fretfulness of the human spirit he'd sensed so strongly at the time. To say yes to Jonathan was as liberating as saying yes to treacle pudding in a saddened world of dieters.

He watched his brother's low, bear-like progress through the water and remembered sitting in just the same spot, seven or eight years ago, before Tela came onto the scene – and William and Jan had been having a discussion about what it was to love.

Jan did love very freely – people, food, cats and dogs equally, the water, the sky for its massiveness, the trees for their deciduousness. So they'd begun talking about what love was and how that one brief word, love, could suffice for one's feelings about a person and also about a packet of fried onions, or a storm, or a poem.

It had started happily enough, but then William had ensnared her in a discussion about love until they had dismantled the word as if it were a building made of matchsticks, one matchstick at a time, dropping, dropping. What is love? – Is it beauty? Is it spirituality? Is it an over-glorified physical urge? What is beauty, what is spirituality? Is it that which is loved? Ah, you define one and you lose sight of the other; you grasp the other and the next slips from your reach. Do you know? Can you say? Can you say for sure? This, for hours, until Jan rose from the boards in silence, said she loved nothing and nobody, not because she was convinced by William but because she was by that point unconvinced by and of everything, had become quite ashen in the face, cried; it was crushing to see such a practical and assured woman cry, to see her upwardly lifted eyes fill with rage and helplessness. She left; if Leonard was right in his remembering, she wasn't present at any of their visits for some weeks.

No, it wasn't that simple. Leonard's memory, flaccid and imprecise as it was, could only render that debate general and facile. It hadn't been. William had spun Jan into a web. It had been an exquisite experience, Leonard had been frightened of the power of his brother's argument, which had in fact said nothing at all, nothing conclusive and nothing instructive. He'd witnessed it compulsively. He watched Jan's undoing as one might a bloodsport – this woman everybody liked so much – and had almost delighted in the elegance of her vanquishing. Could a man fall in love with his own brother? A certain beauty claimed William when he argued in this way, as if his intellect were a favourable light that picked out his humanity and cast his imperfections into shadow. Yes, a man could fall in love with his own brother, he could fall in love with anything that seemed to lend him a brilliance that wasn't his own, and then he could and probably would fall sharply out again. After that debate with Jan, Leonard had called his brother a fucker, a motherfucker, he had said – he remembered because it was the only time he'd used the word and it had sounded ludicrous on his lips. William looked genuinely injured, and said he was sorry if he'd done wrong. Yes, you've done wrong, yes, Leonard had answered, yes.

'Give me your hand,' William said. He'd swum up to the boards and was ready to get out.

Leonard gave his hand and pulled his brother up; he wanted to apologise for how angry he'd been that day over what happened with Jan, which didn't seem much of a crime now when he looked back on it. He wanted to apologise for being absorbed into their parents' doubts and for not defending his brother strongly enough in the face of questions and fears.

'There's tea here,' he said, 'and food inside, and a fire. And a car home when we're ready. Come in and get warm.'

He had a song on his mind, one William had always used to sing. *A spirit that's burning, a heart that is bubbling, saints that are eating and always drinking. Let's go on!* It was strange that the song should come to him suddenly.

He left William swinging his arms, stamping his feet, exhilarated.

Have car – their father's had used to say back in the day – will travel. If the old man had had ideas of a great motorised expedition, a great letting-loose, his imagination belonged to another nationality; no such thing as wilderness or savage land in this little country, nothing one could truly hurl adventurously through – but as they left Shepperton there were patches of rural life that brought those words of their father's to Leonard's mind. The change of seasons could just be glimpsed in furls of red on the sun-facing sides of trees. Otherwise, where there was space, it was shorn golden fields, baled straw, dry tired hedges of bramble, hawthorn and sloe, yellowing grass. William gazed out of the car window with his hands resting on his thighs in such avid surveying of the scenery that it was impossible to know if the avidity was due to complete focus or complete daydream, the here or the there. Not, in any case, in the distracted babble of the in-between where Leonard spent his own days.

'Do you know I almost slept with Tela in this car?' he said.

William turned his attention from the window, then grinned. 'I know now.'

'There was a spring that twanged in the back there. In the end she just couldn't take the whole thing seriously.'

'Really? I can't see why.'

Tapping the steering wheel, Leonard commented, 'I suppose you'd never do a thing like that.'

'Almost sleep with Tela in the back of this car? No, Leo, it would be outrageous, I'm a married man. And there's that damnable spring.'

They smiled, and Leonard could see, even without looking, a light in his brother's eyes, which was to say, a humour and a sudden ease. He said to him, 'If only it weren't for marriages and springs, the world would be so much more fun.'

'And willing partners.'

'Of which for some reason you've never had a lack.'

'For some reason? Look at me, Leo, isn't the reason obvious? Am I not the epitome of manhood?'

William held his hands out in presentation of himself and Leonard might have laughed aloud at the incongruity, intended even as it was. Despite his being a big and present man, there was something so very emasculated about his brother, a tenderness with which he met the world, big blunted features, short grasping limbs that looked made for fumbling and loss of authority.

Leonard said, 'Pa took to asking me all sorts of things about you in that last year – and he actually asked me once what it was that made people fall in love with you.'

'You mean it wasn't obvious to him either?'

Leonard smiled and observed the onset of the city again – fewer fields, busier roads, the multiplying directions of travel. 'Do you know much about Mill?' he said.

'The philosopher?'

'Yes.'

'One or two things.' That meant of course, *plenty of things.* 'Why do you ask?'

'I was just curious.'

'"It is better to be a human being dissatisfied than a pig satisfied" – that was the most famous thing Mill said.'

Leonard contemplated that for a moment and then replied, 'Oh. And do you agree?'

'I think it depends on whether those are the only options.'

'Yes, I suppose it does.'

'Do you think they are?'

'I hope not. A pretty lousy choice.'

'Do you think it's possible to be truly satisfied?'

He shrugged. 'I guess. I have been myself a few times, not that it lasted, but—'

'If it doesn't last,' William asked, eyeing the road squarely, 'is it true satisfaction?'

'Perhaps not,' he said.

What he'd wanted then, if anything, was for William to ask, When were you truly satisfied? Which was to say, for his interest to be personal, not theoretical – not to ask about the nature of satisfaction, the nature, role, impact of humanness and pigness, or to sit and define terms, but to say, Tell me what has made you happy. Something he'd forgotten in their time apart, but had been reminded of with certainty over the last fortnight, was that any conversation with his brother took on the shape of an arrowhead, and would thus taper to some penetrating and often abstract point. It wasn't that he didn't want that sometimes, he just didn't want it always. One had to hold ground against William in a conversation to prevent that, one had to cut off the possibility at its source. And so he just said that: *Perhaps not*, and turned his gaze away.

He glanced in his rear-view mirror and thought of Tela then, not in that clumsy contraction in the back of the car, but halfway up their stairs where she'd used to sit and read in the warmth of the sun through the skylight – big-boned, soft of face. She'd made him satisfied for a while with her luminous interest in his little ways, celebrating the fact that he left an inch of tea in the bottom of his cup and was intolerant of tomato-damp bread and had oddly shaped feet that wore holes in the heels of his socks; all of this was fascinating to her, and in being found fascinating he'd been satisfied indeed, yes, truly.

He asked his brother, 'And do you really believe what you said to your group the other day? That nobody seeks to do wrong?'

Having forgotten completely the reasoning that led William to that claim, it now stood out to him in isolated suspension, proverbial, some sort of koan. *No man seeks to do wrong*. It was Tela that had put the statement in his mind just then, and the small salvation that seemed to come from the idea that she hadn't meant to hurt him. There was a moment of seeing the human world as a bumbling but benign collection of misdeeds and mistakes, without malice or cruelness of any kind, and he found it more consoling than any other previous version of good and ill he'd stumbled on.

'Yes, I believe it,' William replied.

He paused. 'I don't know what I think of it.'

'You mean, whether you think it's true or not?'

'That we're all, at heart, trying to do our best. I'm not sure the evidence would bear that out.'

And the moment he paused the doubt poured in – so Tela didn't mean to wrong him, she was just doing as best she could even if its consequences were painful, so she was quite off the hook, so she, or anybody, could do any number of ills to him, or anybody, and the defence was always there: I didn't mean to, I did it through ignorance – as if the injury didn't matter at all. Then when he pictured Tela on the stairs her softness and peace suddenly offended him, for what right did she have to softness and peace when he suffered!

'I'm foolish to let myself fall so in love,' he said quickly.

'So you're a fool, what does it matter?' It was as though William had expected that statement, his reply fell so seamlessly.

'If I could be more like you I wouldn't be forever falling in, falling out, slicing my heart up at the age of fifty-one – fifty-one, William! Still like a God-awful teenager.'

'Why more like me?'

There was the devoted but distanced love William had for his wife and his children, Leonard thought. And the abstract and almost asexual way he'd responded to Aleph, the benevolent extension of his hand towards the young man's arm in the manner of a god granting favours; solicitous, yet still perfectly wholehearted.

'You're so self-possessed,' he said, 'so balanced about these things.

Got your heart under control. You love the earth, the stars, God, the reliable things – the things that aren't going to desert and betray you.'

From the corner of his eye he saw William smile, and lean forward, aimlessly it seemed, to open the glove compartment. The fixing was jammed and wouldn't give way to his efforts, so he sat back eventually.

'You overestimate me, Leo,' he said, and cupped his hand against his chest. 'I've got a foolish, wobbly old heart that falls in love with every person who crosses my path. Some wobbly old doorknob of a heart that falls off every time someone touches it.'

Leonard raised his brow and smiled. 'I don't believe it.'

'There hasn't been a day of my life that I haven't been in love with somebody,' William said. 'Not a single day.'

They fell silent. The shops pressed themselves outwards in ugly repetitions as if all born of the same limited idea, and all obese with so many objects that the mind could stumble over itself in disbelief. This is what's going through your mind, Leonard thought as his brother stared out of the window at the city. All of this banality and emptiness – what use is it? The suncreams, training shoes, coffee, telephones, holidays, eyeliners, pashminas, dog beds, nose rings, glow-in-the-dark stickers, silk ties, hard-drives, almond cakes, cough tinctures, Bangladeshi curries, Thai curries, Nepalese curries, dummies, washers, balloons, irises, spaghetti, chainsaws. These are for the likes of me, not the likes of you.

It wasn't even their excess that scrambled the mind, he thought; no, just that they existed and that the very energy of human hopes, loves and anxieties passed through them at such speed and so disposably that one never had time to see precisely what it was one hoped for, loved, or was anxious about. Whole cities were built to house such things. The earth itself was buckling under the weight of such things. This is what's running through your mind, Leonard thought; but when he did glance over at his brother at a traffic light, William was regarding it all with the usual largo motion of his head and eyes and the equable curiosity he'd used to give to the wooden puzzle, every time handling it as if seeing it for the first time – for every time it was different, he'd said. The only way to solve it was to come to it assuming you'd never seen it before.

As they drew to a crawl in traffic Leonard tried to wind the window down further, but the handle only turned without leverage. 'Ah well, we'll just have to steam,' William said, and the traffic began to gather up in front of them, to gather up and ruck the thick air, like fabric collected along a needle.

Oh, but it was hot. The next day Leonard went for air at the top of the garden, dusty and with a headache, and watched the first shadows of evening move in.

The Falklands, he'd said to his brother. I never did understand why you joined the navy, why you wanted to be involved in war. They'd gone up to the attic playroom that afternoon to bring down two old mattresses and dismantled bedsteads that had been in there for years, for Kathy had decided that while there was use of a car they might as well get rid of them. But it was deathly hot in the attic and the mattresses were pinioned against the wall by boxes and old bikes and trikes and toys which they were having to pull clear.

It isn't that you've ever been a man who likes war, he'd said to his brother, or cooking for that matter. William replied that he'd always felt it was right to offer help where you could and to nourish others where you could, irrespective of the outcome. He'd had all his life an enormous sense of responsibility for others and for his nation and it had been with pride that he'd worn his chef whites with the Royal Navy lapel. How so? Leonard had said, I thought you believed we're citizens of the world, not of this island or that.

They'd finally excavated to the first mattress and were hauling it out, trying to bend it towards the aperture for the stairs. Do you think being a proud citizen of a country precludes you being a proud citizen of the world, Leo? I don't know, William. Well, what is pride? I don't know – being pleased to be part of something. Does being part of something always make you proud? I don't know; shall we try to turn this mattress on its end and see if it goes easier that way?

By the time they'd got to the second mattress – which wasn't even to have started on the headboards and bases – they'd moved onto the subject of democracy, which admittedly Leonard himself had brought up. If nothing else you could argue it was better for the Falkland Islands to be governed by a democracy than a military junta, he'd said – better for the people of the Islands in any case. Is democracy definitely better, Leo? Yes, if it brought more peace. Does it always bring more peace? Not always, but often. Why does it bring more peace? Because it avoids one madman wreaking havoc with a few million people. A minority rule, a dictatorship? Yes. Whereas a majority rule is likely to be more balanced? Yes. Is the majority usually right? I don't know – it isn't necessarily about right, it's about what people want and need. If what they think they want and need is wrong, does the desire and the need outweigh the wrong? No, it's just— If the majority did wrong, wouldn't that be just as bad, or worse, than an individual doing wrong? I don't know, William.

They'd been pouring with sweat by then and the second mattress was stubborn about going down the stairs. Still the bedsteads to go; if you opened the skylight no breath of breeze came in. All I really wanted to know, William, was how you felt about being in the navy, whether it affects you now, the memory of the explosion in Falkland Sound and all that – it was just out of interest, that's all. Does it affect me? Yes, weren't you traumatised by it? I mean, to save a person's life and to come close to death yourself? We're always close to death. Yes, but you know what I mean, doesn't it change the way you see things? I don't see things in terms of the past. Everybody sees things in terms of the past. Do they? Yes. In what way? Our experiences, we're shaped by them. Shaped how? They influence how we—

Leonard had sat heavily on the mattress on the landing and waved the conversation away. You don't want to talk about it any more, Leo? Yes – no – it's just – He'd wiped the sweat from his temples with a dusty hand. Aleph pulled you into her world, didn't she William? he'd said. The world of dinners with lords and politicians, as if to thank you for saving her. I didn't know you at all then, I saw a picture of you and her once in the paper, at some big swish do – you were more or less in the background, but still. Did I tell you I'd seen it? In the paper! Didn't feel like you were my brother at all, up there in *high society*, up there with the fat men and pampered women. I've always wanted to know you better, to understand you better.

He'd looked up at William who laughed suddenly and said, I was like a fly buzzing round them, they hated me.

He'd made the humming drone of an insect with his tongue against his teeth and then walked carefully down the stairs; Leonard had felt himself sinking deeper between skewed mattress springs, rather as though he were sinking between his brother's expectations. In the garden, as he watched the shade encroach finally across the fence, he could remember William and Jonathan talking coolly once about democracy, and William's fear of what he called collective ignorance. We're given no raw facts to base our votes upon; everything washes up on the shores of our consciousness rinsed and planed by the media. To ask a man for his democratic vote is just to ask him to give back the opinion he's been spoon-fed – and so it went on, with Jonathan adding the occasional note of optimism.

As he clapped the dust from his hands, all Leonard could hear was the buzzing and droning of that fly William had emulated. A persistent buzzing as though afflicted suddenly with tinnitus. Oh, but it's just hot, that's all, he thought, as the gentle sun descended. It's just so hot, and it takes it out of you.

The days passed contentedly. August was drawing itself to a slow, warm close in which the scores of summer were being calmly settled; except for the cluster of dahlias at the bottom of the garden that had recently bloomed, all of the season's explosions were beginning to mellow and turn earthward again. Something felt liberated, or exonerated.

They'd taken the mattresses and bedsteads to the tip, in four journeys, with the bedsteads dismantled and the mattresses fastened to the roof with luggage straps. On the Thursday they'd gone with the boys in the car to Great Monk Wood on the edge of Epping Forest, a carefree, careless day; they'd also spent time in the garden, eaten together, had the two Delohery children from three doors down round for an afternoon; all in all Leonard's questions about William ceased in the languidly full pattern of days.

It was when he'd happened to see his brother on one of those afternoons, going through a drawer in the bedroom as though it were a matter of life or death, that he'd decided to give up doubting him. At first he'd wondered if he'd interrupted William doing something suspicious and he'd moved away from the door without a word. He'd realised then that, despite his indignation at the task his father had set him, some part of him did want William to have done something wrong, one precise thing that could be identified and forgiven and committed to the past so that Leonard – like a detective taking the wife's marital underwear to the suspicious husband with an apologetic sense of victory – could report back to his father's grave and settle the matter. There's the proof of the wrongdoing, shall we now move on? But half an hour later he'd seen William searching through a kitchen drawer, and when Leonard asked him what he was looking for he said Kathy had lost a hair grip, the one with a jewelled dragonfly attached; the boys had bought it for her the year before and its value to her was endless.

William had looked for that hairgrip for several hours, long after the others had conceded defeat, and he'd found it finally on the path near the end of their street, in a little crucible of dust under a hedge. There is your answer regarding William, Leonard had said then to his father's unhearing ears, as William was polishing the hairgrip up on the sleeve of his own shirt – and though of course there wasn't really an answer or a piece of proof of the kind the old man might have been asking for, to Leonard the evidence was manifest and certain. There was nothing to find, there was nothing that William had done that could be feared; there was only fear itself. Yes of course, there were moments – especially in this heat – when William's persistence could irritate, but what of it. There were moments when anybody could irritate or be irritated, weren't there? Could their father claim never to have been guilty of either?

Leonard remembered his father talking about fear often – fear is of the world, not of the spirit, it self-creates and believes its own delusions. In truth it is nothing, and when we gather in the light there is only hope; fear dissolves in the light. It was one of the elements of that faith that Leonard had been able, at least at times, to take comfort from – and thus it was sad then, so sad, that his father, who'd given him that comfort, should have died so afraid and so deluded, barely understanding his oldest son. It wasn't his fault. William, in his absence, left too much time and space for misinterpretation. It wasn't his fault, but he might have known better about his own son. He ought to have known better.

Leonard took the time to catch up with some chores he had to do, some paperwork for his change of address and some concerning the maintenance of the family house until a decision was made as to what to do with it. He sent off his application for probate, and this was a task he'd been avoiding. He knew that when it came he'd be obliged to start discussing with William the divisions of the estate and in this reduction of their parents' lives to material residue they'd have to at last let go – for it was in the owning of what another person once owned that the proof of their disappearance lay, and not the opposite. A life wasn't preserved by the handing down of the house it once lived in, the table it ate at, the mirrors that reflected it; one inherited the bare table and sat at it, and filled the empty mirror with one's own reflection, and thus the death was complete.

The dahlias though – really in all that mellowing off in the garden the dahlias' gaudy coming into colour was unignorable – those flowers that reminded Leonard so much of both his parents. Their strange isolated renaissance near the back fence. It was those that compelled him to take action on the probate, as though in fraternity with the scores of them growing in that dispossessed Edinburgh garden, which would die presumably next year if he didn't take some control over things. It wasn't that he even liked them much, but he couldn't have them die. So he made arrangements to pay a local gardener and handyman to visit the place every fortnight, and he sent off his probate form in the hope that there'd be no hurry in its return.

*

He and William had spoken so little about their parents that it was then a shock, almost as though he'd been spied on or mind-read, when, on Monday evening as the breeze sounded in the grasses below the window, there was a diffident knock on the open bedroom door.

'I found this earlier in one of your boxes,' William said, and he walked in.

He held up a video; Leonard blinked at it. 'You looked in my boxes, William?'

'No, it was on the top. It says *Church* – I was intrigued. Are you angry?'

'No, I'm not angry, not at all.'

Leonard took the proffered video.

'Do you remember, years ago, when Dad opposed having a security camera in his church?'

'I don't see why. The church is surveyed constantly by God isn't it; did he think the camera would see something God wouldn't?'

'You're being sarcastic, William.'

'On the contrary.'

'You're the believer after all. It's me who's meant to be cynical.'

'Because I'm the believer my questions come with impunity.'

'Well.'

They stood opposite one another. Leonard faltered over William's religious flippancy; wasn't he, as the believer, the suppli-cant himself, supposed to be in earnest about God's love, and wasn't it for others to mock? But he liked the mocking all the same, the refreshingness of it. He said, 'In any case, the congrega-tion voted to get a camera for a while, before they realised they'd have to change the tape every five hours and couldn't afford it.'

'And couldn't be bothered to watch it anyway.'

'Probably.' He rattled the video lightly. 'This is one of the tapes of footage. I found it when I was clearing things out from the Edinburgh house.'

'It must be fascinating stuff.'

'It struck me, William, he's on here. We can watch him on here, if we miss him.'

'Let's then. Let's go downstairs.'

'I didn't mean now necessarily.'

'Why not now?'

Leonard was pleased with the suggestion, because he'd envisaged a time like this when he and his brother would be there, in the sitting room watching that footage together. He'd rejected the church so long ago that he felt he had no right to it without William there – and this was surely true. If you had rejected a lover you could no longer expect a right to see her in those quiet and private times. He'd tried, he'd been to the church itself after his parents had died, but he hadn't felt comfortable for a minute, even when he sat and tried to pray. In honesty it wasn't that he didn't feel welcome, but that he did, and then he felt guilty because for all its forbearance he still wasn't going to go back.

When he'd pressed play on the video recorder he sat down in front of the television, his knees drawn up to his chest. They saw the back of their father as he walked away from the camera, having set the video. They saw him leave the church. The angle cut him thin and he looked like a leaf blowing away. Then still, silent footage of the church's tiny interior, grainy and monochrome, from the baptistry down through the nave and into the shadows. For endless minutes the camera recorded nothing but the solemnity of a church's personal life, away from the vicar and the congregation. It was unexpectedly reverent, wholly tender and austere. And it spoke of course of that watchfulness of God, which, Leonard knew, had never bothered his brother in the way it bothered him, the way it bothered most people – religious or otherwise.

In a moment of missing that was so great as to make Leonard feel his stomach had been pulled up to his head and replaced with air and nothingness, he craved another image of his father. He needed him to walk back through the church door. He went to fast forward but William asked him not to, and so they watched each wordless second flip past.

It was a beautiful church, a doll's house, diminutive and fine. For all that, it had the elegant and striving proportions of a cathedral. The camera gave one unmoving view, down and out across the pews. There were inevitable lengths of film that recorded only desertedness, and in that way some ten minutes passed. Of course, nobody would come to the church; their father wouldn't come. He'd set the video precisely because he wasn't going to be there. Personless frames flickered eye-achingly from one ill-defined moment to the next. Leonard forwarded and this time William said nothing. The clock at the bottom right pressed just slightly deeper into the afternoon. Sometimes, Leonard could imagine in the stuttering images their father lighting a candle or straightening the hymnbooks. The old man had objected to the camera on moral grounds, but he'd never had any qualm about the scrutiny it implied of himself; no, he'd lived a life watched by God and he was never alone, all his intimacy was shared with the huge mind, he was two beings at once, not really an individual at all and he didn't let himself go, he'd never even known what it was to let himself go.

As the church became darker and the image less discernible, Leonard stopped the recording and turned the television off.

'He was a good man,' he said, and saw the redundancy of the statement lift William's brow and the outermost corners of his mouth.

'Of course he was, he was born a good man.'

'It would have been strange to see him again anyway. Moving and living.'

There had been that one brief sighting of his back, a stammer of movement. If William hadn't been there Leonard might have rewound the tape to those four or five seconds.

'We're entering an age now, Leo, where everything we do is recorded for posterity; children born today will get to our age and be able to watch a video of themselves taking their first steps, saying their first words. It will stop their hearts growing old.'

'Will it? Can't you have too much of these things?'

William said, with his hands humbly linked in his lap, 'I think it'll stop their hearts growing old.'

Leonard took the tape from the machine and stood. This naïve hopefulness of his brother's succeeded again and again in perplexing him. William was always very positive about progress, about gadgets in particular – if it did a new thing, shed a new light. If it was a mug, but it also had a lid, because the lid was also a small container and there were any number of things you might put in it – a biscuit, the back-door key, if, say, you were drinking tea out in the garden. There was a lot of joy and satisfaction to be found in a thing like that. The great particularity of his thinking cracked when it came to these little pointlessnesses. Leonard had never been able to understand it.

'I'm going to bed,' he said at length, and rolled back his stiff shoulders.

He wanted to ask, even after almost three weeks, Are you sure about me having your room? But he stopped himself. William hated that question, he wouldn't say anything about which he was unsure or offer anything he didn't want to give. And so Leonard just added, 'Goodnight,' and then, 'sleep well, William, and thank you,' and went to leave the sitting room.

'Wait, Leo. I've been thinking more about your query the other day.'

Leonard asked which query.

'I think you asked, to be precise, what pathetic deficit of manhood makes someone kill a chicken. Does that sound right?'

'I can't remember, it was just a passing thought, William. It was ages ago. I didn't expect to be picked up on it.' He said this kindly but with his back foot already out of the door, for some grudging part of him felt offended that his brother was returning the issue to him, second-hand as it were, already used by his students.

'But does that sound like the question you asked? I mean, is that still a question for you?'

'Well – yes—'

'You mentioned something about broken spirits, that a fox wouldn't be broken-spirited enough to kill a chicken for fun, and I've been thinking about that ever since.'

Leonard said lightly, 'I know you have, you talk about it with your group. I can't say I've really given it the same thought.'

'I wanted you to tell me something – do you mean that there's something in the fox that's intact, then, and something in the human that's broken?'

There was nothing in Leonard that was in the mood for a debate, but from the point of view of principle he thought he ought to show some willingness. 'Perhaps I mean that,' he answered. 'I can't really remember.'

He waited near the door for William to speak. William didn't speak, but stared in thought at the carpet while rotating his thumbs one around the other.

Leonard said, 'Yes, then. Yes, there's something amiss in the human spirit. Of course there is, look at us and the way we live.'

'And this thing that's intact in foxes and broken in humans – is it the same thing?'

'I don't know. It probably is.'

'We can't fix something if we don't know which part is broken.

If we could discover what it was that's there in the fox and amiss in the human, what component I mean, wouldn't that help us fix it?'

Leonard brokered a smile for his brother and placed himself on the arm of the chair. 'If I'm trying to sum up what's wrong with it, William, I'd say that it's the mindlessness of it. Somebody doing something just because they can, without any reason or intelligence, just to gain power over another thing. That bothers me, because if we can be mindless about chickens, what else can we be mindless about? Where does it end?'

William narrowed his eyes and regarded Leonard with gentle, summarising attention.

'Oh but it isn't mindless, it's the opposite. It's too much mind, too much credibility given to one's own small mind. And when one pays too much attention to that small mind, one feels small. I suppose the chicken stamper wanted to feel bigger, Leo.'

Leonard smiled with some disdain. 'That sounds altogether patronising.'

'I certainly didn't mean to be.'

'To assume others have small minds.'

'Oh but me too, Leo, me too. We all suffer at times from the tiny mind.'

They watched one another; they'd used to do that as children, outstare one another, and it was always Leonard who conceded first.

William said, 'But then I'm deeply fallible. Maybe it's only me who suffers that.'

'Of course not.'

'Well, based on what you've said I'm going to observe myself, to see my own small-mindedness. To see if there are times that I abuse my power too. Which is to say, to examine my own deficits, my own ignorance.'

Leonard nodded.

'And you, Leo? Do you try to do that?'

'I suppose – I try to be the best person I can.'

William put his hand to his throat loosely and his nod was meek.

'You question me like you question your students, William.'

'Do I?'

'You never used to do that.'

'I'm only interested in what you think.'

'Are you interested in what they think?'

William leaned forwards, resting his elbows on his thighs. 'They don't really think yet, all I do is encourage them to see how much they haven't really thought. They're only like everyone else in that respect, it's just that they're willing to accept their ignorance when it's revealed. I can hardly find anybody else who is.'

In the doorway Leonard slid his hands into his pockets and looked at the mantelpiece clock. 'It's late,' he said. 'Thanks for the discussion – about the chickens. And for the video.'

'Any time. Sorry for keeping you up, I expect you didn't feel like it.'

'Well, it's fine.'

He thought, It's difficult, William, for you to expect me always to be the best person I can. And it's difficult when you tell me I'm not willing to accept my ignorance. Even when he then conceded that William hadn't said that, still he wanted to defend himself, and he struggled not to.

'Goodnight then,' he said.

'Goodnight, Leo. Sleep well.'

*

He didn't see his brother until the evening of the next day. It was around six o'clock when William came home, and he went out into the garden dressed in some old canvas dungarees that Leonard thought might once have been their father's. He seemed brightly determined. His course was straight to the shed at the bottom of the garden, from which he emerged with tools and off-cuts of wooden board.

And with that he took to patching up the shed, which was overhung by the aged branches of two plum trees. Its pitched roof was encrusted with fruit that had fallen each year for well over a decade, and its larchlap walls were firm enough where they saw the sun, but rotted where they were faced to the corner shade. It was at those patches of rot that William was working; he cut away the dry and crumbled wood, and nailed rough squares of plywood over the holes. It was an entirely inexplicable exercise. Leonard thought he looked like a person who was playing a role, so aptly did he fit it – his dungarees, a nail held between his lips and his back bent arduously into the work.

'A chicken coop,' he said when Leonard went to him. He was kneeling on his heels, which was a position unnatural to him, with a hammer clutched in his hand.

Leonard observed, 'I'm sorry to tell you, but there aren't any chickens.'

'I'm going to get some rescued ones from battery farms.'

'I see.'

Well, how pointed in a way, that the plight of chickens should begin to manifest itself in all its clucking, pinioned, featherless lack of glory in their back garden. For all his compassion for animals in the abstract, and for all its principled practice in his life, William had never shown the slightest interest in an animal itself, no, he'd never cooed or stroked or taken delight in a bright eye or a tuft of down or a cocked ear. He appeared to extend to animals the same respectful distance and lack of fuss that he extended to humans; why would he wish to appropriate them, why should it be his right to? And so the endeavour that he was now so fervidly engaged in – sanding, sawing, nailing, all for the sake of housing a few dispossessed hens – caused Leonard to watch with a silently lifted brow and misgivings that he tried his best to curb.

Leonard had, himself, spent the day doing practical things. In the morning he'd cleaned and polished the Austin, so unlike himself, he thought, to tend to a car as if it were something loved, but he'd enjoyed the pointless absorption of watching the blue of its paintwork come up bluer. Later, Oli had come out and wanted to see under the bonnet, so together they'd taken the owner's manual that had been in the boot and had ended up cleaning the worst of the grease from the engine. First Oli got stuck into it with a wire brush and then, when that only revealed the extent of the grease, Leonard had covered the carburettor, unplugged the battery and taken to it with hot water and detergents. This was part of a decision he'd made, this cleaning and tending; he'd decided that he had a short period of time before his probate came through, his final period of time before he was forced to move on with his life. And he would spend that time in suspension and preservation of what used to be – he wouldn't aim to retrieve what used to be, he would just hold its gaze before it turned away and left for good. He didn't even want to drive the car, and anyhow there was nowhere he wanted to go if he did; no, he just wanted to have it there at his memory's disposal replete with ghosts, tank full of petrol in anticipation of final departure, engine scrubbed clean, paintwork exemplary, a capsule in which the fugitive past could stow away until the future finally caught up with it. So he and Oli cleaned it for two hours and went back indoors with their hands blackened and the backs of their necks sunburnt and the wire brush bent to oblivion.

Then he'd been most of the afternoon in the garden fixing the fence where it had rotted and collapsed into the house; a leak last winter, Kathy had explained, pointing to the gutter directly above. She was clearly grateful to him for fixing it and he was grateful for the chance to be useful. He'd also cut the grass, hosed down the lower brickwork of the house where moss had started to grow, and the boys had been out there in the garden with him, playing cricket, engaged in the constant invention of games that they liked to include him in – let's have a conversation where nobody says the word *it*, let's see who can run up the garden in the fewest strides. They were able to count the footsteps in the velvet spring of the newly cut grass. They'd eaten lunch together, Kathy too, on a blanket spread in the shade on the lawn.

Leonard could never quite tell if Kathy knew what her husband did on those days that he was absent from the house. All he knew was that he'd underestimated her; he'd never quite taken her marriage to William seriously – there William and his new wife had stood at the altar, his father blessing a union he couldn't understand – a peculiar union, what with her being twenty years his junior and small and so quiet with her vows, while next to her William professed his with a gusto that everybody had to agree seemed heartfelt, for his eyes shone. Until she became pregnant, Leonard hadn't been able to negotiate the thought of her and William having children, for both were too inward-looking in their absolute and opposite directions to bear their depths selflessly outwards through childbirth. But they did do so, and they'd stayed married, and their peculiar union was more than Leonard himself had ever managed, and humbling to him now that he saw it every day.

In any case, if Kathy was unconcerned about William's outside life, Leonard now realised it wasn't down to lack of interest. She wasn't the kind of wife who'd disassociated from her husband through boredom, saying *yes dear, no dear* to any scale of statement. She was loyal and obliquely devoted to William. Perhaps her lack of open attention to what he did stemmed from the earlier years of their marriage when she might have felt – it had been obvious she'd felt – that what William did transcended her reach, and that for her to intervene on his causes would debase their grandeur. All those people he knew, the politicians and academics and such, the invitations to dinners, conferences, discussions that she'd never accompany him to. He did remember her saying once that her northern accent in the Savoy would sound as wrong as a cow lowing at sea. It wasn't the case any more that William kept the sort of company that she might have to detach from, but old habits did die hard, and no wonder perhaps, Leonard thought, no wonder she still stood back.

He watched William for a few minutes. The truth was that the agenda of the chicken coop was perfectly clear. You brought up the issue of the stamped-on chickens, William was trying to say. And we haven't yet settled the issue, there are still philosophical points up for debate and so much we don't understand, so much ignorance and presuming. With every nail he drove into the wood he was housing the debate, pressing the point into form and reality. Let us see this discussion through – that was what he was saying. Let us bring the persecuted onto the stage so that we can't ignore it, dear brother of mine. *You* brought it up after all; it was your heart that first bled for those creatures.

Oh the chickens, the chickens! How was one supposed to feel about it? Really, one should push oneself to keep caring if one ever cared at all; William was right about that at least, that we shouldn't just brush these things away; we should search and search, as it were, for the missing hairgrip, and not stop until it's found. And there was no point feeling irritated with him for his persistence either, for how could Leonard square such a tight-fisted thing as irritation with what was after all an act of kindness? Yet every attempt Leonard made to open his mouth and say, Let me help you, was staunched at source – he didn't want to help, he found the whole thing a little futile and perplexing. At length he crouched down, clasped his hands together, and gazed at his brother.

'I have got over the stamped chickens,' he said slowly. 'Just to let you know, I've moved on.'

William nodded without shifting his attention. 'Good, I wouldn't want you to be tortured unduly.'

'Meaning?'

'Meaning, good, I wouldn't want you to be tortured unduly.'

Leonard shook his head; those statements could be put down entirely to irony if it weren't for some warm body to them, like the deep resonance of a bell's after-ring firming up the air. Irony would be better, for then Leonard could shrug it off, but instead he was left again with a sort of guilt, that his brother was pleased for him even where he'd done something ignoble. Ignoble, yes – he'd forgotten to care about a squandered hen. But that was absurd because it was just a squandered hen, just a hen, why must he feel guilty!

William was studious in his balancing of nail between thumb and forefinger, and his burying of it into the wood. Leonard patted him on the back, stood and lingered for a moment and said cheerily, 'Well, I'm going to go and get on with some things.' He went indoors. Dusk fell and the duck-egg sky coloured up deeply then darkened, then the first stars appeared and so too did a planet, Jupiter perhaps, low and close in the east. Those fingers, obsessive around the nail, that adamant hammering that cratered the soft dusk, that utterly besetting need to hound, to hound, to send the questions off like dogs in pursuit of answers, a kind of grasping, deranged compulsiveness.

Finally, when the light was too weak to be of use, Leonard went out to him with a mug of tea, at which William downed his tools with what looked like reluctance, and wandered in.

At about nine-thirty the following day Kathy went out with the children and Leonard took his work to the kitchen table to review some of his old lesson plans. He did like to be in the kitchen and he seized those opportunities when the others were out and it was still and quiet. In those rare times of emptiness the utensils and the boys' breakfast bowls and flakes of cereal on the floor testified to life lived at a basic and easy level, and it was to those that he'd glance up from time to time to break, with relief, from reading about the Islamic Hadith or the Unmoved Mover or NeoPlatonism. At times he felt his father standing over his shoulder in the pose of somebody assessing without words, with their fingers linked loosely behind their back as Leonard did with his own students. It was hard to say if he'd be pleased with what he saw. Religion is to be lived, not studied, he might say. But then he might be grateful that Leonard was doing anything with it at all. He tried to eliminate these thoughts and just get on, and he was still working late morning, and quite absorbed, when Kathy came back without the boys.

'Have you sold them?' he joked.

She dropped the bag she was carrying and folded her arms, as if she meant to stay and talk. 'I tried. Nobody would buy them,' she said.

Then she let her arms go and marched from the kitchen to the back garden. He remembered that trait then, of folding and unfolding the arms, as if, in that act of defence, she was always expecting battle. She was out in the garden for a few minutes, in which time Leonard gathered up his notes.

She returned with an armful of washing. 'Are you working?'

'Just going over a few lesson plans.'

'You must know them all by now.' With her foot she scuffed a patch of carpet clear, dropped the clothes onto the floor and knelt to fold them. He knelt opposite her to help.

'I feel rusty after a year off. And anyway, there's always the thought that you might find something in your notes that you missed, or that you've been missing all along.'

'I bet there never is,' she stated.

He looked up at her. 'There rarely is.'

'You teach religion?'

And this she asked him after thirteen years of being his sister-in-law; he well believed that she didn't precisely know what he did. If, when he turned up at her door, all the years of hostile estrangement landed rather messily and indecipherably at their feet, here was one discrete, concrete piece of evidence of it.

'Yes, religious studies, at A level.' As he folded, he avoided any clothes that might be hers, for fear that she would be offended. 'We cover the philosophy of religion, religious ethics. And then Plato, Aristotle, and then a module on Judaeo-Christian thought. The similarities and differences between Greek and Jewish thought.'

'Oh,' she replied neutrally, but didn't look up.

He put the clothes he'd folded – small parcels of children's T-shirts and trousers – on the floor to his left.

'You teach religion but you don't believe in God?' she questioned.

A pause, and then he said, 'Maybe I want to rescue the subject from the zealots.'

'Meaning?'

'Well, isn't it better to have somebody level-headed teaching it? Teaching anything, for that matter. It means I have no agenda, no views to push.'

'Maybe it actually means you have no passion?'

It did seem to be a question and not a statement, so he thought he might meet it on those terms. But when he went to attempt an answer he saw the frustrated pinch of flesh between her brows and was reminded that they'd never got on. Maybe he should be more sparing and careful with their conversation.

'Hardly any teachers have passion after twenty years of it,' he joked.

'Well that's a shame.'

They went about their work in silence for a few moments. Then they both said at once, 'Besides,' and looked up at each other, and smiled, embarrassed. He nodded, you go. But she looked down again.

'Besides,' he said, at length, 'I teach religion as you said, which is about culture. I don't teach God. And even religion I don't like all that much. I fear it.'

She laughed curtly and he shrugged. The conversation had become too high-reaching for the kitchen floor; he wished he hadn't said *I fear it*, which seemed straight afterwards to be too robust a statement for such a brittle relationship. He guessed that Kathy's sense of divinity consisted in prayers made on the move when she needed something or was afraid. Oh God bring this. Oh God take this away. It was too convenient and disposable a thing to be feared, or even thought about in earnest.

'What about William then?' she said, and held his eye. 'You're not alike, are you?'

'What about him?'

'Do you know what I think? That he believes in God just to annoy and upset people. If he'd been born two hundred years ago when it was normal and rational to be religious, he wouldn't be. He just has to do the opposite.'

He smiled, because he'd thought this himself at times, though he no longer did. 'Whereas I'm conformist?'

'Yes, you are. Like me.'

He laid his hands wide on his thighs for a moment. 'I don't know about William's faith, I've never quite understood it.'

'He has a voice in his head, he says, that advises him against doing things.'

She looked at him inscrutably so that he really couldn't be sure whether she found that fact grotesque or amusing or somehow admirable. He only shrugged and added, 'He's always had that, since he was a child. And when he was a teenager his most treasured possessions were those two Salvadorean crosses. If all he was doing was trying to annoy people it was a decision he made from a pretty young age.'

'He isn't like other people,' she replied simply.

Do you think – he was about to say, and he'd already inhaled, brought his tongue and the roof of his mouth into contact to make the *d*; do you think William has any disability, illness? He swallowed the breath that raised the words, because he felt the question was a terrible betrayal of his brother, offensively simplistic, or flaunting a basic misunderstanding of this man they were both supposed to love. They each looked down at their task; he gathered his completed pile into a neat stack and pressed it flat.

'Have you ever worked, Kathy?'

She stood sharply. 'What am I doing now?'

'I meant paid work. Rather than slave labour.'

She bent to collect her pile of clothes and said simply, 'No. And don't assume I'm a slave. The worst thing that ever happened to women was feminists going around telling everyone that women have to be liberated, as if we're caged animals.'

Leonard lowered his head, picked up his pile of clothes and

raised himself slowly. 'I didn't mean—' He looked at her, but she was already given to new tasks. 'In any case,' he said with a sigh. The unfinished sentences funnelled outwards with no end. He took the clothes to the bench along the kitchen table, and then poured himself a glass of water. Kathy put a new basket of clothes in the machine, filled the kettle and began to rinse dishes from breakfast. She used her small body like a tool, all industry and fast blinkered purpose, her plait yielding to the movement of her spine. He could but see her and William in the morning sun whenever his attention was drawn to her plait, and the persisting peacefulness of that image. With the glass in one hand and his teaching notes in the other, he went to leave the kitchen.

'I expect you were thinking then of that morning,' she said suddenly.

He answered, 'What morning?' Because of his thoughts, he assumed at first that she was speaking of the plaits, and the notion that she'd known he was there gave him an over-awareness of himself that culminated quickly in shame.

'We were just staring at the very bit of floor. I think you know which morning I mean.'

He brought his thoughts into balance and glanced down towards the carpet where they'd crouched. 'Oh,' he nodded. 'I wasn't thinking of that.'

'I was so angry with William that day. I could have crushed his head there on the floor. He was lucky it was just a damned cake.'

He nodded again, and of course he understood. He saw Aleph asleep there on the sofa – the whole lengthy extent of her slung down, unwound; and her arm hanging over the sofa's edge so that the back of her hand rested on the floor, as though she were trailing it through water. Her fingertips feeling the warm breath of the black dog that lay silkily stretched on the carpet. And even if he hadn't really approved of her being there it was still a lovely sight, one he'd never been able to diminish in his memory.

'She never struck me as the baking type,' he said, and wished immediately that he hadn't.

Kathy expelled a curt sound that fell well short of a laugh, and wound a tea towel around her wrist. 'The sort of woman who could turn her hand to anything, it seems.'

'Well,' he commented, and lowered his head.

'I didn't really thank you properly for what you did.'

'For cleaning the cake off the carpet, you mean?'

His tone was a little sardonic, in fact, but she nodded sincerely.

'You did thank me, Kathy, and besides I don't think I deserved thanks – in a way I ruined everything. I assume you obliterated the cake to make a point, rather than for fun. Then some helpful character comes and cleans it away before it's ever seen.'

'I wasn't making a point, I have no points to make. I was just angry.'

He said, 'Yes,' rather quietly, and observed in her jaw and throat the faintest shadow of the anxious energy he'd seen that day; how we sculpt ourselves, he thought. We sculpt ourselves over time with our most persistent moods, as though our faces are dunes and our temperaments the winds that blow them into shape.

'Did you ever tell him you'd done that, with the cake?' he asked.

'Obviously I told him,' she replied with a small, arch smile. 'There'd be no point in punishing somebody if you didn't let them know.'

She was right, of course. In the face of her frankness he wondered if the question had been ridiculous.

'Maybe you think I do that kind of thing all the time,' she added.

'Hardly.'

'You stay for one night and that's what you come down to in

the morning. A woman sleeping on the sofa and a cake ground into the carpet. My God,' she laughed stiffly, 'I can't imagine why you ever wanted to come and live here.'

'It was over ten years ago, Kathy. I'm very grateful to be living here.'

'What strange doting things people do for him, Leonard. A woman like her baking him cakes! Her last little desperate attempt at getting his attention.' She chewed on the inside of her cheek and he shrugged, yes. She added, 'I can tell you nobody has ever done a thing like that for me.'

'For me neither.' He smiled. 'But it was probably a dreadful cake.'

'Why did she fall for him, do you think? She could have had any man in the universe.'

'He saved her life – I suppose that colours the way you see a person.'

'Would've been better for us all if he hadn't bothered.' She glanced up with half apology and put a hand on her hip. 'William said she decided she wanted to be a nurse after that. A nurse! A naval chef, a vet, an aid worker – the luxury of the upper classes to dabble with professions as if they're trying on clothes. I bet none of them lasted. Can you imagine her pristine little hand up a cow's rear end?'

He hesitated. 'No, I can't.' Then he added casually, despite what he felt, 'She probably didn't limit her affections to William, and besides, he never reciprocated, he never would – I promise you that's just not his way. There was never a more loyal person—'

She lowered her eyes. 'I know. That's what you said then too.'

'Yes.'

He smiled, and had an impulse to compliment her – your blouse suits you, with the big loose bow, quite Edwardian somehow. You're very stoic, your hair is lovely and long. Stoic!

You couldn't compliment a woman by calling her stoic; Tela would be rolling her eyes at his lack of aptitude for these things. Yet, feeble though the compliments were, they were sincere – he did think her blouse suited her, and her hair was the sort many women would yearn for. More than that, he meant it to compensate her for the continual harsh judgements he'd made over the years, which he now saw he hadn't been qualified to make, and might have been entirely wrong about.

'Do you have something to do today?' she asked.

He assumed she meant, will you be gone from the house today? Will I be free of you? He thought to say by way of apology, I'm back at work soon, then I promise you'll barely see me. Then before long I'll move out, this I promise.

'There's always plenty to do,' he said.

'Oh well, never mind.'

'Why? Was there something—'

'The boys have a friend who lives near the Bellevue,' she said to the objects in the sink. 'William was supposed to pick them up from this friend's house last Thursday and take them swimming. Of course he didn't. Their swimming things are still at the Bellevue – he left them there after his group. He didn't do one thing right last week. He's completely distracted, completely elsewhere.'

The speech belonged to somebody who should look tired, angry and harassed. But in fact she'd straightened, and a certain provoked cheer had entered her voice.

'I can pick them up.' He said it as though the idea had been his all along. He didn't know why he said it that way; too eager to please perhaps, and he disliked himself for it, and for the unignorable triumph he took in that small outdoing of his brother.

She said, 'They need them for swimming this afternoon. William won't make it in time.'

127

'I can get them back whenever you need them.'

'Half past three.'

He nodded. 'Half past three.'

'Thank you,' she replied, and she looked across at him, but only briefly.

A quiet, unassuming Islington, the plane trees, the sycamores, the pushchair wheels running soundlessly over grass, the fleet-footed children in the square. Such an anonymous life William had chosen for himself, to be but one in a city of millions. And also to rarely leave that city and to think it represented the world. Such incuriousness for a curious man, and such an unfretful world he inhabited too, with his abiding family in the leafy shelter of north London. He'd never once made the journey out to Hertfordshire where Leonard and Tela had lived for six years – presumably he'd never seen any real need, since Leonard visited him. I made that journey to work every day, Leonard thought, and was suddenly dumbfounded by that discrepancy of effort.

By the sink unit and cupboards in the Bellevue there was an orange drawstring bag that must be the boys'; he'd seen it somewhere in the house at one point, or maybe hanging on the washing line. Indeed, inside were rolled towels, within which he assumed would be the trunks. There was a carefully folded pair of armbands and three pairs of children's goggles, which he pictured Kathy pressing into the top, and pressing down with her hand to tighten the drawstring.

For all that he'd had no desperation to be a parent he did feel something lift in his stomach when he imagined having somebody to pack a swimming bag for. When he'd used to open his sports bag or his lunchbox and seen the things he needed, his head had been full – at least for a moment – of his mother, or the sight of her hands. These were feelings he now knew were gratitude, even if he hadn't had the discernment to know that at the time. And he thought, How would it be – how would it be to have somebody think of your hands and of your face and to feel grateful – or simply to think of your hands, your face, at all?

He'd no urge to stay there, so he took the bag over his shoulder, and when he turned for the staircase his heart clenched at the sight of a person standing towards the back of the room. He brought his hand to his chest and drank his breath, and as the shock sank away into his lungs, his eyes apprehended his brother's silent sloping figure, back turned, face to the wall, sombrely low lit where the sun never quite reached.

'William,' he said, and snapped the sound through that sombreness. 'I didn't know you were there.'

There was a twitch of movement in the shoulder that seemed quite without volition, more the impact of Leonard's voice on the soft atomic outline of his brother's body. He repeated, 'William.'

Long gone were the days when he'd rush to William's side when he went into a trance, and shake him, *William*, thinking he was dead. He knew he was very much alive, in the midst of life, eyes lit and unseeing, skin oddly flushed and luminous. But still a slow lurch of worry would work across his chest even now.

He waited, and at length William shifted his weight from one foot to another and turned his head. If he hadn't known Leonard was there, he showed no surprise to discover it. 'Leo,' he whispered, 'you caught me at it.'

'I came to collect the boys' swimming bag. You frightened the life out of me.'

William gave a long nod. 'I forgot about the bag.'

That comment sounded unusually defeated in tone, Leonard thought, and he patted the bag briskly to stem the languid mood.

'I'd better get it back to Kathy,' he said. Just before he turned to leave he made the kind of bolstering suggestion he'd never before have condescended to with his brother. 'Perhaps you should go swimming with them – you need to get out. You look pale.'

William gave a declining smile. 'Thanks – but pushing sixty is exercise enough.'

'Right.'

His foot was on the top step before his brother spoke again. 'Before you go, Leo, please sit a minute. I'd like to speak to you.'

Leonard assessed the statement briefly as he might something he didn't recognise, for he wasn't sure if his brother's tone had ever been so complicit, or so heavy with the burden of things not said. He went to the table and sat, as did William, and they were opposite one another as they'd been those three weeks before, with the figs and wine.

William said simply, 'I've wanted to talk to you for a few days. You see, I've been questioned by the police over my possible part in a fire. A month ago a library in east London burnt down, maybe you remember the news? Eastacre Library. It was well known because it was stocked and run by the local community, it received an award of some kind—'

'I do know it,' Leonard said, and pulled back slightly. 'It happened just before I left Edinburgh. They reclaimed an old Victorian schoolhouse – I remember it being started up.' He paused; he did remember that. He and his father had talked about it at its conception a year or two before – a beautifully progressive thing it had seemed then in amidst the various other catastrophes of the world, all the stumbling backwards as their father had put it.

He added, 'Father loved it. When I heard it'd burnt down I was glad he wasn't alive to find out.'

It seemed William considered that information; he peered into the space just before him, then put the fist of one hand loosely into the palm of the other. 'The police suspect arson and want to find out whether I know anything about it.'

'Why would you?'

'Somebody I know is suspected of starting that fire – somebody I know very well.' William's face was only three quarters turned to Leonard, his gaze solemn and dignified. Leonard nodded briefly. 'One of the students who comes to my Bellevue Group. He was questioned and he denied any part in it, but he told the police that I've been mentoring him. Now of course he's disappeared. The police insist that I must at least know where he's gone – I don't know. I haven't a clue.'

William turned and walked across the room to the bookcase, and took a piece of folded paper from the shelf. Returning, and resuming his position almost exactly, he handed it to Leonard.

'It's from a couple of days ago,' he said. 'One of my students gave it to me.'

It was a short tabloid news article, and it was about the fire. Its main focus was the young man, Stephen Malson, and his illustriousness – the son of a deceased lord and the nephew of a conservative MP who'd brought him up from the age of twelve, after the early death of his father and earlier death of his mother. His flecked past was slenderly summarised – his thousand-pound drinking binges, his girlfriends who numbered among them a member of the Italian House of Savoy, his toying attempts to form an extreme left-wing political party, which came to nothing. For a while he'd been a model for an upcoming Italian-Slovenian fashion designer. The newspaper made a great deal of his absconding. In all William was barely mentioned, except to give his name as Stephen's mentor and as the man to whom Stephen had referred in his first dealings with the police. That, and to mention – as though casually – that William had been a Falklands war hero, an expression Leonard found peculiar for all its truth; and to state his age as newspapers were wont to do – in fact to state it wrongly as they were also wont to do, for he wasn't fifty-nine. They might at least get that right; he wasn't fifty-nine.

Leonard folded and deposited the article into William's pocket and stopped short for a moment, staring at his brother's loosely fisted hands.

'You say *of course* he's disappeared, as if that's the kind of thing he always does.'

'He's impetuous.'

Leonard paused.'I saw you outside the house a couple of weeks ago with a man – is that the one?'

With the briefest falter, William looked at him and said, 'Yes, I expect so.'

'And did he start that fire?'

'I don't know.'

'Could he have done it, though?'

'I don't know, Leo.' William shook his head as though he were trying to work it free of his thoughts; he seemed, Leonard thought, perplexed.

Leonard hated that man for a moment, whether guilty or not; even the possibility that he might have done such damage to that sacred little library was enough. He said, 'I don't understand. What makes them suspect him, what evidence?'

'He lives in that area for a start, and he'd been seen around the library the day before, prowling around the back of it as somebody claimed. He admits he was there, though not prowling. Anyway, prowling, walking, running, it doesn't matter – it was suspicious enough to question him, and when they did he had no alibi for the night of the fire itself.'

'Which counts for little – I probably lack any alibi for it. That hardly makes me a suspect.'

'No,' William said, and he took a long in-breath through the nose and closed his eyes on the exhalation. It called up an instant memory of their boyhood, for William used to do just that with the breathing and eye-closing when they played tag or kick the can; William would take his time closing his eyes while the others waited to run, and much as they'd shout at him to hurry, he would never; he would never bend to an outer pressure, though he seemed so compelled by an unnamed inner one.

'But it doesn't look good,' Leonard added, 'that he was seen there the day before. Prowling, or whatever.'

'At the back of the library there are some cedars – two magnificent cedars. They might be the only proper trees that area has, they really are impressive, Leo, just there in all that urban clutter. The point is that he told the police they reminded him of his mother, because they'd buried her remains under a cedar tree at their family estate. It was the anniversary of her death the day he was seen there. I know that part to be true in any case – he talked about his mother a lot.'

Leonard swallowed hard. He said, 'All the same, how dare he implicate you in it?'

'I don't think he meant any harm by what he said.'

Ah, but surely the man meant harm by it, Leonard thought – or why mention William's mentoring at all? Whatever allegiance William had to him was undue and wasted   too much loyalty poured into the wrong vessel, surely too much misdirected hope and goodwill.

William stared at a point on the table and remained wordless. 'And the police?' Leonard asked. 'What did they want from you? What did you say to them?'

'Mostly they wanted to know if I knew where Stephen was. I didn't and that was that.' William shifted his gaze so that it lay steadfast on Leonard. 'There were a few other questions, which

I answered. For example, did I know of any reason he might have started a fire in a library; did I know of any beliefs he held, any motives. Had he said anything to me that made me suspicious.'

'And?'

'He's spirited, Leo, and foolish, and arrogant, and full of ideas and plots and ploys. He wants to change the world. Many people want to change the world – should we be suspicious of them all? When does an idle sentiment count as a motive?'

'You told the police that?' he said. 'That this man – Stephen – is spirited and foolish?

'Yes, I told them what I've just told you.'

'For your own sake, William, you might have picked your words a bit more carefully.'

'But I'm not interested in picking words; I use the ones that drop. I don't have anything to hide.'

'You need to be careful.'

They looked down; Leonard sat back in his chair and his brother was still; such blue eyes, they sometimes worried him with their capacity for blueness. Only three weeks before, he'd slept there on that sofa and dreamt strangely and woken to sirens, and those dreams and sirens still lingered behind his skull as a compressed echo. He felt confused suddenly, as though he were meant to elicit from all that some significance – a foreshadowing perhaps of this news that proved his connectedness to his brother.

He asked, 'Does Kathy know about this?'

Again William nodded. 'She's made it clear I'm to find a new home if this comes to anything.'

Leonard, surprised, sat up a little. 'Well, she's poker-faced then – she's shown nothing of it, she's said nothing whatsoever.' Then he said, 'And will it come to anything?'

'I don't think I've done anything wrong.'

Leonard frowned, and an equal part of him wanted to smile

in panic. Even with the discrimination and intelligence so hard at work in the eyes and mouth, his brother spoke with the innocence of a child, and it was that which Leonard addressed in palliative tones. 'I know you've done nothing, William,' he said, 'but setting fire to a public library isn't exactly a trivial crime. The last thing you want is to be mixed up in it.'

'It's good of you to point that out.'

'I'm only saying.'

William ran a hand down his own right side as if to smooth a crease. 'The police have said they probably won't need to see me again in any case.'

'Then the papers shouldn't even mention your part in it.'

'The papers do what they like if they think they can get away with it.'

Then he was silent for a few moments before he lifted his gaze a small way above Leonard's head. 'Before you start imagining that all this somehow *excites* me, Leo, I might as well tell you I don't like it – a library of all things. It's debasing even to be suspected of it.' He spoke with a lightness that was perfectly serious. 'I'm many things, I know – I'm not a perfect man, but I'm not a hater of humanity.'

'No—'

But what could he say, except that? No – he'd feel debased too in William's position, and he wanted to say, I will stand by you whatever happens. He wrapped the drawstring tightly around the orange canvas of the swimming bag and had the impression of the willing arms of his nephews windmilling through the pool, and the cheeks filled with air, the shouts and laughter and their happiness chopping the tidy water.

'It won't be anything to worry about,' he said, and found himself trying to deflect a more personal concern, that his brother must have been questioned by the police at least once, must have suffered Stephen absconding and whatever loss and trouble that conferred on him, and yet Leonard hadn't noticed any of it for even a moment, not the faintest shade of it.

Thin-lipped, William nodded and sighed, 'By dog,' a light and blaspheme-free curse their mother had taught them when Leonard was too young to know what did and didn't offend God anyhow. He thought it had meant *buy dog* – some strange knee-jerk reaction to any mishap, some punishment, the dog of perdition and misfortune. As with everything else, it had been William who'd disabused him of this myth, and explained to him the true meaning. He hadn't heard him use the expression since schooldays.

In the garden the following morning Leonard pulled up some of the weeds in the raised vegetable beds; they were Kathy's domain and they hadn't been tended well. By the way that she went outside only when she had to, and stayed in the shade even then, it was clear she didn't like the heat, and the sheer length of the summer appeared to have beaten her. The carrot leaves crunched in his hand and the courgettes sprawled wide and parched across the soil.

William had been out in the garden since the early hours working on the chicken coop and there was now a rough framework of one-by-two lengths of wood around which he planned, presumably, to put wire mesh, to make an outdoor enclosure that would attach to the shed. To his credit he'd set about the whole task with enormous practical purpose. Their father had often said that there was really nothing William couldn't do, and do expertly, with enough will – ah, but for the will! It did seem to hold true, for inexperienced though William was with the tools, still he went about the job with calm and dexterity. The heaviness that had been there around his mouth the day before at the Bellevue was gone also, though not entirely. There was still tightness there, shades of unspoken trouble. But it was less so, or at least leavened by the return of some resilient and peaceful bearing.

They worked at their own tasks for some time without any conversation. Every now and then Leonard went to speak to his brother about their conversation the day before, and to say, What now? What will you do to account for yourself? Then he became bothered by his own phrasing, to *account* for yourself; accounting for oneself meant trying to raise one's score back up to even, to zero; to become reconciled with others' expectations. Of course, it implied an assumption of wrongdoing, and he of all people shouldn't assume wrongdoing when his brother needed all the support he could find. Thus, when William went to sit on his deckchair under one of the apple trees, Leonard followed with the intention only of making whatever conversation came and of pressing no points on the subject of the fire.

'I wonder if Tela kept her allotment,' he said to William over his shoulder. 'It'll be death and destruction if she did. She wasn't exactly green-fingered.'

William murmured, hmn. Then he said, 'It's very hard.'

'Yes, yes it is. It is hard.'

That might have referred to anything, of course. But Leonard took it to refer to the loss of Tela specifically. He knew that one of the reasons – even if not always consciously felt – that he sought William's company was for the connection between his present and his past, because William had known her well and liked her, and she'd liked him, and those bonds seemed to have become important among the losses.

William turned his chair inwards. 'What is it you miss?'

He warmed, and he wanted to say suddenly, I love and support you, William, I love you dearly – to let that feeling flow into the accusations against him and dissolve them.

'Her face,' he said after a pause. 'I just miss her face and I see it all the time.'

'I suppose that makes sense. Life marches on, but there. Her face remains locked in one particular moment that'll never pass.'

'Exactly. So I can't move on from it.'

'Do you want to move on from it?'

The question surprised him. 'I don't know.'

'It isn't always easy to answer for our motives,' William said gently.

'I hadn't really thought about it, to be honest – my motives. I just get my head down and wait for it to go away. Sometimes it's the best you can do.'

William nodded and tapped his leg with his fingertips. 'I imagine this face you see is always Tela at her freshest and best, and smiling? No, beaming.'

He nodded, yes, he supposed it was.

'So your loss is always great.'

Leonard nodded, yes.

'Do you think that in reality she's always at her freshest and best, and always smiling? Right now, for example? And in every moment that's passed since she left you?'

He paused, and he directed himself at the fondness in his brother's voice, and away from an edge, a pressing tone. 'Yes, I suppose I do think that. I see her in the river at Jonathan's, coming up out of the water. But I know it's not true, at least not the whole truth.'

'So you choose to think something that hurts you.'

'It seems stupid when you put it that way.'

'It is stupid, but you aren't alone in your stupidity.'

'Well, neither its stupidity or its commonness stops me missing her, unfortunately.'

'But presumably it could. If you've chosen to think something that hurts you, you could choose the opposite, couldn't you?'

'Perhaps.'

'Perhaps?'

'The choice isn't conscious, William.'

'Then is it even a choice?'

'Well no, maybe not – you were the one who called it that.'

'I did, I apologise.' William stretched his fingers back against the opposite palm, one hand and then the other. 'But I don't really understand what you're getting at. If those images of a face flashing up in your brain aren't a choice of yours, what are they?'

Tela's face, Leonard wanted to say. Not *a* face, but Tela's, for that's what we're talking about, after all. He looked at his brother. 'They're the subconscious, I expect, William, just as dreams are.'

William nodded. 'Dreams.'

'And memories, which are also beyond our choice.'

'Oh, really? Just that I read something recently about lucid dreams, that can be controlled. But in any case my information is probably out of date. Things change so fast, don't they – but from your certainty I assume you keep on top of it all.'

Leonard looked down at his shoes in irritation, which he tried to quell. The recrimination was clear enough, but he was too taken by an abstract anger to respond to it. Yes, he thought – dreams, lucid dreams, whatever dream you like; the point is that everything eventually becomes like a dream, doesn't it? The terrible pain of it is that what was once real eventually disintegrates to the touch. Indeed, those short early relationships he'd had as a younger man – they were now so dreamlike he didn't feel entirely sure they'd actually happened, and when he had occasion to remember those times he felt like he was remembering a story somebody else had told him. He looked across to William's bare feet and an ugliness of feeling weighted his stomach, an irritation that met every other irritation that had ever passed through him.

'I just have times of missing the life I once had, that's all.'

There was quiet, and then William said with tranquil persistence, 'So the face that appears to you comes from the subconscious, as if from a dream?'

'Yes.'

'And you can do nothing about that?'

'No. And could you, William? If Kathy left you, could you *do* anything about the torture of it?'

'It would probably be the undoing of me.'

He hadn't expected the candour, and had to right himself against it for a moment. 'We are undone, we're fragile, you admit it yourself. I appreciate that you care, that you're taking the time to help me, but we can't always theorise our problems away.'

'God forbid that we should even try. Better to have them, isn't it, better to accept that they're part of life's rich tapestry and mystery, than to aspire to be without them.'

Leonard gave no answer; he watched instead the loosening of a vapour trail above and stood only for the sake of standing. Since he'd been reminded of that argument about love, with Jan, that dismantling trait of William's had become clear to him. How he could obliterate an emotion held so dearly and feel no shame or regret about that theft, for theft was what it amounted to. The conversation felt suddenly preposterous in the face of greater things, since his brother surely had more real worries than those ponderous ones. It was frustrating that he lacked a sense of scale in this respect. Leonard rested his hands on his hips and stayed just where he was. He felt aimless but unable to go.

He said, 'Actually we seem to have gone off topic, don't we? I thought we were talking about Tela, about things important to me.'

'I'm sorry if this isn't important to you.'

'No, it's just that – sometimes it's good just to talk generally, not to solve anything but just to get it off your chest.'

With a slow nod William seemed to consider this. 'Do you remember telling me about the Oneiroi in Greek mythology?'

'Maybe,' he said. 'It would have been a long time ago.'

'The Oneiroi were the Dreams, sons of Night and brothers of Sleep, Death and Old Age. I mention it because you spoke about dreams just now.'

Well, yes, I did, Leonard thought. And what of it? I spoke about my broken heart, too, but this you seem to have dismissed.

'And well, that Dreams are the brothers of Sleep makes sense. But of Death and Old Age? I wonder why they're not the brothers of, say, Hope and Fantasy? At least some of the nicer things in life. It's always struck me as strange, that dreams, death and old age belong to the same family, as if they run in each other's blood – dreams run in the blood of death and old age, death and old age run in the blood of dreams.'

Leonard remarked, 'It isn't something that's ever struck me.'

'No? You've never considered what dreams might be, and yet you're happy to consign half your suffering to them?'

'We don't all think as you do, William.'

'It's become apparent to me over the years.'

'I can't even work out what your point is.'

William linked his hands in his lap, his feet crossed and his back curved not like an old man but like a child. His face contracted in thought, the brows lowering, the cheeks rising with the studious upward curve of the mouth – not exactly a smile. The jaw tightening as was his way.

'I'm only wondering, Leo – if dreams belong to the realm of death and ageing, and if it's the nature of life for all things to age and die, might we not think that this life is a dream? Might we not look around us at the beauty and the ugliness and think, But what does it matter, for good and for bad it's all only a dream?'

'We might say that, but it would be ridiculous.'

'Ridiculous because it holds no water, or ridiculous because you can't bear to consider whether it holds water or not?'

There seemed little to say in response; just a vague movement of the head.

William added, 'I ask because I'd dearly love to hear your view.'

'To be honest, William, I'm just confused.'

'If we consider that the reality we experience is in fact a dream, then we might stop dreaming, mightn't we? If we didn't want to be tortured by this face flashing up in front of our own, reminding us of our losses, might we just stop dreaming and open our eyes?'

Leonard paused. 'But I say it again, we can't control what we dream about. If only we could.'

'We've no control at all?'

'I don't know, William.'

'You don't know?'

'No.'

'Good,' he said, 'because you thought you knew, and now you don't. Then that's a beginning.'

With that William inclined his head back in contentedness, and closed his eyes, as though something beautiful had been settled between them.

The next morning, in the kitchen, Leonard made his coffee quickly and leaned against the fridge, wondering if he should stay. Kathy and the boys were eating breakfast together and he didn't want to encroach, but neither did he want to leave and seem uninterested, ungrateful, whatever they might think. He held his cup still and listened to their chat and clatter, their pent-up energy breaking across the table.

'Oliver, eat nicely.'

'He put a golf ball in my cereal.'

'Well take it out. Don't put golf balls in Oliver's cereal.'

'I've got a rash.'

'You're a leper.'

'He's a leopard.'

'Stop banging your spoon, come on now, no more sugar, isn't that enough sugar?'

'What would happen if you dropped a golf ball off the Eiffel Tower?'

'Don't you remember, Abe, what happened when we put that tooth of yours in a glass of lemonade that time? Hm? What happened?'

'It wasn't my tooth, it was Oliver's.'

'If it hit a person their head would explode.'

'It dissolved, didn't it, that's what happened. And that's what will happen if you eat too much sugar.'

'And their brains would spray on the pavement.'

'There aren't any pavements in France.'

'Why am I a leopard?'

'I said *leper*, you numb head.'

'He isn't a leper. Let me see that rash, Richard.'

'Is the Eiffel Tower taller than the clouds?'

'It's not a rash, it's just an insect bite.'

'I don't want an insect bite.'

'So eat up, boys. Come on now. Eat up nicely.'

So it was, that Kathy's attempts to drive logic and coherence into the three boys' conversation resulted only in a fourth stream of nonsense. He was only feet away from them but couldn't have felt more displaced. He went first into the garden to see if William was there, but he wasn't, and it was a greyer, cooler day than they'd had for some time.

'He's gone out already,' Kathy said when he passed back through the kitchen on his way upstairs. 'If you were looking for him.'

He thanked her and went up to his room. He'd been looking for William, thinking they might take the Austin for a drive out to Swift Ditch – they used to swim in that Thames backwater because boats had stopped navigating it. Where the Thames looped around in a bow, Swift Ditch cut straight across and created an island with the bigger river, which had appealed to their sense of exploration; their parents had let them think that the trip across the footbridge to the island constituted going abroad. And the optimistic memory of that river was of a perpetually sunny stretch with a sense of unbounded space to it, flat, green and tall with poplars. He'd thought they might take their swimming things and chance the water after all these years, but of course William was nowhere to be found. What was it that made one seek the company of those who didn't want it? Really, a contemptible childhood weakness for approval, doglike in some respects.

In the end he took the car east across London to the long residential street in Plaistow that housed Eastacre Library. Architecturally, everything was so out of place that nothing looked out of place, for on that one street there were the weathered Edwardian terraces, the nineteen-fifties houses clad and flat fronted, the high rises and the modern complexes of cramped flats; and also of course the remains of the Victorian schoolhouse once filled with books on handmade sandalwood shelves, with handwritten indices of each and every item in stock, kept in shoeboxes elaborately painted by a local Bangladeshi woman. Those were the details that had remained most vividly with him when the fire was reported, the loss of the handwritten records, the sandalwood shelves, the painted boxes.

Above the burnt-out oak doors the carved datestone read 1886. The walls stood but the roof was gone, leaving a collapsed ribcage of wooden joists; the terracotta bricks had mostly blackened and as far as he could see all the windows were out. How like a ruined body it was, as if defensive from a beating, staggering about on its last legs. It didn't pay to use the word tragedy too often, but what had happened to that building in front of him was a tragedy; gone the shelves, the books, gone the buoyancy and togetherness of a community. He remembered seeing news footage of the street party when the library had opened a year or two before, and how by then it had already captured something good about the mood of the nation. There could never again be a more colourful scene than that, with the prismatic array of Asian and African and Caribbean dress, the Chinese in their electric silks. They'd hung paper lanterns along the streets and wound lights up the trunks of the cedars. The mayor of London attended and some local celebrities, for it wasn't a trivial thing, this success that had been achieved by a group of people without money or power.

It was really nothing short of enchanting to Leonard now, as he stood before the little that remained of the building, that inside that old Victorian schoolhouse a deprived community had accidentally amassed one of the richest collections of literature in the country – books in English, Punjabi, Cantonese, Urdu, Sylheti, Bengali, the Caribbean creoles; great works of literature that had never found their way to British shores, pulp fiction, rare books of illustration, folklore and fable, children's books that were a hundred years old, passed through generations. Almost every member of the community had donated almost every book he or she owned; books had been sent from families in the homelands, some of them heirlooms. They had items that the British Library itself coveted, amongst those a Qur'an that had a rare double frontispiece of exquisite Islamic art never seen before, and in light of those treasures the British Library had donated funds to pay for security equipment and impromptu shelves that could be suspended from the ceiling by pulleys to house the expanding collection; Leonard remembered on the news footage a young Jamaican woman in carnival costume hoisted up on one of those shelves with an armful of blue and yellow paper butterflies that shimmered under spotlights as she loosed them down into a sea of clapping hands. He remembered that image so well because Tela had watched it with him and said it was one of the proudest days in London's history – as if it were the butterflies that had been the inspiration for such pride, not the hands, nor the books.

He stepped away from the building; it was cordoned off and boarded up in any case, and there was no going inside. The dissuasion was emphatic, placards everywhere that warned of unsteady masonry and broken glass. If his memory didn't fail him, the reason the community had seized control of the old schoolhouse in the first place had been because a boy had died there. Standing derelict for decades, in an urban area with few playgrounds, it must have been a magnet for children. You could wait twenty years for the council to do nothing or you could do something yourself; you either left the place derelict or made something of it. Probably books were all they collectively had to spare, so they spared them, and there it began. He'd never liked to be defeatist or to think fatalistically, but he couldn't but wonder if some things were never to be changed, no matter the fight and the energy invested – for less than two years later derelict it was once again; gone the sandalwood shelves and the painted boxes and the Jamaican folktales, the butterflies, the lanterns. Painted blue and large on the burnt bricks: *Thee only we serve; to Thee alone we pray for succour.*

*

My brother, he thought. I know you've nothing to do with what has happened here. But why that conversation yesterday in the garden? All morning he'd thought more than he'd like to of that useless conversation, and of how it had come apart in the way of the vapour trail. It had started as one straightforward thing with a single trajectory and then had begun to break from itself until it was no longer clear, and one could no longer be clear about it. He couldn't even call it an argument, it was just a sourness. Something fresh going off.

He was frustrated, no, hurt – for though William had been that way with people for decades – questioning them, undermining them, like a child asking Why? Why? Why? – he'd never been that way with Leonard. Leonard had been the single exception and the exceptional exception; his brother. They'd shared their conversations and related in lightness, in talk of rugby, in a certain mind-reading, in a private language, in playing games, like whistling the shapes for the other to guess. They'd had their own way of relating that was particular to them and from which all others were barred. And really, if he were to be truthful with himself, if he stopped looking for the bright side, that had simply gone. Now it seemed that when William expressed his frustrations with him, it wasn't with him, Leonard, as an individual, but him as a representative of the world at large, the world whose blindness William was losing patience with. Leonard had become *people*, no longer a minority of one but the front-man of a dull majority.

There was something that he kept coming back to, though, in that conversation in the garden. Twice in that discussion William had apologised, and though it had been in sarcasm as it always was when he was trying to outwit somebody, it hadn't been, in that case, only sarcasm. Something in him had seemed wholehearted, as though he really were sorry, as though he didn't want to be having that discussion with Leonard at all; he just couldn't help himself. In all the world Leonard was his final bastion of tenderness and of surrender to that last perfect unquestionable thing – familial love. He didn't want to treat it like everything else, but he'd come to the end of himself and could no longer stop it.

Well, maybe that was how he felt. One couldn't tell, one could only make up truths from what one hoped. Maybe William had no sense of the end of himself, of his finitude, and of those things that required preservation and care.

Several days later the hens arrived, five of them, each strangely alien and uncomprehending in appearance. William released them into the outside run of the coop he'd built which occupied the back quarter of the garden. He'd laid down several bowls of water and grain for them, built perches into the coop and filled a large cardboard box with straw for warmth and nesting at night.

They stood somewhat bewildered, but with great hope. Heads cocked, one claw lifted and drawn up to the body, delicate and anticipatory. They were featherless in patches, one of them more so than the other four, and the feathers they had were reedy and rigid or grew in tufts around the head and thighs. Their skin was bruised and rubbery and they were lump-chested as though a tumour grew there. William told him it was no tumour but just the pouch in which they stored their food before digesting; when the feathers grew back it wouldn't be visible any more. Leonard was glad of the fact – even knowing they were normal, he found those exposed pouches disheartening and didn't like to look at them. The five poor creatures picked uncertainly on weak legs in an almost comic parody of what it was to be a hen, scrawny-necked and pebble-eyed, with their combs large and listless on heads which drew into aquiline little faces. Ridiculous, they were, but pitiful and endearing, lifting their claws as if the earth were hot coals, and blinking at the sunshine.

The boys stood at the wire mesh and watched them for a few moments as they scratched about in the dust. They noticed everything about the chickens that was grotesque and abnormal – their heads like the Venetian masks Kathy's sister had got for them, their flesh like old ladies' tights, their robotic strut and peck. Kathy told them to be nice about the unfortunate things; William told them they should be however they were and say whatever they saw – there was no point censoring a child's imagination or of teaching them how to be nice, especially not for the sake of an indifferent chicken. Niceness for its own sake was a thing that had far too much importance in the world, he said. She flapped her arms at her side, put her hands on her hips, but said nothing. Leonard often wondered how she would ever uphold her reputation as bickering fishwife if she never did bicker; he thought he even saw her smile slightly under all that surface indignation, and turn her face up an inch into the generous warm midday.

It was the last day of August and the sky was shedding thick, bright light. The apples were reddening, and the pinks and scarlets of the dahlias were blasting hot. William had on his usual crumpled summer linens, but had supplemented the outfit with a bright blue sunhat which sat large on his head, and which he kept adjusting with contrived vanity. And as if they'd woken up that morning and decided to try out different personas, Kathy wore a red cotton dress Leonard had never seen her wear or imagined she would ever wear – knee-length, sleeveless and almost frivolous. He noticed for the first time that the skin on her thin arms was beginning to slacken with age and that the muscles in her neck, always long, were becoming sinewy; still, she was more attractive than she'd been when younger, more grown into herself. It seemed they were all elsewhere, in some corner of Africa or plump in mid-America, spliced from time into a simpler past. It was only the radio, which Kathy had brought out onto the back patio as she hung out the washing, that made any effort at signifying the times.

'More fuel protests,' she said to him. 'Bad time to acquire a car.'

'It's okay, that car runs as much by the grace of God as it does by petrol,' he replied.

'Well then you're doubly scuppered – I wouldn't rely on the grace of God either.' She smiled and pegged a sock to the line with a quick plunge that reminded him of a heron ducking in for a fish. Then she glanced up the garden towards a heedless William, picked up the empty washing basket and said neutrally, 'Was it you who wanted those hens?' When his response was emphatically no, she took a few seconds to look puzzled, then responded, 'If they start laying it'll be eggs every day for the rest of our lives.' She stood for a moment gazing into the tail end of her comment, then went indoors.

The police came later that day, pacing into the colour and warmth of the back garden. Leonard was sitting on the lawn when they rang the doorbell, fixing the broken pivot on Richard's Tonka lorry so that it could articulate again, while Richard watched him lever the metal back into shape with solemn attention. The other boys had gone to kick a ball around with the Delohery children. William was sitting deep in his deckchair with his hands clasped, watching the hens, and had been that way for over an hour, lost to his thoughts. It was Kathy who got up and answered the door to let them in, two police officers, one male, one female – and when she followed them out into the back garden it was clear she hadn't meant for them to make it all the way through the house, they should have waited by the front door. Richard should never have seen them. Leonard saw her draw the back of her wrist quickly across her forehead, exasperated and hot.

The two police officers waited on the patio. William went to them and offered his hand to shake, then took them indoors. About five minutes later he came back out to where Leonard, Kathy and Richard were gathered in false relaxation on the lawn, talking in aimless and awkward tones about anything but the pressing matter of the police officers inside the house – they'd murmured about the behaviour of the hens and the strange low purr that built in their chests as they pecked for food, about the divots in the dry lawn from the boys' cricket, about lawn feed, about hosepipe bans.

'They just want to carry out a search,' William said. 'We'll wait here, they won't be a minute.'

Kathy made an instinctive, protective move towards the back door. 'Search for what?'

'I've no idea.' William crouched by her and took her hand. She squeezed it curtly then got to her feet without another glance in the direction of the house, and herded Richard to the back of the garden with her.

Leonard said nothing to his brother. He patted his arm, which was meant to suffice for support, and maybe did. The police could search the house twenty times and they'd find nothing. If they'd been looking for some overt thing that proved William's degeneracy or advertised his career as an arsonist they'd leave empty-handed; and if for something else, trails of thought, hints at habit, they must have been disappointed at how scant the trails of William's life and how resistant those few existing trails were to forensics.

They might have found hanging in the wardrobe neat and limited collections of the calico shirts he wore, which were off-colour, but beyond that didn't condemn their owner at all. They might also have found the sandals whose soles were pressed into deep bowls at the heel and into ravines at the edge; perhaps from there could come a forensic guess – these sandals have been worn for many years, by a man whose weight falls backwards and outwards. This might have added to their knowledge, but not to their wisdom. What else would they have found? The Hacker Gondolier and the vinyls of plainsong, and of *Don Giovanni, Manon Lescaut, Lucia di Lammermoor*. The little black and battered any-year diary he kept but wrote nothing in, as if he just liked a way of visualising the passing of days; the three keys on his key ring – front door, back door, Bellevue; the Salvadorean crosses, the brain cross-sections, the gallery of children's drawings. Really there was barely even one single man within these few objects, let alone a particular man who could be suspected of having done a particular thing.

Before they left, the police checked the newly converted chicken coop. The creatures looked on in nervous dismay; once again, Leonard thought, it's the dumb hapless hens who are at the brunt of it. No sooner are they released to freedom than their sanctuary is shuffled inside out by suspicion and human rot. But sure enough the police left with nothing, concluding their vague visit with a vague promise that that was everything they needed. One had to wonder how nothing could be everything they needed, unless it confirmed to them the little doubted fact of William's innocence. And yet if they doubted it so little, why did they persist with him? In any case they left, and the late Tuesday afternoon resumed its appearance of normality.

*

William asked him, as he came in, 'Where have you been all evening?'

'Down into the city, for a walk,' he said. 'I treated myself to a polystyrene tray of Vietnamese noodles on a bench by the river.'

'They were good?'

He hesitated. 'Seven out of ten – I couldn't tell what kind of meat it was supposed to be, which always makes me nervous.' He sat on the armchair opposite his brother in the low light of the back living room; the portable TV was set up ready, he guessed, for the recording of the Wasps game that had been played that weekend; it was just a pre-season friendly, hardly significant among the other events of the previous week, but, in a gesture that touched Leonard, Kathy had recorded it for her husband all the same.

'The moon was beautiful, though,' Leonard added, 'over St Paul's – low and full. I had one of those rare moments of feeling at home.'

'We wondered where you'd gone. Kathy cooked for you just in case.'

'Sorry, I should have said – I just felt like getting out.'

William switched on the lamp next to his chair and sat upright in its light. 'Leo,' he said, mild and plain, 'I've had plenty of time to think about this issue with the fire, what it could mean, what could happen. I know Kathy's worried.' His thumb twitched at that as if with a low electric shock. 'But somehow the police coming here today has put my mind at rest, if that doesn't sound idiotic – what I mean is, I've nothing whatsoever to hide and nothing that can be discovered. The entire police force can come and live with me for all it matters to this case. I'm not concerned, and I don't want you or Kathy to be either.'

Leonard shrugged his acquiescence. 'I know. In a way I've thought the same myself.'

And he had; there'd been a moment as he'd stood on Jubilee Bridge quite still while the city's footfall made music around him, laughter everywhere breaking through the evening like an unburdening, and some strange levity had almost physically lifted his chin. It was both futile and last-ditch for the police to come and search the house, the innocent old upright house. My brother is as guileless and shameless as the full moon, that's what he'd thought. If I know him at all, then I know him in that respect.

'I gave the police a note earlier in the week – Stephen sent it to me.' William cocked his head after speaking that. 'It said very little, it didn't even say where he was, but I thought it would be wrong to keep it from them so I handed it over.'

'He sent you a note?' Leonard leaned forward in his seat. 'To here?'

'To the Bellevue.'

'From where?'

'It was postmarked southern Italy, but Stephen knows people in Italy – the police doubt he posted it from there himself.'

Leonard's sigh rose in anger and fell in distraction, and he passed his hand quickly over the chair arm to brush away something that wasn't there. That man's selfishness and ignorance, he thought, it knows no bounds; he needn't have ever mentioned William's name, let alone be sending conspiratorial letters to him, and as for why William had ever befriended him or seemed to think so much of him, it was impossible to say. Impossible, really, to know what thing it was in a person – beyond his or her humanity itself – that would be beguiling to William or worthy of his respect. Whatever it was, Leonard suddenly felt he didn't possess it himself – that edge, that degeneracy that gave heat as it burnt out the soul. Whatever it was, he didn't feel it was something he'd ever have.

'You did the right thing handing it in,' he said to his brother finally, and draped his hand round the curve of the chair.

'There wasn't ever a dilemma, I've got no interest in protecting Stephen if he's done wrong.'

'So you think he has done wrong?'

'The note said that he was well, and that he didn't regret what he'd done, and that he only hoped it wasn't reflecting too badly on me.'

Leonard squinted into that little revelation with some disdain and disbelief. 'Which is basically an admission.'

'It sounds that way, doesn't it? The police certainly read it that way.'

'Well me too, and it changes everything.'

'What does it change, Leo? What difference does it make whether I'm not an accessory to a crime Stephen committed or not an accessory to a crime he didn't commit? In either case the truth remains unaffected, doesn't it?'

Leonard looked down at his lap. 'Why are you so calm about what's happening? Apart from the fact that you're somehow implicated, don't you care that one of your students and friends – I presume friends? – has done something sickening? A library! A library – and what for? What could he hope to gain?'

'I care when *anybody* does a stupid thing, whether or not they're a student of mine.' William looked up at him with an intent frown that buckled his brows. 'A person's relation to me has no affect on the rightness or wrongness of their actions.'

Leonard tucked his hands tight into his front pockets and stood without a response.

'And as for being implicated, Leo, what Stephen has done is a matter for the law, and his reasons for doing it are a matter for the same, to be settled not by me but by lawyers. If I've unwittingly broken a law in any way, that's for them to decide, and I have to trust in their greater wisdom on the subject. Do you see? It's being dealt with on exactly the level it should be, so I'll lose no more sleep over it.'

'For most people that lack of control would be a cause for worry, not for comfort.'

'Why? Don't you trust in this great edifying thing we call the legal system?' With that impassioned but lightly teasing smile in his eyes, William brought his hands to a demure entwinement on his lap. 'Aren't we told in every way that it knows best and will protect us? Aren't we relieved to live under its vast wing?'

Leonard said, 'You mock, William, as if this were some amusing thing happening to somebody on TV.'

'I wouldn't find it amusing even if it were on TV.'

Leonard asked after a pause of some seconds, 'And Stephen? Do you miss him, now he's disappeared?'

'Yes – I miss every human heart that's ever crossed my path and gone again.'

'Whenever I ask you a question about a specific person you give me a general answer – you miss everyone, you care when anybody behaves stupidly, you love everyone. But I'm asking you about a single person, not everyone.'

'I don't see single people, I see people, I don't love or hate discriminately, I just try to give myself equally to all for as long as what I give is wanted. And always, Leo, always this act of giving is vulnerable and my heart gets knocked about. But you ask me to get bogged down in the details of one person and to break my heart against another heart as if there were one person alone in the world who could make me happy, like every poor doomed soul stuck in an opera; to go mad – going mad is a sign of humanity after all. Would you like me to go mad?'

Leonard bit his lip. 'I thought you liked opera.'

'I love it for all that.'

'And I don't ask you to get a broken heart, or to go mad.'

William's look examined him uncomfortably and precisely. Leonard ventured, 'And our parents then, you don't miss them in particular? They're just people?'

'They aren't *just* people, they are people.'

If it hadn't been for Kathy coming into the room at that moment Leonard would have chased that comment, for whatever mighty and all-purpose notion his brother had of *people* it couldn't have accommodated their own parents sufficiently, or William's wife, or children – nor, surely, himself. It was beyond Leonard to accept that. But Kathy came in carrying Richard whose breath was an audible rattle in his chest. William stood to put his hand to the child's back, and kissed his temple.

'Couldn't he sleep?'

'His asthma is bad tonight,' she said.

She handed the child to William, who took him full-armed into the bulk of himself and cradled his head.

Kathy tucked her dress behind her knees as she sat. 'It's bad timing – he's supposed to be back at school tomorrow. We can't let him go if he's like this.' She'd let her hair loose so that it fell to her waist – such an impressive head of hair, strong and silken, so surprising to see it that way thick across her back. Her voice quiet and considerate, she said, 'I think he's worried about what happened today. He's a sensitive child. It all troubles him.'

'About the police?' William asked at normal volume, and she pursed her lips in a silent ssshh, and shook her head in a bid for his discreetness. She really hadn't acknowledged Leonard until that point, but then she glanced at him to seek his support, or so he presumed. He gave it with an uncommitted smile, but he felt embarrassed that for the first time they were acknowledging the issue at hand. It had been a week since they'd had news about the fire, and Kathy had known longer; yet even with the police there they'd gone on as if there was nothing to mention. He blamed both her and himself equally for their cowardice. He asked, 'Is he okay?'

William ran his hand over the child's head and asked in turn, 'Are you okay, little man?'

Richard nodded through a murmur and clung his arms around his father's neck.

'Did what happened today trouble you?' William said, and though Kathy inclined her head in exasperation William didn't look up to see it nor remove his attention from his son. Again Richard nodded. 'Are you worried about the police coming here?' The child nodded.

Kathy said, 'You're making things worse.'

'Things mustn't be hidden, nothing good comes from making a taboo of an issue.' Once again he dipped his head to Richard's. 'What worries you?'

'Leave him be, William, he isn't well enough.'

'There is evidence these days, Kathy, that children are human beings.' William was serene in the face of his wife's anxiety; he looked at her and back to the child, and concluded, 'Whatever worries you, there's nothing in the world to be afraid of. I promise this; all is well, all is well.'

Tela came on Thursday evening.

'It's someone for you,' Kathy said, as if she didn't know who Tela was. And maybe the forgetting, or misidentifying, was genuine, because Tela was the very last person any of them expected to see, and she was dressed in an obscuring ensemble of clothes that made him wonder if she'd worn everything she owned at once. It was true that at the turn of

September the weather had shifted quite distinctly, becoming greyer and fresher – a relief to him – but it didn't quite merit that level of wrapping up, he thought. The silk scarf around her neck and the wide velvet hat made her face loom in pale astral suspension from her body.

'Tela, come in, please don't stand there.'

'Thank you.'

In the hallway she removed her jacket; she took the hat off and unwound the scarf, and there was the full bright oval of her face exposed in muddled blonde hair, that small upturned nose, the pointed chin.

She asked, 'Is that the old Austin I saw outside?'

'It is.' And he was about to explain that he had it on loan, but then saw an utter lack of interest on her part to have any more detail on the subject.

He always thought she was slimmer than she proved to be. In his mind she was skinny and juvenile, when in reality she was thick around the waist and thighs. He used to make this error of judgement even when he saw her every day; each morning when they parted she would become sylphlike to his lax imagination, and each evening when they came together again he would have to accept, in a way quite gladly, that this wasn't so. It was her face that fooled him. It was elfin and freckled across the nose, and the blue eyes had mischief. In the eyes, nose and mouth, and in their coming together, she still looked twenty-five.

'You're wearing so many things,' he said. 'What will you do when winter comes? You'll have no distance left to go.'

'I'll stay indoors.'

'You will not, I've never seen you stay in one place for more than fifteen minutes.'

'Untrue.' She smiled and looked down at the carpet.

He too looked down and put his hands in his pockets. I'm

the cat and you the dog, she used to say. I go out and explore my senses, you stay in and loyally wait. He'd never known how he felt about that, it seemed unfair, as if he just had to sniff her coat and extract the world from those scents she'd rubbed up against, and that this would be enough for him. His only portal into the wideness of the world, and it would be somehow enough.

Then William appeared in the hallway from the kitchen and her face lit. 'William.' She raised her arms as if in embrace and then went to him and kissed him on the cheek. 'You look so well.'

'And you, my dear. As beautiful as a child.'

Silence for a moment, and then William added, 'Why don't you get on with things? We'll bring you coffee.' He motioned towards the door on his left, the back living room, where Leonard had been when Tela arrived.

Leonard moved towards them. 'Thank you,' he said. And then to Tela, 'Shall we . . .?'

Tela nodded. They went into the room alone and Leonard closed the door behind them. She sat in the opposite armchair – William's chair by the window with its half view to the garden. It was only eight-thirty but twilight outside now – the disintegration of their hot summer was most marked in the onset of evenings and the rapid damp cool that came down on the tail of sunset. The aspen in the back garden had started to give astonishing colour as yellow as sunflowers, which they could see dusk-muted through the window.

When Kathy came in with the tray of coffee she didn't stop to make conversation, she simply put the tray on the occasional table, smiled, let her gaze linger for just a moment on Tela, and then left. Tela poured coffee for them; she had never waited for others to take charge.

'I haven't been here for a while,' she said. She walked over to hand him a mug, then returned to her seat.

'Eighteen months, two years?'

'I'd say something like that.'

'We came here on Boxing Day once – was it two years ago?'

'Yes, you showed us how to play that card game – the one Jan taught you.'

'Skruuvi.'

'Yes, Skruuvi. With the Bolsheviks and the, what were the others?'

'Kotkas.'

She ruffed the hair at her neck with her fingers so that it loosened. 'Bolsheviks and Kotkas. That was too complicated for us.'

'Well, I taught you the modern rules. They're more difficult – in the old rules you're not obliged to bid a Bolshevik. Do you remember that part? Maybe I should have stuck to the old rules.'

'Ah.' She drank her coffee and crossed her ankles.

'Those are sweet shoes,' he said. He was sure they hadn't been in the pile that had reduced him that day when he left her house. They were red and like ballet shoes, and had a single strap that circled the ankles. They weren't at all in keeping with the thick black tights underneath them, or with all that relentless clothing.

She looked down at them and twitched her feet. 'Thanks, I got them recently.'

'They suit you, they make you look like something from a fairytale.'

She laughed and put her hand on her belly in protectiveness, and it occurred to him, Dear God, this is why she's come, and why she's so blossoming, I know what she's come to tell me. Her hair had grown and was lovely – loose straw-coloured waves that went spirited and tangled to her mid-arm. He refrained from saying something about that too, that her hair, as well as her shoes, was sweet, or nice, for those words weren't really the kind of words for her, and besides she'd always hated his compliments. Whatever he'd said from whatever corner of his heart, she'd found it incomplete or insincere; if he'd killed himself for love of her, that, too, would have probably struck her as disingenuous or uncommitted.

'You must be wondering why I'm here,' she said.

He didn't reply, but took his cigarettes from the bookcase next to him and removed two from the pack. He threw one across to her. When she refused he would know if his intuition was right, for she never refused cigarettes. A reverent and committed smoker; it had been because of her that he'd started in the first place and had come to think of that activity as life inherent, life and freedom and happiness.

But she did take it, she balanced it between her fingers and waited for him to pass her a light. At that he almost rose to lecture her: Tela, you can be so irresponsible, you're not in a fairytale no matter if you look like it, why have you always had this destructive streak as if nothing and nobody is important to you? The torrent continued in his throat and heated and burnt it.

'Well,' she said, 'in part I've just come to see how you are, and because I miss you. And I want us to be friends. In fact I need us to be friends.'

'Right,' he answered. He lit, and threw her the lighter.

'How possible is that, do you think?'

'To be friends?'

'Yes.'

'Not yet, Tela—'

'But given time?'

'Yes, given time.'

'Good.'

'I don't blame you, by the way. It was me who abandoned you. What can I expect if I desert you for a year? And all I ever did

162

was make myself a parasite, living in your house, attaching myself to your friends. I think I thought it would prevent you from leaving me, which I suppose it did for a long time. Then the parasite left and you realised how good life was without it.'

She raised the cigarette. 'Is there an ashtray?' It was almost a whisper. He got up and took his ashtray to her, which necessitated staying there himself. He knelt on the floor, at the greatest distance possible from her chair; he propped the ashtray on the arm.

'No, you weren't a parasite, it was just that I met somebody else. There, it's said.'

Before he could think it through he interjected, 'And now you're pregnant.'

She broke into shocked laughter. 'Am I?'

'Aren't you?'

'Is it? Are we playing the question game?'

He paused. 'No, we're not, Tela. It isn't a game.'

'I'm not pregnant, Leo.'

'I thought that was what you'd come to tell me.'

'I'm forty-two, being pregnant is one of the less likely things to happen to me.' She smiled. 'I'm more likely to have a heart attack than a child.'

Leonard heard the front door close and he assumed it was William going out. 'So you have somebody else?'

'Well, not really, he's married. Everybody of my age is married, you see. But I'm afraid I fell in love with him and—'

'Let's not talk about it,' he said.

She gave him one of her looks of perplexity and impishness; oh he wished she wouldn't – that little puckering of her features that made her appear a teenager only half comprehending the adult world. Hopelessly dear and sexual, and he wished she wouldn't do it. 'You don't want to know at all?' she asked.

'I don't, Tela, because all the time I was away I knew you would fall in love with somebody, and it's all right to know some things in the abstract as long as you never actually run up against them in real life.'

She flicked her hair over her shoulder and leaned forward with a sort of urgency. 'That's exactly what you do with everything. That *exact* thing.'

'What exact thing?'

'You avoid subjecting your beliefs to reality. That's exactly what you do.'

This wasn't very exact to him and he wished for an example, or a different observation altogether. He thought she might continue, because she was still leaning forwards with her cigarette pointed at him and her mouth half open, alight with revelation. He wanted her to go on; if there was anybody in the world whose eyes he might see himself through honestly, it would be hers – rigorous as her vision was, but wild enough to tuck away his petty wrongs and his silly flaws and dream him up into something altogether bigger and better. He wanted her to say, And if you wouldn't do that, that *exact* thing, you would be perfect, and I, for one, would be with you right away. With that, the riddle of his entire personhood would be solved, and everything would come to him.

Despite wanting this, it wasn't the case. She sat back and said, 'I understand, though, why you wouldn't want to know about this – other person. To be honest, it's a tawdry little story, sleeping with a married man who isn't ever going to leave his wife.'

'Yes, well. Maybe it's tawdry and maybe it isn't.'

'Maybe.' She bit her lip as she nodded. She was obviously sad. To see her vulnerable was of enormous consolation to him, so that he could quiet the jealousy that had begun to pitch its wail deep between his ribs and instead want to take her in his arms in reassurance, and in longing for something greater for both of them.

Tela put her cigarette out before it was finished, one of her odd profligate habits. 'Well, if you don't want to talk about that, we'll leave it. But I'm just asking you not to blame yourself, it was me who abandoned you. I probably would have fallen in love with someone else at some point even if you hadn't gone away.'

He did wonder if this was supposed to make him feel better, but he said nothing. There was no malice motivating the words.

'The other thing I came about was this,' she said, and she drew a piece of folded paper from the breast pocket of her top. He took it back to his chair with the ashtray and settled. It was a newspaper clipping from the *Evening Standard*, and stated details of the police investigations into the fire in a series of calm facts; a mention of Stephen and William, their ages, the absconding. Sixty-two, it said William was in this article. Leonard looked up to point this out to Tela then changed his mind. In exasperation he put his cigarette out and folded the article again in half.

'It was something of a surprise to me when I saw it,' she said, and she wrapped her small hands around her cup.

He hesitated. 'Shall we go into the garden? I'll show you the chickens.'

She turned to the window with a look of faint disapproval, for it wasn't warm and there were only a few torn patches of sunset remaining to the dusk. But she stood and they went out, through the kitchen where Kathy, who was decanting into a bowl the leftover bolognese from dinner, stepped quietly aside for them. He led her up to the enclosure where one of the chickens was still questioning the dry ground for food; the others were collected in the coop and their outlines could just be seen cobbled together in closeness. Even in two days they'd changed, he thought, gained in confidence and found balance and movement on their feet, a certain pleasure and purpose in life. There was a slight drizzle and Tela crossed her arms in front of her. It wasn't that she seemed cold so much as bereft of disguise, with her hat, scarf and jacket hanging in the hallway. She inclined her face towards the wire mesh but her features didn't animate, rather held themselves just so like frozen cream; she was rarely reluctant, but she was reluctant then.

'They came the day before yesterday,' he said, and qualified, 'the chickens.'

'Oh.'

'They were rescued from a battery farm.'

She stepped forward and said with interest, 'That's why this one looks so scrawny then.'

'Do you think it's wrong to kill a chicken?'

'Pardon?' She turned her face to him in the scant light.

'Do you think it's an abuse of power to kill a chicken?'

'What does this have to do with anything?' She shrugged, but when he didn't answer she said, 'Well, it depends why and how you kill it.'

'In what way does it depend?'

She didn't answer him, she just smiled and tipped her head back to the dimming sky and a low, robustly waning moon sheened with clouds.

With more intent, he asked, 'Do you think a chicken killer has a broken spirit?' And he took a step closer to her. 'If he has a broken spirit, which *part* of his spirit is broken in particular?' Standing right at her side, he ran his index finger down the mesh. 'Well?'

She sidestepped him and arched her brow high. 'How should I know?' she replied.

'No.' He crossed his arms. 'How should you know? How should

anyone know?' He shook the newspaper clipping in his hand. 'Believe me, that's what this whole business is about – William getting obsessive about his ideas and being unable to let anything go. If someone shows so much as a passing interest in a subject he'll pursue it until they wish they'd never mentioned it.'

'I don't know what you mean.'

'Look, somebody he knows well, and discusses things with at length, has burnt a library down. Do you know William once put a match to one of my books, I remember it well – it was *Under Western Eyes*.' Tela shrugged at that, and he hesitated. 'We were youngish, you know how it is. We were drunk and we'd been talking about revolutions and whether you can really change anything. And there I was waving around my copy of *Under Western Eyes* and spouting some opinion or other – and he took a match and said I'd be better off setting fire to the book and thinking for myself.'

She raised a brow and looked away. 'Did he burn it?'

'I put it up my jumper.'

'And on the back of that you think he'd help burn a library down?'

'Of course not.' He overlooked her disparagement and only uncrossed his arms and shoved his hands into his pockets. 'My point is that you can imagine the conversation, can't you? At his youth groups. Debating the topic of words and meaning and books and wisdom until everyone's blue in the face and somebody decides to stop thinking and start acting.'

Tela pulled her chin back towards her, shortening her throat, saying nothing.

'It's not that I think he suggested starting the fire, of course he didn't. But was he an accessory? Perhaps – perhaps it could be interpreted that way. I don't know the law, Tela, but I know it's not as simple as William makes out. There aren't just two states of right and wrong, there are degrees of things.'

Still she said nothing, though there was a rather small shake of her head. Are you judging me? he wondered, and wondered also if he should be saying any of this to her when, by her own choosing, his world was no longer any of her concern and his thoughts no longer her privilege or problem.

'Is he getting advice from anybody?' she asked.

'No,' he said, in such a way as to imply, of course not; William must do everything his own way. She crouched and pushed her fingers through the mesh to flick at a piece of lettuce that had become folded up against the frame. She began clicking her tongue at the hen; 'Here, come here, little lady, eat this.' The hen ran towards her with mechanical speed and dug her beak into the flaccid, pale leaf. They watched her gulp it as though drinking deeply.

She said, 'My – this man – this man I'm seeing is a criminal lawyer. Would you like me to ask him about it? Perhaps he'd speak to William and let him know at least what the law is.'

There was a stale moment between them. She leaned her head against the wire and clucked at the hen, while he remained with his lips pressed together staring at the overhang of the roof on the coop and a single drop of water that had gathered itself from an hour of drizzle, and held itself suspended there.

'William won't accept it, I shouldn't think,' he said. 'He has disdain for all professionals – he's not going to accept advice from a lawyer over some crime he's certain he has nothing to do with. As far as he's concerned this is a matter the lawyers fight out among themselves. He'll let them decide his guilt, but he won't take their advice.'

'He is going to need help, Leonard. You could ask him at least.'

'Fine,' he said more gently. 'I'll ask him. Thank you.'

She took the hand he offered and came to her feet. In the short eye-to-eye exchange he felt the here and the now and the great heaviness of himself, the strange arbitrary fact of himself, and it embarrassed him. He said, he knew unwisely, 'A lawyer, then? That's nice.'

'Is it nice?'

'It must be terrible for you, to play second fiddle like that.'

'Nice or terrible? Make up your mind.'

'Some things can be both by turns.'

'There are worse positions to be in. I think it would be worse to be his poor wife.'

He nodded and regarded her for a moment in the confused light of dusk; while shapes came specifically, it was hard to judge where in space those shapes were, and harder still to read the depth of her expression; but he knew there was some playfulness behind her words for he could hear a light trill, a sort of dance, that old girlishness that might after all never leave her, no matter her point in life.

'I have to get going,' she said. 'But it was good to see you.'

'And you. Thanks for dropping by.'

'I didn't even ask you about Edinburgh, or work, nothing.'

'We'll have to meet again soon then,' he said, despite himself.

She nodded. They went back indoors, through the now empty kitchen and to the hall. The scarf, the hat went on. 'Say goodbye to William and Kathy for me. And let me know what you want to do about my offer.'

At the door they kissed on the cheek, exchanged a few more quiet and inconsequential words, then she went out of the door and he waited on the front step while she made her way up the short path and right towards the main street.

Somewhere in the early weeks with her she'd once turned away from him naked to show him the part of her body that was invisible to her. She'd asked him to describe it and so he had: her strong compact back and the fine roundness of her shoulders sloping away, and the slight lean she took to the left, the freckles and markings, and the small, deep V at the top of her buttocks, a muscle there that twitched, cheeks that spread very sweetly and pinkly, the flat plains and then steep depths of her thighs, which were short and strong. Because he had seen in detail what she couldn't see, he owned it in a sense, she said. So it was for him to take what he owned, which he did at length in an inept and self-conscious way, and with increasing euphoria because he hadn't known it could be that way. Her face was never turned towards him. So with her back to him he was having sex with somebody who wasn't her, somebody he'd invented for himself.

And now he'd seen her back exiting the house and the garden to become naked, maybe even that very night, with another person, and still he wished her well, and was grateful to her. He shut the front door finally because the chill of the evening was coming in, and that poor child's cough sounded damply from upstairs. Tela had smelt as water tastes at the clear and deep part of a lake, he thought. Could that be a smell? It was the first time he'd been able to identify it. It seemed that it was on him, on his face and neck, or perhaps it was just the darkness and opening out of autumn.

A little after daybreak he got up, and at about six-thirty went out. Now that the children were back at school the house stirred early – Kathy would rise to get the boys dressed, give them breakfast and make them lunch, William would rise to walk them to school, and Leonard found himself up as if his own psyche were so accustomed to school terms that no circumstance could override that hardwired urge to be up and be out.

He went for a walk along Regent's Canal; it was a place he'd seldom been to and never at that hour, in that state of stillness and suspension. He passed along the leafy stretch east of Islington Tunnel where the morning water was black and the reflections grass green. Most of the narrow boats signalled not a breath of life, but a light came on in two or three, which rocked in the water as their sleepers moved through the cabin. There was occasional clanking from within, or clipping of crockery, and the beating of ducks' wings on the water, and these sounds were more music than noise; they described the silence more than they broke it. If one could separate out all the heard sounds, he thought, beginning with the sound of one's breath exiting the mouth, and retreating out to the hush of traffic at the furthest periphery, one could measure the depth of space one stood in. Layer by layer, the expanse could open out with one's own ears at the centre like small beings doubled over in attention.

He walked on into a treeless stretch of path. Tela would be burrowed down in bed somewhere with her hand to her chin and her jaw tense in sleep, still two hours from getting up. So fast asleep when, already, queues of cars were mounting at the petrol station he'd walked past on his way to the canal, where people had woken up fevered with a cause – he'd heard on the radio as he got dressed that the fuel blockades were increasing in size and strength at the ports. Tela wouldn't know about it and nor would her fanciful idealism allow her to care. So long as there were the red shoes, he thought, and velvets and silks cheap from the market and the place on the stairs in the sun, there was no cause for worry in her world. *Oh come on*, she'd used to say when he commented on the way education had turned into little but a pen-pushing exercise or on how the population was growing too large or politics too back-handed and war too ready; *Oh come on*, she'd say, and tell him to enjoy life more, to which he'd object. He did enjoy life, but that didn't mean one had to pretend it was perfect.

Besides, his fear was vindicated; they were alive in the new century but not especially well; there was this thing with the fuel, and people so immensely worked up about paedophiles that they ran left, right and centre trying to avoid them, and the continual effervescence of war in the Middle East, air raids in Lebanon, more needless deaths on the West Bank, systematic torture of Palestinians; rivers were polluted, the skies and seas; he didn't sit and worry about it all but he saw it nevertheless because he wasn't blind, and refused, unlike her, to pretend to be so.

Every age thought itself to be at the cusp and the breaking point, didn't it, and saw in itself a significance that didn't belong to the previous age? But theirs really was at a cusp in the sense at least that a new century had rolled into being under their feet and tipped them into a definite point in the future – the twenty-first century, whose existence they'd used to accept in purely mythical and hypothetical terms. They weren't modern any more, they'd exceeded their modernity. The triumph of their times was that they'd created for themselves a world intrinsically impossible for them to understand. Was he right to say that sometimes he could feel the panic? Something new was expected of them, but they'd developed no new skill with which to bring it about. Through scientific genius they'd been able to conjecture a reality textured with sights and sounds beyond all expectations, running at all angles from this reality, reverberating along shorter and longer wavelengths; and they knew that man was imprisoned inside his five human senses and could experience barely any of it. The burden of that knowledge was endless frustration, for what was it to have a brilliant human mind when its utmost brilliance lay in conceiving of all the things of which it would never be capable?

The Depplings had been a good and loving lot; oh they had, they'd been wise observers of the world, and careful partakers. And before he died, their father had got himself paternally anxious about the current state of things, as if he didn't like to leave a world he felt was in trouble and might need him. Here was a brand-new century so untouched and offering of itself. Yet what was man doing with it? There were wars darkly flourishing all over the place, and it wasn't that the ever-pacific old man condoned an open war, he condemned them all, but those new ones fought far away and for obscure private gains were insidious and alarming. Nobody told the truth; maybe they never had, but now that there were so many more people than before there were, by pure statistics, so many more lies, and lies had a critical mass at which they became so complex they started to look like the truth even to the liars themselves, so there was little distinguishing between fact and falsity even if one maintained the will to.

When Leonard comforted his father by taking him out to see the new dahlia stems and the cresting vista that fell in bounty from the bottom of their garden, the old man's breath would even out and he'd concede that everything did seem all right after all. The cows and sheep were grazing right enough, and the streams ran with unerring ease and vigour, and the west side of Blackhope Scar caught the glancing gold of the sunset just as always. Yes, everything seemed robust and unending. Then they'd go back indoors and whatever they did with the rest of the day it would culminate in the lighting of the fire, even in the summer, and some cooked meat for dinner with a supermarket-bought hot sponge dessert, and those intimate things would do for a while by way of comfort.

But one time his breath didn't even and when Leonard took him back inside from the garden he picked up the three-dimensional puzzle of William's and worried away at it for the entire afternoon. When Leonard asked what was wrong, he shuffled a copy of *Scientific American* a few inches across the floor with his foot, towards Leonard, and started saying how he really didn't much like this thing with Schrödinger's Cat and its being dead and alive at once, nor the idea of waves being particles and particles being waves, and multiverses bothered him even more than ignorant atheists – though he didn't mind at all atheists who'd taken the time to think things through. He was all for science and progress, but what was this wretched world that this wretched cat lived and simultaneously didn't live in? We were being stripped of our certainties and it was monstrous – for the world was there for touching and seeing and sensing and then, ultimately, for knowing, for *knowing*, and for giving oneself to in love and grace, whether with God or not. This was for him an issue beyond religion; however one comes to know the world, one must find a world that is knowable, otherwise we might as well be amoebas inhabiting a Petri dish.

The more restless he became on the subject the more avidly he threw himself into his home-brewing sessions, in defiance, Leonard supposed, of that despised cat and its profound underminings. He busied himself even where poor health made busyness awkward and he would get preoccupied and gratified by the rules and methods of his brewing guide. By the last few weeks of his life he'd started to make some very competent ales, bottles and bottles of which were lined up in the cellar. Watching the news became for him at once an obsession and an intolerable affliction, for he was shrewd and knowledgeable about current affairs and thought he saw the whole globe heading towards an impasse. The first year of the new century was, he'd said, a littered mix of earthquakes and meteorites, crashes and explosions, and ominous politics that would do nothing enlightened for the world. The death of some two hundred Nigerian villagers was one of the last news items he heard – they'd been scavenging for gasoline from a leaking pipeline when it exploded. They scavenge because they're poor, he'd said, they die because they're poor, all our livelihoods depend on things that cost money, all our needs have been put just beyond our fingertips. It's a question of who can stretch the furthest. The rich can stretch the furthest, poverty is rigid, only money makes one elastic; love used to – no, love still does, but society pays no heed to love any longer. Those villagers could not live on love. Nor were they – like that cat – both dead and alive at once. They were squarely dead and definitely dead and dead without quantum consolation, and the sooner we stopped trying to confuse one another with impossibilities and accepted the flat reality of things the sooner we might start to rebuild this broken world.

He'd gone uneasily back to his brewing with sallow but resolute face. A man needs *certainties*, he said, tapping his brewing guide; he needs determined outcomes that are within his reach. All this horror and muddle and hopeless stretching, a man needs somewhere to stop and *rest*. Leonard could see there was no point in taking him out into the garden that afternoon so he just brought him tea and helped him decant his brew into the stoppered bottles and carry them to the cellar. It was the day following the tragic fate of those villagers that the old man refrained from the news entirely, and went out alone to check how the dahlias were budding, then came indoors finally to die. Up I go, he'd said on one of his last breaths, the words diffusing in front of his lips like seeds knocked from a dandelion; so sweetly said, with a whispering childish pout.

The canal path opened out at Wenlock Basin, where the water was now black with the shadow of the warehouses and mills that bordered it. The quietude Leonard had felt just fifteen minutes before had dispersed with the terrain-change, from the jade overhang of trees to the high-rises butting up against a white sky. In fact it was still relatively calm and quiet, with the weeping willow stretching sentinel over the narrow boats curved around the corner of the basin and the water disappearing eventually away into trees, creeping away into shallowness, and the tall city beyond with its distant wakings. If his quiet was gone, the change was probably in him and not in the world of the canal. His father's anxious visions had never transferred to him before, but they did so then when he stood at the mouth of the basin. There did seem to be more than a sense of the blind precariousness of things – that basin, that open fan of boats, the canal as it took a slow looping journey down to the Thames, those Victorian warehouses and mills, and skyscrapers, all of them supposed evidence of man's industriousness and innovation and his ability to make permanent, yet all of them were in truth nothing but his limitations made matter, rather like the elaborate creation of a child who has inclinations but no plans, because she doesn't yet understand enough of the world to plan for it.

He understood then what his father had been craving, that resting point at which he could stop and say, Well at least I know this. When at sea in a storm, at least you know which way is north. Times were changing. Of course they always changed. Still, one couldn't always *feel* that, not in the way he could feel it then. The fact that everything was built in the spirit of certainty only highlighted the fact that nowhere could certainty itself be found. Each man made up his mind based on another's guesses, and held to it as though he'd mined it himself from the pure well of truth. And so he must, he must. Even if there were no pure well of truth he must act as though there were. There must be a place, or many places, to stop and rest and say, This is what I know. Every belief must constitute a place of rest, else the journey ruins one.

And it was impossible in all those thoughts for Leonard to bury the picture of his brother standing somewhere along this arm of water, one solitary and slightly ghostly figure asking the world to admit its ignorance. Rest nowhere, entitle yourself to no surety. Nothing but the absolute truth counts for anything, a half-truth or a benign ignorance is as good as a lie. Why did his brother have to think and talk that way? *The truth* – as if there were just one truth, towards which all outcomes were pulled gravitationally. Do you think, William, you're the chosen one bearing a light too bright for others to look at? As if there were even such a thing as this light and this absolute end. His demands sheered against the human need for peace and quiet, and if Leonard was only beginning to see the extent of that now it wasn't because he was only just realising it, but because he was only just remembering what he already knew and had wilfully forgotten through love and loneliness. This time for which he so pined, when he and his brother would lock in elegant and expansive debate about any issue that so presented itself, this time he so wanted back had never existed. When he considered it, all that had ever happened was what was happening now – those spiralling and self-limiting conversations they had in which his brother would force every one of his concerns into oblivion.

He turned away from the view of the basin and began to go back the way he'd come. By the time he passed the boats along the green stretch by the bridge, their hatches were open and their inhabitants up or on deck, their radios playing, their dogs loose, and their days very much begun. Were these the people to whom William spoke when he came down to the canal? This young woman here with the dark hair and wide articulated smile who acknowledged him as he passed, or this short-haired woman on deck who had some capable, intelligent look to her that extended even to her simple sleepy back-stretch, or that stocky no-nonsense man with her, opening the engine hatch with pillow creases still imprinted on his cheek? Had William broken into their spare and unassuming lives with conversation and questions; had he told them what he felt, that it wasn't just idle to live by blind acceptance of the way things were, it was inhuman? Had he told them that – that in their accepting contentedness they were inhuman?

Leonard realised that he was more worried about this fractious lack of fit his brother had with the world than he was about the specific problem of the fire, for he seemed to believe that nothing more could or would come of the police investigations, whereas William would never stop being who he was, and there would never be a point at which he'd find himself at home in this world. And here was a sad fact which ought finally to be acknowledged rather than wished away: it wasn't the exact truth that Leonard had found his dead father cradling three photographs as he'd told William on the day of their reunion; he'd been cradling only two – one of his wife and one of his youngest son. As for the picture of William, it had been Leonard who'd taken that off the sideboard and put it on the dead man's lap with the others. He thought of that then as he passed up onto the road from the canal, and of the distress he'd felt. There was a moment at the top of the steps, where the main road washed past thick with morning traffic, when his sense of his brother's presence behind him was so strong he had to turn round to prove to himself he wasn't there.

With a face as open as a meadow, William folded the newspaper article carefully as it had been and handed it back without a word.

'So will you agree to see him?' Leonard asked, and William answered that he would.

'Let the person who knows the law take care of the law,' he said, with a shrug that combined at once nonchalance yet also an earnest deference to wiser views. So Leonard nodded, and in the wake of William's surprise compliance he contacted Tela on Friday to say they wanted to take up her offer. William called the number she gave and was offered the swiftest of appointments, so that on Monday morning, after William had taken the boys to school, they were making their way to the man's law firm.

Leonard had expected from his brother anything but agreement; in truth he'd been steeled for a laughing refusal or a cross-questioning on the role and point of lawyers or another deconstruction of his own emotional predicament where Tela was concerned, and this meant that when straight acceptance of the offer came his relief was all the greater for it; somebody was going to take that edgeless extent of opinion and misunderstanding around the arson and was going to quantify it.

He waited outside in the street in the sun; it was a bright but cooler sun that gave sharp and chilly shade. By the time William returned to the double doors of the law firm, Leonard had bought a paper just a few doors up along Charing Cross Road, read all of it he wanted to read, rolled it up and had taken to hitting it gently against his leg too many times before he noticed his thigh become irritated by the impact. It was only when William appeared that he realised his own absent-mindedness and ceased the hitting. With a nod but without a word, they set off slowly up towards Covent Garden and progressed along the sunny edge of the shadow that cut the pavement in two.

'It seems straightforward enough,' William said, 'If I'm an accessory to Stephen's crime, then usually Stephen would have to be found guilty of that crime first.'

'Of course.'

'And to be an accessory who gave support and encouragement,

rather than some actual thing, there would need to be clear evidence that I did that – clear evidence that I gave support and encouragement for that *precise* crime.'

'Which you didn't.'

Leonard walked with his gaze turned out openly to the street, the buses and cars, and suddenly the sun was gone and the light reduced to one fallen, motionless, shadeless gauze.

William worked his way elegantly past the others walking along the pavement; he wasn't an elegant man, but he did have a defining ease of movement, born of confidence, born, Leonard had often thought, of a deep, defiant assurance that he was safe in this world; the assurance became all the greater, Leonard thought, whenever he was in fact least safe. 'It looks as though there probably isn't enough evidence for a case,' William concluded.

'There you go then.' Leonard said that as though the point of the exercise had all along been to reassure William, not himself.

'Of course he doesn't know the details of my case – he's not my lawyer. He was just giving general advice.'

'Even so.'

Leonard refrained from asking what he was like and whether good-looking or especially charming; and he tried not to be indignant about having to take advice from a man who was having an affair, as if he'd never have it in him to do such a thing and as if, in doing so, it impeded a person's moral position on any issue, one's judgement and worthiness.

The sun came out again as they passed along into Shaftesbury Avenue, where the fine lacemaking of branch shadows on the road was obliterated and restored, obliterated and restored by the rolling tread of the car tyres, and by their own walking.

William transferred his hands to his sides and his heavy features flickered rapidly with that tree-filtered light. 'We used to speak for hours, Stephen and I,' he said. 'About education, among other things. I pressed him for views – he's one of those men who can't bring himself to think twice about any issue that doesn't affect him. He had an education, he'll never have to work for a living, why should he care? When it comes to it he's a spoilt child with a beautiful face that'll get him far. I pressed and pressed him to think about it. I was direct, I didn't shy away from the topic.'

'You don't shy away from any topic.'

'You've no idea how much I hold back, Leo, no idea.'

'Well anyway,' he replied quickly, 'none of that makes you guilty.'

'Then I'll take your word for it, but the thing is complex. You've been trying all along to tell me how complex things are, and at last I see you're right – although now you seem to have changed your mind.' William glanced at him with a quick smile. 'I assume I'm innocent because I meant no harm, but is it enough to mean no harm? I didn't mean for a match to be struck, I certainly didn't mean for a community to lose its hope, as they so like to point out it has.' His look pierced Leonard, so intense it was, almost frightening in its sheer force and integrity. 'Yes,' he said, 'the law is clear – either there's enough evidence or there isn't – but the law is just the surface of the water, and nothing that happens there happens on its own – the colours, the swell, the bubbles that break, they're all caused by things above or below the surface – and I don't know enough about those things.'

It didn't seem to Leonard that his brother was anxious about this question of guilt, but rather that he took immense interest in it, as though it were to him that wooden puzzle that needed to be solved. Leonard told him, kindly, firmly, 'You don't need to know about all that. All you need to know is how the surface looks, and in your case, now, it looks fine. By all accounts it looks fine.'

'So you think everything has become simple?' William replied.

He exhaled and thought a moment. 'I meant that facts can be complex, William. But now we have more idea of the facts things are simpler – all the abstract things that happen below the surface don't matter once the facts are straight.'

William nodded long with his gaze tilted slightly skywards.

Leonard added, 'You don't have to settle every single matter just to settle one single matter.'

'Don't you?'

'No, you don't – will you just accept what I say for once? Will you accept a straight fact?'

William slowed his step and looked at the ground, then nodded and patted Leonard on the back. 'That man's probably not worthy of Tela, in case you wanted to know.'

'I don't want to know.' Leonard half smiled.

'Then I won't tell you about the gaping hole I saw in his soul.'

'Oh, come on. Hole in his soul! That seems harsh, William, the man's just helped you – whatever he's like surely he doesn't invite a judgement like that.'

'Every single thing that comes to us we invite, or else it wouldn't come,' William stated coolly.

That's nonsense, Leonard thought, and found that his irritation had begun to flare up so quickly these recent days, as if it were forever awaiting an opportunity. So he said it: 'That's nonsense, William,' and tried to keep lightness in his voice. 'People don't invite bullets through their heads or earthquakes to their villages. There are just some things that happen, some of them are lucky, some aren't, there's rarely a logic.'

Leonard glanced across at his brother, who only nodded his inscrutable response. Their walk continued sober and docile. A gaping hole in his soul, he thought, and despite himself the comfort he took from that was great, great indeed.

In the camera's gentle and motionless vigilance of the church, the large oak door on the right stood now ajar, pushed from the outside by an unknown hand that never ventured in. Leonard watched it open as though a ghost had visited, and the daylight bled onto the screen in a wide blinding bar down the door's edge. The sense had always been there, even as a child, that it was impossible to intrude on a church. You could only enter if invited – but you were always invited. And you could bring your disbelief and it would take it from you tenderly, thus proving with deep tacit quiet that your disbelief mattered not at all and caused not the slightest offence to the greater truth that was.

There the church waited in its state of eternal hospitality. Everything that came over its threshold it received and met on its own terms. Eternal, maddening hospitality. One wanted to shake it and to place a question at its core, but it always had a comeback: you're right to question, the Lord made us capable of questioning Him, that is the most beautiful proof that He exists. That stoicism he saw in the shifting frames of the church he saw too in his brother, and sometimes it was unbearable, sometimes he wanted to shake him up.

So then, it was with some relief that he gave William the four separate newspaper articles he found in the days that followed – three in the London press, one in the national – and observed a slight drawing back, a slow muted shock work its way over William's mouth and eyes, and then a silence. There was no quip or sarcasm to follow, and no dissecting discussion. It was low-minded to feel relief at that response, but Leonard did, for it was a response he could understand and reach out to.

Though judicious enough in what they said, the newspapers had found fascination in this story of the fire – such a feckless, wealthy young man as Stephen Malson, and so colourful and photogenic, so that the picture of him and William at a party in a room Leonard couldn't recognise gained greater space in each of the four sucessive articles. They made much of his absconding, as if his swift flight from their shores were part of Greek myth.

One could sense that there was far more the papers would have liked to say had the liberty been theirs – to have revealed William as some eccentric who'd spent twenty years of his life in the navy, a war hero, an anarchist, a philosopher, who'd famously had a close friendship with the beautiful Aleph Keillor, daughter of Lord Keillor, who'd provided her bail money when she was arrested over the Poll Tax riots. Yes, to say: Here he is again at large and on the rampage! Here he is, the possible lover of Mr Malson and suspected of aiding him in the arson attack on Eastacre Library. It was a seductive story in its way, even Leonard could see that. William had known his own small amount of infamy those fifteen or so years before when involved with Aleph, and he'd presented himself always as a scrupulous, principled, high-minded man; there was nothing the media liked more than to expose the black truths about those who seemed white.

He watched the surveillance of the church on this night without expectation of seeing his father; the things that he'd held on to just a month before he now found lacking relevance, for there'd been such change in the intervening time – nothing had changed outwardly it was true, but everything inwardly. It was as if William was a house of cards they'd been watching all their lives with breath held or drawn lightly, and finally a card had fallen; thus it was as if something inevitable was beginning to happen. Leonard rose from his kneeling position in front of the video and went upstairs to the toilet; he remembered then that their father had used to refer to the media as a swarm of flies, an infiltration into all breathable air and a steady hum, a maddening hum, you could swat and swat but it made no odds. Still its vile infiltration. The house was dark and would have been quiet but for the occasional cough from Richard's room. It was almost one a.m., and, by the time he'd been to the bathroom and was about to go back downstairs to stop the video and get a drink to take to bed, the child's coughing had become insistent. He went into his room and saw an outline of Richard in the darkness; when he turned on the lamp he saw that the boy was sitting up in bed pulling anxiously and sleepily at his pyjama top. He sat on the mattress edge and put a hand on each of his shoulders.

'Can't you sleep?' A barely audible no, but a firm shake of the head. 'Do you need your inhaler?' A nod, and the child pointed towards the shelf at the far side of the room. Leonard brought the inhaler to him; the child knew perfectly what to do, there wasn't any need to interfere. The small mouth closed in on the plastic and he breathed in and held the air in his lungs, then out, patient and adroit. 'Leave that here by the bed,' Leonard murmured when he'd finished. 'You should always keep it near you.'

He lay the child down, covered him over and turned out the bedside light. He was careful not to disturb the piece of wet tissue paper on which some broad beans were germinating – a school project probably to show how committed life can be regardless, for there they were, beginning to shoot towards the lamp's limited bright arc.

It was only then, without the light and beyond the rattling and purring of the breath, that Leonard noticed the sound of the rain, steadily torrential, and surmised that the sound must have been there all along, as roaring and peaceful as the pour of a waterfall. He stroked the boy's head for a minute or so, and when his breathing was at last even and his head shut-eyed and tranquil on the pillow, he withdrew his hand. He wasn't to leave, however; the moment he stood to go Richard detected the movement, woke up and clutched his fingers in a bid for him to stay. Thus he stayed, stroking the small forehead and looking straight ahead of him into the darkness.

There was movement some minutes later on the landing, and then the landing light went on. It was light-footed movement, not William therefore – and soon enough Kathy pushed open Richard's door which had been ajar. He whispered, 'Kathy,' so as not to startle her, and he prepared for her bemusement or annoyance at the fact that he was in there with her sleeping son. But she stood in the lit doorway and put her left arm across her chest, as if it were bare, and took in the scene without a hint of reproach. She was wearing a blue nightdress which came to her knees, royal blue, not at all transparent, and yet modest instincts led her hand to cup the outer curve of her right breast. Her hair was out of its plaits and hanging rather piously in one twisted rope over her shoulder.

Leaving the door open and the light falling in, she came to the bed and sat at its far corner with a hush of cotton and a faint scent of soap.

She asked, 'Have you been in here for long? You should have woken me up.' He told her no, not long, just minutes. 'He's been bad recently.'

'He has,' he said.

'I worry about him missing too much school.'

'If it can't be helped, it can't be helped.'

Kathy just nodded. 'He'll catch up anyway.' She nodded once again. As it was Richard had only missed the first day of school, the day Tela came, and he'd rallied in the interim as if school provided him with relief – he wasn't an extroverted child, and if he was like William had been, by all accounts, at that age he probably enjoyed the solitary escape of being one among many and of losing himself in all the conundrums of sums and ancient empires and how a broad bean grows and a chick hatches; the luxuries of pure, unburdened consideration. Yes, Richard was like William in that way – an interested person. It didn't particularly matter what the thing of interest was.

They sat quiet against the wash of the rain. 'Heavy,' she murmured, looking towards the window as if she could see through the curtains. A wet, dark world it was outside, with the gutters flooding and the rain one continual tide of sound – no thrumming, no sense of its divisibility into drops, no sense of its ability to stop, nor its will to. It had been the driest summer for years, and now it was easy to think that a loss was being made up finally, and that it might rain for a decade.

Richard murmured in his sleep and Leonard was too self-conscious, with Kathy there, to do what he'd previously done – stroke the child's head and press away the frown between his eyes with the light kneading of his thumb.

'I hope you don't mind me being in here, I didn't want to wake you all up.'

'It's fine,' she hastened. 'Thank you for doing it. Were you asleep?'

'I haven't been able to sleep.'

She nodded. 'The noise of the rain.'

It was nothing to do with the noise of the rain, but he moved his head as if in confirmation and left the comment alone. Downstairs the surveillance of the church went on soundlessly on the screen in its constant minuscule shifts, its constant accumulation of time on the camera's counter, in a kind of watchfulness of them, he imagined. A benign observance. And somehow, while that video played, the house seemed at rest. He asked, 'Is William awake?'

'Of course, I'm not sure he ever really sleeps.'

Leonard looked down at the slumbering child in recognition of this fact, that his brother was awake but not present, and not the one who'd come to the boy's aid when he coughed – and Kathy must have inferred his thought for she said, with a squint that was almost conspiratorial, 'I told him not to go to Richard. I don't like him to look after the children when they're ill.'

Her gaze was fixed on her son, a sea of love so buoyant that it held aloft any anger, any frustration or resentment, held it up against itself.

Leonard said, 'William used to look after me when I was ill; he brought me sweets – we had an uncle who worked for Trebor, and we'd get enormous bags of sweets that were supposed to last us the year. William would give me his entire rations, all of them. One time when I was about five, when I had tonsillitis, scarletina – something like that – he sat by my bed all day and unwrapped the sweets for me one by one. Aniseeds, fruit chews. And blew on my forehead to cool it down.' Leonard smiled mutely and caught her eye. 'I used to get the most ridiculous hot heads. A one-boy portable heater system.'

She returned the smile, but it was curbed. 'And then he grew up,' she said.

'You're thinking of how he was with our mother.'

'Your mother was dying of cancer and he took it on himself to try to argue her out of it. *Argue* her out of it! As if she'd let something simple get out of hand. As if it was *unreasonable* to him. Do you think you can reason with a disease?'

Leonard was quiet; no, he didn't think such a thing, and his heart was wrung out when he remembered the prolonged blink his mother had developed when she was in pain or anxious at that time, a blink of such stolid religiosity, a *do with me as you will* look. How she'd said, I'm dying, William, I have a terminal disease. Dying isn't a failing particular to me. And how finally she'd been driven to such despair by her son's questions that she told him to go away, anywhere, so long as it wasn't within her range; she'd asked her beloved oldest son, in whom she'd had so much faith and trust, to get as far away from her as he could.

'Maybe it was just his way of coping with her death, Kathy,' he said. 'He was very close to her. He wanted to save her, just like we all did.'

But he knew that wasn't the long and the short of it, and Kathy knew it too. She was right, William had made no secret of the fact that he considered illness to be unexpressed emotion, unexamined thought. That was really all – and one could fall back on the expertise of a doctor but unless the mind permitted recovery it wouldn't come; the mind was a force and great lunar pull on the body's tides, and to try, in the fatal manner of King Cnut, to head off the tides without recognising the high, glowing gravity of the mind was to enter into an endeavour that was sure to fail. If you wanted to change your mind William would provide endless help, but if not he'd no patience, and barely anything to offer. Love the person, love the person always and absolutely, no matter how sick he or she is, but never give credence to the sickness, never accommodate its tremendous, consuming demands.

Kathy had set her face into a resilient frown and tilted her head to one side to observe the rise and fall of her son's chest. 'Did he have some of his inhaler?'

'Yes, just before you came in.'

'Good.' A gratified look passed her face, and then she set her head straight again, now with some resolve. 'You see, Leonard – if you don't mind me talking like this about your mother – well, she believed that it was God who'd entered her and rearranged her cells and given her cancer, and being God's work there was no way of arguing with it. No, she just had to die of it and keep her chin up like a good Christian.'

He let his fingers move through the silk of the child's hair for a moment and watched her. 'Yes, it's true, I've thought of it myself. Religion killed her, made her give up. It makes me hate it.'

'No but you see, don't you see?' She let her arm drop away from her chest for the first time, and the back of her hand rested loose on the bed. 'Her view's no different really to the atheist's view – yours, mine. If I got cancer I'd think something big and unbeatable had got inside me, and couldn't be argued with. I wouldn't call it God, but it would amount to the same reaction. Wouldn't it?'

He lifted his hand from Richard's head and ran the back of his index and third finger slowly across his own mouth and let them rest at its corner, bent at the knuckle. He thought, Yes. He conceded a nod.

'You see, whereas William doesn't take that view,' she said. 'Because he believes that God's infinite peace and logic can't create cancer. And so the cancer doesn't come from God, but from a *straying* from God, from God's will. All ills are a wrong path chosen, and to get better you just go back the other way. Nobody else I know – religious or otherwise – thinks that way, thinks there's a *choice*. Because he's hopeful you see, he's so *hopeful* about humanity, he wants so much from it because he believes it's capable of being great and wise. *Wise*.' She lifted a hand in disbelief at that word. 'And the problem is, it isn't wise, is it? We're better to accept its limits and live with them.'

As a speech, Leonard thought, it was a strange mix of reverence and ridicule, of deep understanding and rapid capitulation. Where she became more animated her voice didn't rise but fell into a harsh whisper so as not to disturb Richard, which gave the odd impression that her most vehemently held beliefs were secrets to be imparted guiltily. In any case he hadn't appreciated that she might understand her husband; no, he'd thought she rubbed along with him in ignorance, and that the ignorance was what preserved them. He was surprised and didn't know what to say.

She adjusted the straps of her nightdress with a distracted nervousness. 'I want to ask William to move out for a few nights.'

'Why?'

She shook her head and her jaw tightened. 'I just can't stand it – the newspaper articles, the scrutiny. I don't want it to touch my children's lives.'

'But you do know the truth?'

'Of course I do. And what difference does it make?'

They said nothing, and while doing so gazed into one another's laps, those peculiar spaces that were a dark, shapeless neutrality, a part of them that could just as easily have been a part of anybody. He shifted his hands from there, where they'd loosened into a bowl, and placed them at the back of his neck. She shifted her gaze away in turn.

'I would leave here if I could,' she said suddenly. 'I miss the countryside.'

'You don't like London?'

'I don't feel like I live the way a person in London should live. I always feel provincial.'

'You're not provincial—'

'What I think I mean is, I don't live in London. I live in this house. My world is five people. Six now.' She glanced up. 'I like mountains, I like lakes.'

'You could visit some. Why don't you? A holiday.'

She nodded. It wasn't a pitying or tragic gesture, he was glad it wasn't those, but he wished it could have divested itself of that enduring air of bitterness. He sympathised, of course he did; she lived in London for William and she lived without the possibility of leaving. William would never leave – Leonard had no inclination to lure her into discussing impossibilities. But a holiday? Why not? And she could go out more, day trips, she could see hills if not mountains, and rivers if not lakes, or the Heath or Kew at least, or up to the Fens just for the difference of it; he could go with her if William wouldn't, he wondered if she knew that was possible.

'It would be good for Richard's asthma,' he said. 'To go on trips more often, or even to get away for a couple of weeks.'

'Yes, it would.'

They both watched the sleeping boy as if remembering finally the reason they were sitting in conversation at that time of night. She laid her hand on the small hump that was her child's feet. 'We should get to bed. He's sleeping fine.'

They stood carefully and the bed shifted and regained equilibrium. Kathy left the door open. On the landing she seemed panicked all of a sudden by the exposure of her nightdress, though it exposed nothing. Her hand went to her neck and fingers curled around the hemline. 'Sleep well, won't you,' she said, and he said he would, and wished her the same. She went into her bedroom, opening the door just wide enough to pass through it, then closing it tightly.

There he stood. He returned downstairs, and the video was still playing out the gradual, cautious drama of light as it inched through its daily rhythms. The church door was now closed and that blinding shaft of light gone. Who'd closed it – had it closed on its own, in a wind the camera couldn't perceive? The same wind perhaps that had opened it? Leonard might have rewound to find out, except that the mystery only bolstered his view that all churches were haunted – they were haunted by God, and the religious feared and took comfort and went to the haunted building to ask for favours in return for their belief. They asked for God to go lightly with them and spare them cancer, a terrible accident, a lost child, a natural disaster. The religious went to church to stay close to the enemy. That, he'd always felt, was the truth of it.

But in an instant, and only for an instant, he saw it all quite differently, as William saw it. God had nothing to do with that building that the camera so phlegmatically revealed. He wasn't the Lord who indiscriminately gave and took away, and who made life-shaping, life-shattering decisions for the mortal on a whim, or on a piece of divine reason too abstracted to understand. No, God was a piece of pure philosophy just as zero was a piece of pure mathematics, put there to serve myriad functions. Not in the slightest way was it there by default or thoughtlessness. God wasn't a totem, an idol, an excuse, nor even an explanation in itself, but a philosophical principle that William had interrogated like any other, asked questions of, asked for logic and consistency from, weighed it, worked it, asked it to earn its keep, and had found it to be a formula that made sense of so many of the world's structures that he perceived.

We are born from unity, we divide into isolation. We winnow ourselves out from the thing that first made sense of us and then expect to find meaning, yet a fraction makes no sense without the number of which it's a fractional part. We see loss, feel grief, give ourselves illness, we're cells that have over-divided and we call the division growth; the only real growth is in the return to unity, God, the unifying principle.

Tired to his core, he turned the video off. The rain still poured as he went upstairs, and in bed as he tripped down into the deep open shaft of sleep he kept thinking that to divide by zero was

193

to end up with infinity, as was to divide by God. To divide by God, to divide by God, over and over he thought it without sense; to divide by God; I must tell my students that the way to pass their exams is to divide by God. Then he must have slept, for it was morning.

The rain didn't end when the sun came up. It fell throughout breakfast and coursed suddenly out of the gutter in through the open kitchen window. 'Well, that's the plants watered,' Kathy said, and latched the window closed. The local radio reported flash flooding across London, and Kathy listened with her finger to her lips. They looked out of the utility-room window to see the saturated garden and the flooded pots and half-filled wheelbarrow. The chickens, by now more respectably feathered, pecked at the seed floating in swampy ground. On the radio people called in to report the water they could see, the roads, the roads were rivers, things harmlessly left out from the summer were drifting down the streets. These observations were much laboured, as if in marvel that the newsworthy past had intersected with the present, so that what one stood in now was an unusually remarkable moment.

The rain continued long after breakfast, rinsing the window of Leonard's bedroom. When the letter came in the post shortly after lunch, granting him probate, it was sodden in its envelope. It offered him an appointment four days hence – which would be Monday – so that he could sign the necessary document. For the time being, then, once it had dried he folded the letter into the manila file he was using for all current business, which in fact only contained at that point the various matters of probate and inheritance tax – dear God, not much going on in life, he thought.

Through the rain he made his way up to the local supermarket to fetch some basics; it was only a fifteen-minute walk each way but in that short time, walking up the main road, he could see the state of things. The petrol station he passed was one of the few still open in the area, though even then there were signs to say that purchases were rationed to a maximum of five pounds, which would get you nowhere much further than home, he thought. The queue of cars that trailed from its forecourt was easily three hundred metres long and had to be managed by police. Queues of people on foot, too, shouldering the downpour while they waited to fill canisters.

The roads were noticeably quieter but not calmer, and they ran with rainwater which plaited in a fast flow along the gutters and gushed upwards from drains. Litter ran in the flow, and a plastic headlight cover, a wing mirror, an item of clothing he couldn't identify, a plastic toy rabbit that belonged to either child or dog. He'd never seen so many police on the streets or so many small protests dotted strategically. The wetness magnified sound so that he was subjected to a wall of continuous noise – the protests, the traffic, the sluicing of groundwater and the rapid hammering of rain on the umbrella he'd borrowed from Kathy.

As the day wore on the rain was such that the back garden, and consequently the chicken coop, had become waterlogged. Together, in the interests of the hapless wading birds, he and William took a large tarpaulin from the shed and covered the roof of the coop. They secured the corners with terracotta plant pots.

'It'll stop it getting worse at least,' he said to his brother, and they retreated sodden to the shed to escape the downpour.

He exhaled a bubble of laughter – it was something to do with the vision of them both stooped in that shed with rain dripping from their eyelashes and their clothes clinging to their bellies, those too-big bellies that the ageing man always does his best to hide. Too late for that now – the rain had made them come clean about it. And there'd been all the things he'd had in mind about their mother's death and about going away somewhere on holiday – lakes, mountains – about the mysteriously opened and closed door of the church, yes, about God or whatever it was, and all of that had amounted to this: two grown men in a shed, stooped, soaked, heavy-bellied and frowning through rain-drenched lashes for the sake of five chickens! Laughter began spilling from him unchecked, and in turn his brother's face broke into a smile too, then laughter which multiplied laughter, until neither could stop nor really account for why they'd started.

Then, in the midst of that amused wheezing William started suddenly and boldly to sing: *L'amour est un oiseau rebelle*, with a comic gusto, *L'amour est un oiseau rebelle, que nul ne peut apprivoiser, et c'est bien en vain qu'on l'appelle*, and Leonard joined him in that operatic rendition, though with a thinner and raspier voice. *Love is a wild bird that none can tame, and you can call him but it is in vain.* Their mother had used to sing it as she cooked and their father had said she'd make a good Carmen, with her Mediterranean skin and the shocking amber eyes that could fell an empire. It wasn't that she was ever beautiful exactly, but she did always snag people with those laughing eyes as if to say she wasn't yet finished with them. They would all join in with the singing then; or maybe they'd only done so once or twice, but in any case Leonard remembered it as if they'd been through the Habanera in their kitchen every week.

They sang it above the rain with exaggerated seriousness and stamped their feet between verses – William's velvet baritone and Leonard's attempts to stay in key. Contained by the shed, Leonard thought their voices might actually sound quite good, quite impressive, what with the rain's percussion behind them. Then between their voices and the rain came another sound which they didn't hear at first. When, gradually, it broke through, it made a word – William, *William*. Then Kathy striding up the garden hunched against the weather, shouting and irritated at being unheard: 'William, for God's sake, there's a *phone call* for you.'

Leonard stayed outside to close and bolt the shed while William ambled in, unhurried even then. When he went into the house himself William was still on the telephone and Kathy was waiting near him in the hall with her arms clasped around her.

'The police,' Kathy said quietly as Leonard made to come through from the kitchen. William had always held the telephone oddly, Leonard thought, with a light grasp, in the manner of somebody who is picking up an object they'd rather not hold. And he'd speak down it with a faint frown which Leonard took to signify puzzlement – he seemed to say, Isn't there a better way to reach one another than through this bizarrely shaped instrument? In this case, as in most, he made minimal response to whoever spoke to him at the other end. There was no point standing and watching, Leonard thought, better to go and get dry.

It was some ten minutes later before he came down, and he found William in the kitchen drying his hair with a bath towel; Kathy was making a pot of coffee, towards which she gestured by way of asking if Leonard wanted one. He nodded.

'Stephen has been found,' William said. 'The police have him in their custody. And as a result they want me to go back to talk to them tomorrow morning.'

How strange – he'd felt closer to William out there in the shed quarter of an hour ago than he'd felt in a long time, and now he couldn't think of a single thing he could say.

'I could come with you if you like,' was all he managed eventually.

'Thank you, Leo, but it's fine.'

'Well, if you change your mind.'

Leonard glanced at Kathy and went upstairs again to his room. He thought little, nothing, of that development with the police because he didn't know enough about the law to know what it amounted to. He couldn't bring his thoughts to it in any conclusive way. His worry, if that's what it was, bore itself out in a pressing clarity that they should all get away, as he and Kathy had discussed late the night before. Away in the car – all of them, drive up north for a few days, a kind of freedom.

The bedroom door opened then and William came in wearing dry clothes, pushing the door with his foot and carrying two cups of coffee. He passed one to Leonard and sat on the bed, his bare feet rooting to the floor as firmly as a magnet finding iron. They drank for half a minute in silence, until William said, 'What is this that's happening?'

'I don't know, William.'

Their bafflement at the situation eased it; it made no sense to them, which was proof therefore that they had nothing to do with it in truth. It sat among them in their household as a stranger they had to tolerate, but only tolerate, never fully accept. I'd better go out to the car, Leonard thought, and check it still starts after all this rain. It was important to keep the car running; the car, the car, an unreasonably significant glimmer of hope and a little provision of fate.

With a short sip of coffee, William said, 'I'm just very happy you're here.'

Leonard moved his head slightly and gave a small, grateful smile. They drank again and looked, without speaking, at the tens of children's drawings on the wall which were so endlessly fascinating to Leonard, and endearing. They went on like that for five minutes or so; Leonard began thinking again of their mother, who'd occasionally received drawings just like those from the siblings of the babies she'd delivered. She'd brought life into the world every day for thirty years. The most robust and unshockable woman, who'd gradually grown larger and larger as if to depict symbolically all the flesh she'd plied and roused into life. Midwives weren't ones to worry about the sound of a woman screaming or a man weeping, or the sight of torn muscle and the feel of blood and placenta coagulating on fingers. But one didn't pull a life safely from the womb just to have that life squandered by lawlessness and misdirection, nor by misery, nor by regret. Run-ins with the law weren't what all the hope should come to. She'd tell her children at night; don't go off course, my darlings, be good, be happy.

It was impossible to know what William was thinking, whether similar thoughts, or thoughts about Stephen, the police, anything else. Whatever thoughts they were he was deep in them, and then suddenly clear of them, for he stood, said, 'I'll go and help Kathy,' and left the room as quietly as he'd entered it.

It was almost eight o'clock by then. Leonard went out to the car. The rain had eased and the patches of evening light had opened up in the sky. He tried to start the engine but it turned over weakly without starting – not the battery then, but beyond that he was at a loss. It took him a minute to realise that the gauge was showing the tank to be empty, when he was sure there'd been half a tank of petrol at least when he'd left it. Well, what else could he have expected in the middle of a fuel crisis, when he'd even heard on the news that people were siphoning one another's fuel? Of course they'd siphoned the Austin's. It must have been one of the few cars old enough to have no lock on the fuel cap or some particular valve, and if he'd had the wits about him he might have known to expect it. He tried not to feel panic, for it was nothing. Really, it didn't matter, this whole idea of going away didn't matter at all. But he went indoors heavy and with a sensation he'd sometimes known with Tela – that another thing had happened that couldn't unhappen and which led to a place of diminishing hope.

In the kitchen he found Kathy on her own negotiating a large stir fry around the wok.

'I sent William and the boys away,' she said, 'there's not room for us all in here.'

'Can I help?'

'No, go out to the garden and tell them it'll be five minutes.'

He went out into the dusk. William was crouching at the chicken run just as Tela had done a few evenings before, and his sons were standing around him, their fingers hooked solemnly into the wire. When Leonard approached they looked up and then back to the run.

He said, 'Dinner will be ready in a few minutes,' and William thanked him. Two of the hens must have gone into the coop for the night, and the other three were clearing up any last remnants of food from the wet ground with their cooing and clucking. It was chilly suddenly and the sky had cleared to a crisp navy.

'Well, boys?' William asked, so that it was evident they'd been engaged in some conversation before he came outside. 'Your uncle here seemed to think that the deficit was reason and intelligence. What do you think he means by reason and intelligence?'

The boys had all glanced at Leonard by now, standing as he did behind them. They usually had such restless energy, moving like light around their father's stillness. But they were subdued, yes, as if tired or bored, and Leonard wondered if they hoped for him to divert the conversation. He guessed, of course, that they were talking about the chicken stamping and he resented being quoted on something he'd said so flippantly or so long ago, if indeed he'd even said it at all. He couldn't recall what he'd said.

The boys might have been excited by the tale of the killed birds at some point, but surely not any more. Dismayed, he took a few steps away and craned his neck back to look at the emerging night sky.

'Do we think,' William continued, 'that a person who stamps on a chicken's neck for fun lacks reason and intelligence, at least for that moment?'

The boys agreed with their father, and a new question began. Leonard wandered the length of the garden, its rambling fence and cover of fruit trees. It hardly seemed like a garden in the middle of a city, so full and still it was in the quiet dusk, its trees bloated with soft fruit. Much of the fruit had fallen and fermented. It was a mystery, why William felt he had to chase down every topic of conversation even with his own children, when what the boys wanted to speak about was Lego, trains, the Black Seas Barracuda pirate ship Oli was building, and to do so without having to enter into moral examination. More than that, it was a mystery that these narrow, inconclusive, pinching questions about the chickens should still be what occupied his mind when he had the police to confront in the morning and a serious conviction inching ever nearer to his door.

He knew the boys would come up the garden at any moment; if he could say comparatively little about them as people, he knew at least that they were human and that therefore at any moment they'd break free of their father's curiosity and come racing up the garden in release. He wondered why William was so unable to let a thing go. The chickens, the damned chickens. A tree could let its fruit go. William should let the chickens go.

'We have to take the time to understand a thing,' William said then a little louder, and he'd stood, and his trousers were loose around the knees. 'Until then we have no way to judge it.'

Leonard watched him walk back towards the lights of the

house. Presently the boys sprang into motion and there was a rush of arms and legs and push of energy up the garden, and the questions and the nature of things and the search for universalities collapsed into a three-child brawl on the grass.

Kathy's voice sang through the house in anger. To alien ears its rant might even have sounded comical in its steep lilts and sudden torrents, as she went about railing against her husband's failings, pointing out her own constancy and undeserved loyalty; she drew his attention to his joblessness and his meddling and his lax, liberal parenting, his incompetence as a son, his unworldliness, and the worry lines he'd etched on her brow.

'Then you speak to the police and don't even bother to *defend* yourself,' she shouted, and the after-ring of her sentence hung isolated on the landing where they stood, outside Leonard's door, until the lack of response forced her to take up again, 'I've been steadfast, I've stood by you, nobody else would have bothered, you *ape*, you forgot to evolve, and still I've stood by you.'

Against this William's voice was even and calm, and he thanked her, thanked her and thanked her over and again, and told her she'd been steadfast alright, as steadfast as a thirteen-year drought. She told him to get out of the house and, as far as Leonard could tell, he conceded with grace and good humour. Leonard could imagine his brother taking Kathy's hands and regarding her with his wide, kind face; in times of contrition or defencelessness, all that was ugly about him shifted into a form of extreme attractiveness that had nothing to do with eyes, nose, mouth – how could anyone explain it? It had just always been that way ever since Leonard could remember. The world simply fell away from him, all its weight and judgements. Leonard knew that was how he looked to Kathy at that moment, and she had to be pitied, for what defence did she have against it? Then his voice came without either attack or self-pity, saying that he'd leave the house for as long as she wanted him gone.

'You don't have to emigrate, you just have to get out for the day,' she said, both bitter and forgiving. 'Just get out from under my feet for a day.'

Leonard heard his brother's footsteps diminish on the stairs but didn't get up to the window to see him leave the house. He dropped to the floor the short stack of newspapers he'd bought that morning and leaned forward heavily on his knees.

By force of habit the papers usually ended up on the kitchen sideboard where they'd stay for a few days until they were thrown out or assigned for some other purpose – to protect the table from the boys' games, to wrap vegetable peelings in. These papers they'd collected that reported on Stephen and William were surely too poisonous for the kitchen, so he took them down to the back living room and put them by the armchair.

He looked out of the window at the aspen and beyond that to the chicken run. The reports that morning said that later that day Stephen would have to appear in a magistrates' court charged with arson, having been harboured by acquaintances at an undisclosed location for the past four weeks – and presumably William knew this from his interview with the police, but he'd said nothing about it when he'd got home that lunchtime. The most Leonard knew was from the argument he'd just heard and from those articles there, those paltry articles.

William had sometimes said, regretfully, that the world came to know itself not by inner knowledge but by the media it watched and read, a distorted mirror that gave its image back wrought out of all shape; it was as senseless to believe this image as to believe a person who tells you your leg is straight when you know, even with your eyes closed, that it is bent – you know because it is your leg, because there is an internal system that brings you that information directly and without distortion. It's senseless to believe the distortion, but still you do.

Leonard nudged the papers aside with his foot, for he didn't want to resort to those distortions where his own brother was concerned, and to have to triangulate his knowledge of him with the local newspaper. Why will you not tell me what's happening? he thought. He imagined the gathering warmth in the sun that he'd felt on his forearms and the back of his neck that morning a month before in the square, when the protests had been beginning. His skin had received that warmth with gratitude and without question. All he wanted was to receive his brother like that, and to be received thus. Directly and clearly. To know that on this earth, which contained for him no other family, there was his brother whom he could receive simply and with all the ease of warmth from the sun. Not just through the eyes but on the back of the neck, the back of the knees, the crown of the head, the crook of the arm. Just to receive him, with the blind side of the self. For his brother to confide in him, and to know he wouldn't be judged.

Still, at least the several articles that had appeared that morning didn't mention William much, and where they did it certainly wasn't to say anything new; the press was far more interested in Stephen. At least the attention had been deflected from him, that was no small thing. As for Stephen, it was plain he was a fool; Leonard cared nothing for what happened to him.

Above all else Leonard wanted to move the car. That night there'd been two dreams of a similar kind; in the first he urged William to run away, and the whole dream was spent in circular petitions and frenzies that fed themselves to the point of sickness. You should go, before they catch you. Go, *run*. I cannot leave London, William had protested calmly; God means for me to be here. Go, run, go. I cannot. You must. I cannot.

In the second he urged the same, and this time William, Kathy and the boys did go, with their cases stacked on the roof of the car. They were going to the countryside. It was a striking and simple dream and full of hope. When Leonard woke from it he pulled himself up in bed and was convinced by its wisdom and by the need to do something towards it.

For forty-five minutes he queued in a petrol station forecourt in Clerkenwell, with a petrol can he'd found in the shed; of course there was going to be no such family escape to the country, but in any case the Austin had to at least be capable of moving somewhere, for its trapped position outside the house had become, overnight, unacceptable to him. All those dreams of liberty running through its contours, and the peering headlights, its sprightly form like something spring-loaded, all this was of absolutely no use without even a negligible little swill of fuel in the bottom of its tank.

Finally he put his five pounds of petrol in the can, bought a local paper and walked the mile or so back home. He rounded the corner where the main road gave up its noise and motion abruptly to their undisturbed street, and he saw William approaching from the house, a distinctive figure in his linen trousers and a blue shirt, and that loose and ambling gait.

'I have petrol,' he said when they were close enough to hear one another, and he lifted the can with tentative cheer.

William put his hands in his pockets and asked, 'Is that cause for celebration?'

'It'll be priceless, this five pounds' worth, if things carry on the way they are.'

William gazed at him without much expression, neither inter-ested nor disdainful. He did pass his gaze over the paper folded in Leonard's other hand, but then shifted again to make eye contact.

'Did you know there's a fuel crisis on, William?'

A warmly mocking question, and William replied, 'Really? Which channel?'

Leonard smiled and looked aside. Even with the witticism, his brother's company that day cast a shadow. Never did it do that; it often brought a person up short, sharp, like something caught under a midday sun, but it never threw itself long and lean in that way. 'You're out somewhere for the day?'

'To Jonathan's,' his brother said, and turned his eyes very briefly to the sky. 'Swimming opportunities are running out.'

'Run out, as far as I'm concerned.'

'Well, you don't have my padding.'

'I don't have your madness, William.'

For a moment he wondered if William was going to invite him to Shepperton, then he realised that he probably wasn't, and that the answer would be no even if he did. Sometimes it just was that you were going where you were going, and it wasn't possible to change direction for somebody else. Besides which, he'd feel obliged to go in the Austin if they went together, and then Jonathan might ask for it back. He wasn't going to use that treasured ration of fuel just to have to give the car back.

'I'll see you this evening then,' he said.

William nodded and levered his backpack more firmly over his one shoulder. 'I will, Leo. Enjoy your day.'

They parted, and Leonard made his way back to the house. When he looked behind him towards the main road he saw the back of a man in ill-fitting blue and white, moving a little tenderly as if his joints pained him. Dear William – when had he got old and careworn; what could be done to help him when he didn't even perceive he needed help?

When he got in there was nobody downstairs, though he assumed Kathy was home because her shoes were by the door. The boys would be at cricket by now, he thought. He put the petrol can and its meagre contents in the shed and stopped to check on the hens. How well they looked, their feathers glossed and luxurious around their necks, and those humps on their chests indiscernible. Bizarre, plucky little survivors that they were; perhaps it was easier to survive if you had no concept of death – there was no pulling through to be done, or mental rallying in the face of annihilation, you just carried on as you always had done thinking your life was one long, unthreatened day. Back inside the house he put on enough coffee for two, and it was as he sat and opened the newspaper onto the table that Kathy came into the kitchen.

She didn't speak, but sat next to him on the bench and looked over his shoulder as he inspected the news articles. It was there, on page two, news of Stephen's court case the day before.

'They didn't release him on bail,' she said, as though that gave them the answer to various questions – when in fact they didn't know what any of it amounted to. The man had pleaded not guilty and was due to face a trial, but because of his previous absconding the courts weren't going to risk letting him go in the interim; so there he was, William's protégé, in police custody.

Kathy pushed herself to standing with her hands. 'It's because he had no mother.'

How to respond to such a statement without knowing where exactly it had come from? From her scorn, from her pity? Leonard looked down at the article and at the picture of Stephen that seemed to have become the standard, one taken slightly from above, with his gaze upturned to the camera, so that there was a look of mischief to the wide eyes and tapering, rather fey chin – and in shot, just, his elegant fingers holding a cigarette.

Kathy said, 'A father gives morals, a mother gives empathy. If you don't have empathy morals are useless.'

'Yes, perhaps.' He took the coffee that she'd offered him. 'Do you think that's the case with you and William?'

She sat across the table from him, and for a moment he thought she'd answer, since she gathered in her breath and tilted her head to the side as if making way for a declaration. Then she asked, 'Would you say I'm a good mother?'

'I don't think any child could hope for better, Kathy.'

Maybe it was that his answer was completely unhesitant and genuine, for she smiled involuntarily and reached her hand forward so that her fingers touched his knuckles where he clasped his mug. 'You're kind,' she said, and withdrew her hand again.

'You've given your children your life.'

She looked up at him, shrugged, and looked down again.

'Do you doubt it then – that you're a good mother?'

'It doesn't matter.' She shook her head quickly and briefly. She brought her hands, interlocked, to her chin. 'I'm going to go and see him – Stephen Malson, I mean. As a mother and a woman, I'm going to go and ask him to have some thought for others.'

'I think you should stay out of it, Kathy—'

'Well that's fine, it you think that.' Without much pause she said matter-of-factly, 'William was upset this morning when he left.'

'Yes.'

She seemed so distracted, he thought, slipping from one topic to another like that as if they each laterally depended on one another – Stephen, empathy, mothering, William – and maybe they did depend on one another but he didn't know what to say beyond that – yes, William did seem upset.

'On Friday, when the police questioned him again, instead of just saying he had nothing to do with it he started trying to split hairs with them over the meaning of words – but you know how he is. He didn't even *try* to defend himself.'

'Maybe that *is* his way of trying to defend himself, Kathy.'

'Then he'd better get a lawyer fast,' she said sadly, 'or he'll find himself up to his neck.'

He closed the paper and put it aside, and some moments passed without comment. Then she finished her coffee, put the cup in the sink and said she'd go and get the boys from cricket.

He walked with her, a half-hour walk each way through the cool damp streets. The temperatures hadn't recovered again after the heavy rainfall and leaves had been lost on the planes and beeches on the roadsides. He told her he'd cook, and on the way back he detoured from her and the boys into a butcher's where he bought a joint of lamb for marinating and slow braising; along with that he'd do cumin-spiced aubergines, some sweet potato with paprika, shallots, spiced red lentils, so that there'd be plenty besides the lamb for William to eat. Something bolstering at that, food to banish the world, as Tela had called it. It was the recipe he and Tela had regarded as their dish, their trademark. The two or three times he'd made it in Edinburgh his father had loved it too, and it had brought him strange deep comfort, the smell of the meat in the house which mixed with the brewing beer, the dark tender strips of lamb falling from the bone, the juices, the cinnamon, cumin, garlic and allspice.

But as it was he'd got only as far as turning the oven on and preparing the lamb when the telephone rang, and Kathy came quickly into the kitchen to say that William had had a mishap in the water. A *mishap?* Jonathan had to save him from drowning, Kathy said, and she appeared almost incredulous at the idea, for these simple human vulnerabilities didn't really befall William – accident, illness and drama; he was fine, Jonathan stressed, but he couldn't very well come home by train in that state. So Leonard put the lamb in the oven – it would take four hours to cook; he went to the shed, took out his petrol can and poured its contents carefully into the Austin. He fetched one of his own thick jumpers for William to wear, and he called Jonathan back to tell him he was coming, but that it would take him easily an hour in Saturday afternoon traffic, perhaps an hour and a half. He asked to speak to William, but Jonathan said it would be better if he just got there.

So he edged his way out of the city and the Austin's engine growled like a famished belly; the old thing could give up the ghost any moment, he thought, and realised how naïve his thoughts of exodus had been if this was the vessel to take them. Near Marylebone he came across a group of protesters who'd sat cross-legged on the A40 in fluorescent tabards, and for a few minutes of waiting stationary for something to happen, he considered turning back for home in defeat. In time, at the point at which the small reinforcement of police began to move in on them, they stood and moved to the roadside with a perfect, defiant choreography.

He ebbed out through Shepherd's Bush and down the airy stretch past Kew Gardens. William, nearly drowning! Endlessly up and down William would swim as a teenager, up and down Swift Ditch with an interrogative breaststroke that cleaved the water wide for his passage; and their parents didn't know where he'd picked up that tenacious habit, but his sustained stroke would sometimes attract smatterings of spectators along the bank by the rangy poplars, people who'd been for a walk and come back an hour later to find him still ladling the water aside in his cupped palms as if he were trying to empty the river. It wasn't swimming at all, it was just floating with sheer dogged endeavour that, though definitely admirable, nobody could see the purpose of. In all of that there was never any question of him drowning. It was as though he had complete mental control of that trench of water, that he'd pitched his intellect against its textures, its weeds, its floating minnow skeletons; it was outwitted by him, and it gave itself up. Swift Ditch was wild compared to the slim ribbon of river at the end of Jonathan's garden; it was, yes, almost beyond the imagination for William to have half drowned in that.

Jonathan had said he'd leave the front door on the latch; Leonard pushed it open and went through to the living room and back doors. The little house smelt of cooking, and there were empty plates and used cutlery on the carpet by the lit fire. Jonathan stood just inside the patio door with a glass of wine in his hand, wearing a fleece, his hair flat to his head where it had slowly dried. He was looking out onto the decking where William sat. The sight shocked Leonard in fact, because he'd expected his brother to be by the fire. But no, not at all – he was outside on the edge of the boards with his legs crossed, wearing nothing but the underwear he'd swum in. A bright green towel was bundled behind him where it had fallen, presumably, from his back.

'He's been sitting out there like that for well over an hour,' Jonathan said.

'What happened?'

'I don't know exactly, all I know is that he almost drowned. Perhaps he got cramp – he stays in there for half an hour, forty minutes. It's really too cold to stay in that long. Even Jan wouldn't.'

Jonathan spoke in his usual grave, placid manner, his arms crossed in front of him and his gaze fixed immovably on his friend outside.

'You pulled him out?'

Jonathan nodded vaguely. 'I only went out there to take him a glass of wine – if it weren't for that he might be dead by now.'

'Won't he come in?'

Jonathan shook his head.

'He needs to come in and get dressed.'

'He'll come in when he's ready.'

'I expect he was ready an hour ago.'

'He's not a child, Leonard.'

How is that relevant? he thought. Children aren't the only people who need to avoid hypothermia. But he'd no right to be angry with the man who'd got in that brown water and pulled William out; what he should be expressing was gratitude if he expressed anything at all. He collected up his brother's clothes that were laid over the arm of the chair, just inside the patio door, and he added to them the jumper he'd brought from home. It was true at least, what Jonathan said about William staying in the water too long. William's proficiency there was born of fear-lessness and indifference to discomfort more than of skill; he'd take no account of his age when he set out to do what he'd done as a fourteen year old. If he got cramp he wouldn't necessarily know what to do, and if he got too cold he'd register it only at some part of his brain that had no capacity for response and which would bear it a little longer and then a little longer. The rest of him would be heedless, that old slow reptilian heart sliding up and down through the water – foolish man. Foolish man! Leonard went out to him, dropped the clothes down and put his hands on his shoulders.

'William, come indoors.'

William was staring ahead at the water in what seemed to be one of his trances. He blinked, and there was a vague twitching of muscle across the flat plane of his cheek, but otherwise he might have been in a deep open-eyed death. With the towel that was on the boards, Leonard covered his back and tried to rub some warmth into it. There was a cup of tea, now cold, by his thigh. Well, at least Jonathan made some small effort; he shouldn't have let you sit out here like this though, Leonard thought. Your skin cold and white as used tissue, look at you, suddenly an old man, look at you shivering.

More urgently this time, he said, 'William.'

William blinked again, turned his head slow and fluid as though it were afloat in soupy water, and picked up the cup of tea. The towel slid again from his back. 'Leo.'

'What happened to you?'

'I think I just – panicked. I swallowed too much water.'

'Why did you panic?'

William shook his head as though he'd perplexed himself beyond expression, and Leonard considered whether to challenge him; eventually he only offered his hand. 'Come on, get up, your clothes are here.'

If his brother had ever before confessed to panic, or seemed panicked, Leonard certainly didn't remember it. The boy at Swift Ditch never swallowed water, such a thing was impossible for his conquering little self; what was more, the man who'd grown from the boy at Swift Ditch never swallowed water, for then he was conquered, and the man was unconquerable. He didn't panic, his calm was an ocean. A mouthful of river, Leonard thought, did nothing to drown him. He noticed the fierce redness of his brother's hands and feet, the toes purplish around the nails, as their father's had been in the mornings of his last weeks – death coming, he'd thought when he first saw those damask toes, even though their colour might have been quite harmless, and he was always glad to get socks and blankets to shroud them from view.

Jonathan came outside and together they helped pull William

up; all his great solid weight, pale and heavy, his shoulders trying to straighten again from their buckled tension, his legs – from that foreshortened perspective – too small and too short so that he appeared froglike. And then when he was on his feet he took his shirt from Leonard, clutched it in his hand, and said, 'I'm sorry you had to come, that was your precious five pounds of fuel.'

The apology wasn't flippant or joking; then, visibly distressed, he pulled the shirt over his head. Leonard picked up the towel and the cup, and waited for him to be ready.

The city that passed the car windows as they drove home was the city they'd lived in most of their lives. In William's case, all his life – apart from his time in the navy he'd rarely left and never gone far; he'd never considered leaving for any real length of time. Maybe their parents had taken them on trips when they were small children, but he'd never go on a leisurely trip by his own doing. It looked to Leonard like a stressed city, one at odds with itself; inevitably the fuel protests would come to an end, but where would there be any sense of victory on either side? As far as he could see the majority of people hated the government and the majority of people in government acted as though they might hate the people. The skies were bright and dark and cloud-scudded in an ever-changing chilly light that held too many dimensions and not enough fastness or balance; where to put one's sights and attention and focus, what to think, what to trust? One moment you were staring out of the car window searching for sunlight, the next you were squinting against it and holding your hand up against the glass.

The next night Leonard, unable to sleep, got out of bed to get water. He'd been lying awake thinking about the lamb, of all things. He thought of its sacrifice, which felt, to him, guiltless, for it was given in the most free and complete of ways. It wasn't that one creature was plucked in reluctance from the teats of its mother but that a whole species had come to exist for the purposes of being eaten – it had given over its mortal purpose to that cause, it existed for that and it was bred for that, and if the sacrifice had been unwilling it would no longer have bothered. And when the family had licked their fingers of spiced grease the night before he'd felt an immense gratitude for that creature and all its kind, who'd brought about a sense of wellbeing in the Deppling household for one night.

That day had been cool and cloudy again and William had sat outside in the back garden for most of it; Leonard had hardly seen or spoken to him. The ever enlarging stack of newspapers they'd collected between them in the last two weeks was larger still, by the side of the armchair in the back living room, mutinous, it seemed, against the peaceable row of records. Leonard didn't know who'd bought them that morning, but he decided against looking inside to see what they said. All he knew was that if they were on that pile, they related to the fire in some way, and he was beginning to lose taste for the subject faster than he could gain curiosity.

He'd taken William a nectarine at one point during the day, and one for himself, and tried to make light conversation. His brother had very little to say. William never suffered from guilt, but even by comparison to a person prone to it he seemed to feel disproportionately guilty about the use of the last few pounds of petrol, for when they'd got home from Shepperton the gauge was back in the red; it didn't matter, Leonard said. Better that he had it to use than not, and he could get more. I'll get you more, William had said. Leonard had insisted that he didn't, not least because his brother was sniffing and nasal with a cold. It was so rare for him to have a cold that Leonard struggled to remember the last time, perhaps as far back as his teenage years. In spite of it, later that afternoon William had gone out with the petrol can and come back some two hours hence, sloshing whatever quantity was in the bottom of it. The Clerkenwell garage was closed, he'd told Leonard, no more fuel there. He'd had to walk out a mile and a half towards Holloway. Leonard thanked him and put the can in the shed. In the evening there was a family dinner together which was hijacked as usual by the children's conversation and in which both he and William said little, and that in total was all they'd really seen of one another.

He went quietly downstairs. He was learning to be considerate of the fact that Richard woke easily, and when he woke he'd often become anxious and the cough would start. He put his feet down carefully on the treads. The darkness had seemed to curdle the day's freshness and leave the air in the house close and pressing. The lamp was on dimly in the kitchen. He hadn't expected anybody to be up, and when he saw his brother there, standing at the ironing board where an old suit was draped, nothing could have appeared so incongruous to him. William was dressed in the linen trousers he'd been wearing the last few days, but his top was bare. He lifted the iron up from the sleeve he was attending to and his smile was a half measure, unforced, but unavailing. There was a hunted look to his expression, one that Leonard found so unsettling and strange that he couldn't bring himself to speak, except to say limply, 'You're ironing' and for William to return, 'I'm doing well. I've only been going twenty-five minutes and I've almost finished this sleeve.'

Drinking back a glass of water, running another, Leonard stood for a moment.

'May I ask why you're ironing?'

William stood the iron to the side and ran his hands along the fabric. It was his wedding suit, Leonard was sure – he recognised the heather-coloured silk lining which had matched his own tie. 'You may ask,' William replied, and the low light gave his face a false leanness and the sobriety of an oil painting, an old Goya portrait, a Rembrandt, gentle but intransigent, his frightened smile mustering up shadows around his eyes. He meant by his reply, You may ask, but I can't answer. Leonard could think of no response, so taken aback he was by the fear in that smile.

He went back up to bed. There should be nothing very alarming about the sight of a person ironing, even if the sight was uncommon; one shouldn't lose sleep over that. At first Leonard had thought his brother might be preparing to go to the probate meeting with him the following day, but the idea stood up to no scrutiny. In truth Leonard knew what occasion William was ironing for, and of course his brother knew that he knew. There wasn't any need to say. Unless he was greatly mistaken, it was clear that, following William's questioning on Friday, he'd been asked to appear in front of the magistrates. He sat on the edge of his bed, and then he coiled his irritations and worries inwards with the pulling up of his feet onto the mattress, and he dug his feet between the springs.

In the morning he stayed in his room until he heard the front door open and close, and he watched William walk down the short garden path in his suit. It was surely the only suit he owned, and being thirteen years old it had lost its sharpness in the cut and fabric; it hung badly around the thighs and the jacket pulled slightly at his waist where he'd put on weight. A little awkward right-sided shrug as he went to open the gate, a step that had lost its rhythm; his hand, having hooked the gate, went for the pocket and then retracted when it found it was still stitched closed.

Kathy had already gone out an hour before to take the boys to school, and she hadn't yet come back. In the silence he dressed in shirt and tie as he might for work, because he really didn't know how one was meant to dress for a probate meeting; perhaps he should be smarter – there seemed to him an immense responsibility in taking on his father's entire estate, everything that had formed his life, the material outcome of every decision he and their mother had made. And all the more immense, too, for the fact that William had renounced his right to take grant of probate and left it all to the youngest son, the little brother, the one who'd never used to see himself dealing with anything.

He cleaned his shoes a little, since they needed it anyway, but his sense of occasion was overshadowed by the constant knowledge of his brother in his pressed trousers and his flowerless buttonhole and that cold he'd contracted, trying to straighten his question mark of a back against the wooden pews of the court – and in relation to this it was difficult to feel that his own dress, or responsibilities, mattered in the slightest that day.

As it was when he arrived, the Commissioner was dressed no better than him. You could easily be offended, he thought, by how informal the man is and how routinely he shakes the hand, takes the seat, passes The Oath and a pen, and offers the New Testament. For a matter of seconds Leonard paused over that offered book and wondered if he should swear on it even against his better judgement, as a final act of respect for his father. But he said instead that he wasn't a religious man, and would prefer to make a legal affirmation without the Bible. The Commissioner swiftly cleared the New Testament back to the drawer in his desk.

When he came out of that bloodless little room fifteen minutes later it was into a dry and softly autumnal mid-morning, and it struck him that it was done. He now owned all that his parents had owned, which felt curiously like the final gene had mutated and he'd become nothing more and nothing less than all they'd once been, having thought himself unique and self-determining for so long. The seed of his utter generalness had been growing in him and finally he'd reached out his hand, taken oath, and its first shoot had sprung forth between his earnest, pledging fingers.

He waited at home. It was lunchtime and Kathy was still not in. He went about harvesting the few onions that had survived the summer in the allotment, and earthed up some potatoes. Picking through the packs of seeds he'd seen in the shed when he'd put the petrol can there, he chose spring cabbages and made a sowing. The little he knew about gardening he'd learned from his father, and most of that concerned the things that needed to be done at around this time of year – yes, it had been September the year before that they'd spent all those hours outdoors, when his father had still been fairly fit and able. How he missed the mountains whenever he thought about them, and the light and the rainbows breaking loose of black clouds, and that garden sloping – as his father had said – like a big open palm. He put the tools away, collected the weeds and old vegetables that he'd cleared and threw them in for the chickens.

At almost two o'clock William arrived home, and from the garden Leonard saw him come briefly into the kitchen then walk out again. Five minutes later, when he hadn't reappeared, Leonard went upstairs and knocked on his door.

'Are you all right, William?'

'One minute,' his voice said, roundly and clearly.

So Leonard went to his room, and shortly after his brother came in wearing a shapeless shirt and some grey cotton trousers, his feet bare. His wedding suit lay over his arm.

'I wanted you to know that there's enough evidence against me for a trial, so I'll be getting a date through to go to court. I thought it was important to tell you first.'

Leonard leaned back against the chest of drawers behind him, and he said without accusation, 'You haven't been telling me anything, William, not even about going to court today.'

They looked at one another and William seemed to assess the comment as if he were sympathetic to its tacit point – that had Leonard known about what was happening he might have done something to stop it.

'I haven't been myself, I've been scared, I've behaved in a way that deserves no respect, and I'm sorry. I am, Leo, truly sorry.'

'It's not that I want you to be sorry, there's nothing shameful about being scared.'

'But it's shameful to let your fear take over.'

Leonard shifted to stand by the bed. He thought, Nonsense, nonsense to talk of shame and fear like this, and he regretted that awkwardly intimate space into which their conversations so readily crowded themselves; no way out except more intimacy, more frankness and more examination.

He said, 'So you've been charged, released on bail?'

'Yes, charged with accessory to arson.'

'How long will it be before your trial?'

'I don't know, it might be weeks or months.'

'I don't see how there can be a trial, evidence, anything. I don't see how it's come to this.'

'But of course it was always going to come to this – I'm an ugly man in a world that loves beauty.'

'It's nothing to do with beauty.'

'I'm a persistent, annoying man.'

'The issue is a fire, William – not persistence or ugliness.'

Leonard closed his eyes for long enough to lose exact sense of where his brother was in relation to him, or how much space there was between his head and the light fitting, or his calf and the bed; a good, momentary loss of context that made him reluctant to see again. In the silence he noticed his brother's smooth breathing; the cold seemed to have left him, and indeed, when he opened his eyes he saw a face that was flecked again with colour and the beginnings of health or hope, a new buoyancy.

'You have to get a good lawyer, William. We have access to the inheritance now, we can use any amount of it on that, I don't mind – use it from my pot so that you can keep yours for Kathy and the boys.'

'In honesty I'd rather splash out and buy petrol instead, thousands of cans of it, just to drive round the square for the rest of our lives. It would do just as much good.'

'You make everything so difficult for yourself.'

'What is it they say? A jury consists of twelve people chosen to decide who has the better lawyer. I'm not interested in that kind of justice; if I've done wrong I want the wrong to be found out and not disguised by the best legal mind money can buy. Do you think that's an idiotic view?'

There wasn't anything Leonard could say so he shook his head in tiredness. William stepped towards him then and his instinct was to move back, an instinct he checked through shame. It would be best now to take his brother's hand and forearm in a gesture of solidarity and faith, but he couldn't do so.

William laid the wedding suit on the bed. 'The evidence against me is all in notes Stephen wrote in our meetings. You see, I'd been speaking about books once, and Eastacre came up because it was around the time it was in the news. I said, in the context of a bigger discussion, that the best thing for that community would be for the library to burn down and for the people to speak directly to one another instead, unmediated, looking one another in the eye.'

William had been gazing at the suit, but then he looked up.

'Leo, I believe we should speak if we want to communicate, not write. We should speak directly. That way we can be the guardian of every word that comes out of our mouths, and if somebody wants to bend what we say, we can gently straighten it again. But if a word is written it can travel thousands of miles and years from its creator, and any amount of bending can happen. We have too much hope for the written word; that was my only point. Too much hope for it and too much faith in it. No wonder we misunderstand each other and lose one another in translation.'

'And they have that in Stephen's notes – you saying that the library should be burnt down?'

'Out of context, with a separate agenda. But I'm almost pleased, because doesn't the misinterpretation of it exactly prove my point?'

Leonard nodded and, with a sigh, put his hands in his back pockets. 'Surely Stephen couldn't have taken that as a cue to burn it down himself.'

'Surely not, otherwise I might not have said it. But with hind-sight, I suppose Stephen was waiting for life to happen to him, waiting for the opportunity. If I brought the group an issue to question, he'd conclude that because we took so much trouble to question it, there was no answer possible. When we discussed sin, and I left him in a position where he had to admit there might be no such thing, he took that to mean it doesn't matter what you do, since it won't be sinful. The police showed me some of the notes, I read them – and that was all he took from our meetings, from every discussion we ever had about justice, politics, art, education, science – he interpreted from it a moral void. Not a moral guide, but a void. That void can be filled with either hopelessness or anarchy. If you want it to, it gives you licence to do anything you like.'

'You speak as though you assume he's guilty.'

'But I don't occupy myself with thoughts about his guilt – *my* guilt is my worry. I didn't aid Stephen in that fire and I didn't know anything about his plans. But it looks like I did lead him into thinking it was fine to do whatever he liked. I don't think that's a crime, but apparently it's not up to me to pronounce the verdict. And the point is that maybe I'm wrong anyway – we all have these blind spots in ourselves that are the areas we can't quite turn our necks to see. If I'm wrong and it is a crime, then I need to be shown, otherwise I'd have to act as though it's sometimes preferable to remain blind than to see truth. If I act like that I've lost the very thing that makes my life worth living. The belief that happiness and freedom come only from knowing oneself.'

There were tears in his eyes – they were always moist, as though constantly stirred by sensation, but just then they were tearful. I could never feel moved to emotion over such an abstract thing as self-blindness, Leonard thought, and struggled as he so often did recently to find a fitting reply, or a worthy one. But William moved abruptly to take the suit from the bed, and he held it out.

'I want you to keep this. Then, when I need it again I'll have to come to you for it. I'll have to ask you, and that way there can't be any secrets or darkness between us.'

Leonard stood motionless. 'You keep it, William.'

'I'm asking you as a favour – will you, please?'

'I can't see how me having it will help.'

'Nevertheless, I'm asking you.'

He was reluctant, but he nodded at length. 'I'll hang it up,' he said, and he took it out of his brother's arms.

He'd woken dully for the few days that followed and felt heavy and mindful of something holding him down. As soon as he opened his eyes he'd suffer the recognition that William had a tether at his neck and the tether seemed to extend around the house, constricting and bearing down on the adults of the family. He wasn't to change address, nor to visit Stephen, nor to run his groups; fortnightly he was obliged to report to the police to prove he'd not absconded. He wasn't to leave the country even to go on holiday with his family. It wasn't the conditions themselves that bothered Leonard – if only the courts knew the irony of those constraints, for to confine William to London was to confine a bird to the sky after all. It was the imperious fact of the constraints that made Leonard wake heavily; the incrimination of them.

At times Leonard would go from his bed to the window to see William and the boys leave for school, the boys' glossy heads appearing into view just below the window where the flowers needed cutting and then moving apace down to the gate, so unconscious of themselves, Abe's overlarge feet treading down the sprawled growth along the path, and he wondered how they'd be affected by what was happening, or what he himself would do or tell them in William and Kathy's position, or indeed, what they had told them already.

Often when he woke he was thinking too of his father. He'd been reminded of an evening in which the two of them had been watching the horrors of the news, and the old man had said, Do you think this is sinful, what's happening here? And it would be a murder or a bomb or a kidnapping. Sinful enough, Leonard would remark – then he'd hear about how William would claim otherwise, William would think the murder or the bomb wasn't sin, but just fear. In fairness to the old man, he only worried about these things because he cared; he did care what his oldest son thought, because he respected him and hoped for so much from him. So it was a matter of deep concern to him that those two metaphysically different terms, sin and fear, which were looked on quite separately by God, should be conflated like that by William. For sins were of the world and to be punished, whereas fears were of the spirit and to be comforted, and to give the opposite response to either was to increase the potential for both.

If truth be told Leonard hadn't given the discussion another thought until his brother had spoken a few days before about the evidence against him. But that morning he'd woken with it fronting his mind and had gone for a walk feeling unsettled. When he came back he put away the breakfast dishes and went upstairs, and up again to the playroom where he could hear movement.

He knew it was his brother, since the boys were at school and Kathy had gone to the library; she'd been spending her time there lately, those few mornings when she hadn't come back when expected. She might never have told Leonard where she'd been except that she'd been coming in one day just as he'd been going out, and maybe she'd felt that her lack of anything to show for her day's outing might recriminate or rouse suspicion. She'd taken to sitting in the study area of the library reading, she told him. There wasn't a reason; she could read just as well at home. It was probably stupid, she just liked it there. It wasn't stupid, he said. He'd done it himself in Edinburgh at times and it was peaceful, among the people learning Russian, looking at maps from the 1870s, hunching over medical textbooks, among their coughs and sneezes, their wonkily worn glasses, the musical tinning of their headphones. It really wasn't stupid to escape into the world like this for a while.

As he pushed open the playroom door he called, 'William?' He went in and his brother was filling plastic coloured boxes with all the loose items on the floor, the building bricks, puzzles, cars, balls and the rest.

'Tidying up after the animals,' William said, glancing over with a smile. 'I expect you're desperate to help?'

Leonard took in the bedlam of the room. 'Desperate,' he replied warmly, and began picking things up himself and tossing them into the boxes. He added, 'I thought they were supposed to clear up after themselves.'

'Leo, if you had children you'd know it's like asking the sea to clear up after itself. It will, when it next comes in, but in the process it'll leave a shore full of itself again. It's in its nature – nothing to be done about it.'

'Ah, the utter thanklessness of it!'

They exchanged a smile and Leonard knelt on the floor to get to some of the odds and ends under the old school desk that had somehow found its way up there. There were marker pens, scissors, glue, brushes, a battered old papier-mâché frog's head the size of his own, straws, cardboard, a jar of dried paint. And he found the Game Boy he'd bought Oli three or four years before, and underneath that the remote-controlled car – the *Panther 2* – that he'd given one of them, he couldn't remember which. He separated out the pens and brushes and put them in the desk, and added what was left to the boxes.

It was hot and stuffy in the attic, and it smelt of activity and endless preoccupied endeavour. He stood to open the skylight, then knelt again. He said, 'William, what do you mean when you say there's no such thing as sin?'

William looked up with a cocked brow. He had, rested on his palms, the impressively constructed pirate ship which he'd been inspecting, as if trying to see how his sons had managed such a thing. 'I only said it's possible there might not be.'

'Only, I can see how a statement like that could be misinterpreted.'

'Yes, I can too.'

'Father was bothered by it.'

'Then it was a gift to him. I love to find myself bothered by

226

something, it means there's some stone unturned in my thoughts. It calls me again to question.'

William placed the Lego piece with care on top of one of the full boxes and he pushed the box behind him towards the wall.

'You're so scrupulous, William.'

Coming to his feet with quietly cracking ankles, William brushed off his trousers and began gathering up the pieces of train track that littered the floor. He said, 'What *is* sin, Leo?'

Leonard glanced up to the skylight and back. 'But he was right, wasn't he? Father, I mean. I see him there in his old armchair picking at the fabric, worrying about it. But he was right to worry, his fears have come true. Haven't they? In speaking that way to Stephen, in saying there's no sin, only fear, you take away any sense of punishment, of consequence.'

Without visible injury or annoyance, William straightened from his task. 'You tell me what sin is then – if you know, tell me.'

'In the Bible it's temptation – temptation to do what we know is wrong.'

'What tempts us?'

'The fruit, the woman, the money, the prize – everything tempts us, what chance do we stand?'

'Why do those things tempt us?'

'Because they make us feel better. You might not suffer this yourself, but for some of us life is made worth living by these – pathetic little reliefs.'

He said it without rebuke, he really meant no rebuke. It was only said in truth, for when had William ever succumbed to temptation, when had he ever been weak?

'I suffer it all the time,' William said. 'We always want to benefit and to make gains for ourselves through what we do. Nothing could be more natural.'

'So then sin is trying to benefit ourselves?'

'No, otherwise we could do nothing but sin. You'd be right, what chance would we have?' He said lightly, 'I am many things, Leo, but I am not a Catholic. God forfend.'

They'd both stopped what they were doing and had come to be looking at one another, Leonard kneeling on the floor, his brother standing with pieces of train track in his hand.

William said, 'Do you think the chicken stamper's end objective was to kill a chicken?'

Leonard broke into abrupt laughter. 'I think the chicken stamper's end objective was to drive me insane with questions about chicken stamping.'

'Then let's hope he doesn't achieve it.'

'I'm sorry.' He picked a staple from the carpet and opened it out distractedly. 'No, I doubt that was his objective. I agree with you, I expect he thought it would benefit him somehow.'

'Make him feel more powerful, as you said before.'

'Perhaps.'

'Do you think it succeeded? Once he'd performed the Herculean feat of slaying a chicken, he felt better for it, more powerful, more in control of his life?'

Leonard didn't see a need to answer; for a moment he felt he might reach out and take his brother's hand. It's all going wrong, he wanted to say. For the first time he actually brought himself to imagine the figure of their feted culprit, his lean frame, his clenched teeth, and how he might have stared at the creature giving one final quake of life under his boot and felt his own throat tighten with what he could only put down to a sense of victory.

'What if sin is just this?' William asked. 'Just this mistaken belief that something is going to bring us some gain? What if it doesn't spring from a piece of dark devil-given apparatus in our souls, but just from ignorance, and from that, fear?'

They remained where they were with nothing to say. William took a tissue from his pocket and blew his nose. It might have been because they were among these pastel plastics of childhood, and all this will to play at any cost, but Leonard was prepared to accept what his brother had said. He remembered the boys when they were toddlers and all their terrible screaming self-interested havoc which, rightly of course, nobody thought sinful, and for which they earned not one second of real reproach. As their knowledge of the world improved, so too would their behaviour, nobody doubted this. They were forgiven their ignorance, soothed for their fears, encouraged to learn what they didn't yet know: encouraged, soothed and forgiven. What went wrong then? At what stage did the dimpled child, with his several ignorances and fears shackled to his leg, become the lean adult who murdered a chicken; at what stage did he no longer deserve to be soothed and forgiven?

'William,' he ventured. 'When Father died—' He was going to say, when Father died he didn't have your photograph on his lap. He held back and looked lopsidedly at his brother.

'When Father died?'

He shrugged and smiled. 'No, nothing, forget it.'

The confession had been motivated by a compassionate feeling that wanted to express how William, himself once a roseate, angel-faced child, had been wronged by the family. But there was nothing to gain by saying it, since their father too, presumably, had acted only through fear himself. He too had probably been a bouncing bright impeccable infant once. Forgive all of us, then, for the terror and the mistakes – for ultimately what else could one do but forgive?

William crouched for the rest of the pieces of track and didn't press for an explanation.

'Perhaps there's some comfort,' Leonard said, and he sat on a low stool the boys had made with building bricks, so low that his knees came almost up to his armpits, 'to think that we're all ignorant – to make sense of the world that way – perhaps there's comfort in that. I'm ignorant myself and I know I mess things up all the time. And the thing is that if I do some small thing, tell a small lie to protect someone,' he looked at his brother with thoughts of the photograph, as though that candid admission of his capacity to lie was as good as the undoing of the lie; and he looked down again, 'then I do it through ignorance and fear, just as that person killed a chicken for the same reason, just as a person can instigate genocide for the same reason. And I know that they're not the same, but somehow, William, there's a common logic to it. I suppose you've been telling me this all along, and it's what you've probably told your students.' He looked up to see his brother regarding him with so much attention of the sort he'd so rarely reciprocated. 'But I can see what you mean.'

With barely a beat for breath or thought William asked, 'Why do you think they're not the same?'

'What – the small lie and the genocide? Does it need saying? I don't wish to plunge us all into despair, William, to think that if we lie or even crush the neck of a bird we've as good as killed a race of people. Like you said, we're not Catholic.' He raised his brows; on balance, probably unfair to Catholics, he thought, probably crassly simplified. But all the same.

His brother asked, 'What if those actions are exactly alike?'

An oblique breeze through the skylight lightly lifted William's hair, the only movement in the airless room. Leonard didn't answer.

'Would you find that repulsive somehow, if I said there's no moral difference between doing somebody the smallest discourtesy and committing genocide?'

Leonard watched his brother's hair move in that fine, thoughtless dance and he said, 'Repulsive – no, I just wouldn't know what you could mean by it.'

'Maybe you think that we measure the sinfulness of something, by which I mean the ignorance and fear of something, by the harm it causes. If you tell a small, merciful lie that isn't very harmful, it's less bad than telling a big, harmful lie, which is less bad than killing a person, which is less bad than killing a number of people. But this isn't the point I've ever tried to make, Leo.' William crouched and sat back on his heels, with his shoulders steeply sloped. 'Yesterday Oli smashed this train track up in a temper because Kathy asked him to do something he didn't want to do. He mustn't behave this way, we think – if we let him behave this way now, without respect for orders, he might grow up to do far worse. These are acorns that grow into oaks – don't we think that? Nip them in the bud. But what if smashing the train track isn't the acorn, but the full tree itself? What if something is wrong by its ignorant and fearful nature, rather than by the amount of harm it does? In which case, any ignorance is fully and equally wrong. What Oli did yesterday isn't a step towards chicken killing and genocide, it's the entire journey.'

Leonard wrapped his arms around his knees and turned his attention up to the passing scenery beyond the skylight. From that perspective, gazing up and out well clear of any horizon, there was no sense of city and one could be anywhere. He'd brought the subject up because he'd been worried about what William might have said to Stephen that could have incited him; and now he didn't know at all if his brother's take on the subject comforted the worry or inflamed it.

'It's a theory,' he said and he saw that William was perfectly still, holding on to those pieces of track. So then you've punished Oli as if he's killed someone? he thought. He brought his forearms to lay flat across his knees and remembered William sitting just like that as a child, clutching some toy or puzzle in concentrated silence, and whether it was a memory or not – whether just an imposition of the present onto the past – it gave him love for his brother that belittled the questions. A love that was peripheral but immense, like a mountain range seen from the corner of the eye.

William said, 'We wouldn't have to wait for horror to happen, if we could see the full extent of sin, as it were, in a childish tantrum. We could address it at every turn. We wouldn't blame God, we wouldn't have all this religious nonsense about hell and the work of the devil. If we could see ourselves plainly as children lost in our ignorance of the world, but all the same capable of learning, I believe we could heal ourselves.'

'Yes,' Leonard answered, and he lowered his head.

He lay in bed reading, half attentive to the words on the page and half elsewhere. A fox barked, and instead of dismissing it as he always did, he thought about the chickens and whether they'd be safe out there in the enclosure. Should he get up and check? But he wanted to stay in bed. Why should he care, what concern was it of his? He was tired and so much wanted to stay in bed.

For here is the thing: you may not care about a chicken, but ultimately you are forced to care about a chicken. That dark ego in your machinery is careful to tell you that you and the chicken have shared fates that stretch even beyond the common fact of your endangered lives and certain death and lame physical assailability. You share a logical fate, for if you've not thought enough about the chickens it means you've not thought enough about any of the issues related to the chickens, which are the issues of life, the complexities of life that encompass everything from the progress of frost creeping over a leaf to the progress of a civilisation creeping over a continent; and on the way, the fates of the composite things, the lives of the people, the things that bother your own wellbeing.

You don't care enough to think about them and so you're not something worth caring about yourself; no wonder you've become this dead human weight, no wonder you're alone!

You're trying to read and thereby shut me out, says this persistent ego. You can go back to reading your book in hopelessness, but bear in mind a point of salvation, which is this: the one thing, the one small but deep thing you have over the chicken is your capacity to be considerate of it, to protect it. Of course you would never crush it with your own boot, but will you get up now, out of bed? If you will not get up in the night to check it's safe from the fox, you're not safe from the fox either, your soul is finally a chicken's soul and you must only hope that someone greater than yourself will protect you when the time comes. But of course you don't believe in anything greater than yourself, so you are entirely without hope of deliverance. Lie down then, pretend the fox doesn't bark; read your book.

This thought process happened to Leonard in one single moment between hearing the fox and closing his eyes in fatigue. And there in his mind, behind his eyelids, he saw himself some three decades before staring at a plate of macaroons while his brother held forth with a rally of questions about the nature of the mind. All that provoking thought, and the most Leonard could do was hanker for another biscuit and wonder if it would be rude to reach for one. It was sometimes that way with his brother, that in comparison to him he felt like a blunt stick that had found its way into a quiver of arrows.

He reopened his eyes and put his book down, for he hadn't taken in a word of it. William would say, Good for you, Leo, it's all fearful drama in any case, and he would likely throw it over his shoulder with a comic flourish. Richard coughed in the next room, but it was a low and somnolent sound that had no urgency to it; and there, by contrast, the fox bark kicked once more against the warm hum of late-night city traffic and planes – a high crack of sound that was persistent and needy; hungry for a hen, Leonard thought. Fine then, I will get up; even though I know very well that there's mesh all the way around the coop, I will get up and atone for my inept and lazy mind, my misplaced yearnings, my insignificance. He went to the bathroom which had a view over the back garden. Through the open window he saw his brother down there, a crouching bare-torsoed figure made liquid in the moonlight, stooped at the mesh and silver-backed like a fish. He was binding up the loose corners of the coop with something, some extra mesh or wire, fastidious and searching with his fingers to check for breaks in its resistance.

You are too slow, says the languishing ego; you might have guessed that your brother would show the better vigilance. Still, you did try. You were beaten by a better man, but you did try. Leonard took himself back to bed quite sick of things. Poor hen, he told himself, and felt more empathy than he could account for; her simple existence is threatened by the fox's hunger, the thug's foot, the philosopher's mind. Put your head under your wing, poor stupid creature, sink your beak in, close your quick eyes to the moonlight, hope to be alive still when morning comes.

He'd hung the suit in the wardrobe as William asked; an empty request in a way, given that William could in principle go in and take it any time he liked. But the more he thought of that simple thing his brother had asked him to do, the less empty the request became. There was no question of William going in and taking the suit without asking him, because he'd given his word and his word was as stone; you're the gatekeeper, is what William had tacitly said, hadn't he, when he laid the suit on the bed? You're the gatekeeper and I don't want to pass anywhere without you. It was hard to think of another time in their lives together that William had dignified him with such a position, and now it had come it put a strange, dragging weight on him. It was hard to accept himself as William's gloomy usher to a courthouse and, if the idea could even be entertained, to a prison cell – though indeed, he didn't ever entertain that thought for long, for he couldn't.

But the papers had begun taking an increased interest in deeper points of the Eastacre fire, though passing off their views as a kind of abstract musing that didn't relate necessarily to Eastacre itself. The report that most troubled Leonard was the one that urged readers to cast their minds back to the Bonfire of the Vanities, to the Nazi book burnings, to the fall of the Royal Library of Alexandria. Consider the historic role of libraries in the emancipation of the human intellect and the democratisation of knowledge. Consider the destruction of books as a tyrannical act against freedom and democracy. And so it went on, et cetera et cetera, in this way. Leonard read the article when the paper came through their door, before breakfast, and as soon as he'd done so he dropped it onto the pile in the back living room so that William could be spared its views.

Didn't the report seem a bit jubilant when it made its references to these things? God knew there was enough strife in the world without trying to drag the evils of the past back into the present. If one national paper had begun to seize this topic – the latent fascism and despotism of burning books, the attempt at quelling and crushing the human spirit – he knew that others would take up that theme too, because so it worked, in themes and fashions. The men responsible for book burnings in the past have been recognised as the enemy of people's hopes and achievements, the report had said, in the vein of the worst despots who'd lived.

It was worrying, the building of that wave that was unfurling towards William. For even Leonard could at times make out the vague shape of his brother's perceived guilt. The one subject he knew his brother had addressed with Stephen was contentious enough, and there must have been many more like it. Which was to say, if William thought that lying gently to a friend, committing arson and spearheading a holocaust were, morally speaking, all of the same scale, and all childish errors, there were any number of ways that message could be heard and carried forward into life. Wouldn't it seem preposterous, even monstrous? And didn't it have a harmful corollary, which was to say that it was no more wrong to commit genocide than to be generous with the truth about the number of photographs on a dying man's lap? One could see how an impressionable mind, looking for provocation, might take this kind of assertion the wrong way and be misled, and how his or her moral compass might be confused. Leonard had said it to his brother; William had seemed to consider a debate, and had then said simply, Yes, it could be taken that way I suppose.

At breakfast that morning William prayed. First he'd fetched the boys' bags, books and sports kits and put them ready by the front door, then he sat on the end of the kitchen bench where they all ate in a rushed and barely seated muddle of food, school ties and toy dinosaurs, and he linked his fingertips in his lap, let his chin rest towards his chest, and closed his eyes.

Later that morning, when William had got back from walking the boys to school, Leonard found him standing by the armchair reading, with the pile of newspapers at his feet.

'You shouldn't read those, William, they'll ruin your day,' he remarked, and came to stand near his brother with a coffee he'd poured for him.

He expected, when William turned to him, to see that fearful shrinking back he'd seen the night before last with the suit ironing, or the dismantled, vulnerable look William had acquired lately where uncertainty provoked the muscles around his mouth and eyes into faint twitches. But there wasn't such a reaction – no, William just glanced over his shoulder, extended a small smile that was reminiscent of his smiles as a boy, turned back and submitted a fingertip to a line in the article he was reading.

'There isn't any proof that the Library at Alexandria was burnt down to destroy the books – not even proof that it was burnt down on purpose, actually.' He was gentle and placatory. 'Some say it caught fire accidentally when Caesar sent fireships in on an enemy fleet in the harbour. But even that isn't known for certain.'

Leonard paused, and he nodded. He might vaguely have known that fragment of history himself from his teaching, now that William had come to say it. 'You're right,' he answered. He passed his brother the coffee.

'I suppose the thing is that we should strive to get things right, rather than settling for part-truths just to prove a point.'

Again, William's words were firm and sweet-tempered. He folded the newspaper and laid it down on the arm of the chair, then thanked Leonard for the coffee, which he took in both hands.

Leonard left him there. A little later he saw him hanging washing out on the line in the garden, then he saw him kneeling on the grass cutting chicken wire with a pair of snippers and measuring it up roughly against gaps in the dividing hedge. Did he not know the damage of articles like that? Did he not know that if there was one like it there could be many, and that it was troubling if the press decided to continue on that path? Though that particular article didn't reference him or Stephen at all, it was more damning than any personal slander – it elevated the fire beyond matches and flames and into the realm of tyranny – despotism as they'd put it themselves, despotism that followed a dark lineage back through the hands of oppressors and zealots – and in this light therefore William wasn't being charged with speaking a few inflammatory words that might or might not have led to this or that outcome, but with the continuance of an entire tradition people feared and hated. Our democracy is threatened by acts like this, it said; and with it your freedom, your children's freedom, your right to your own history, your own language.

Yet William had read the article with care and showed no anxiety. Indeed, early that evening Leonard went past the back living room while William was sitting in the light of the lamp, reading through the pile of newspapers, and when he'd finished they'd been folded and stacked on the armchair itself, and William had gone to wash up after the day's meals with a distinct quietude, as though each article had increased his resolve and his calm.

And then on the Saturday an article appeared in the national press that took the hope out of Leonard's heart. It was short enough and factual to an extent, and not in the least impassioned if you took the words on the page at face value. It simply reported that William had been charged at Highbury Corner Magistrate's Court with accessory to arson for the fire at Eastacre Library in Plaistow, back in July, based on evidence of his ongoing mentoring of Stephen in controversial doctrine, which the younger man had said influenced his thinking.

The article drew no particular bias on this, yet it made a final and evasive observation of the fact that William had spent some time in his younger life in a psychiatric ward with symptoms of a possible personality disorder. The reporter's point wasn't clear; did she say it with censure to suggest William's views were so bizarre they'd even had him sectioned, or with some mercy to suggest that his views might be so bizarre because he was mentally unwell? Mercy or otherwise, it was unjust, Leonard thought, unjust, irrelevant and should never have been mentioned.

'They can't write things like that,' Leonard had said, his heartbeat quickening. 'They should retract it, it's unjust; it's illegal.'

He'd sat with his shoulders tensely hunched, looking up at his silent, unflinching brother.

On the Saturday night, before going to bed, they stood in the kitchen getting water to take up. William, in what seemed to be his only verbal response to those articles, said with the true pitch of a question that had yet to be answered, 'If A causes B – even if it really does – is B its *fault*? Is a flood the rain's fault?'

Leonard didn't answer, but took his brother's glass from his hand and filled it at the tap.

William prayed a great deal as that week passed, both alone as usual, but also in the midst of the family as he'd never used to do. There was suddenly a receptiveness in him, as though he were opening his airwaves to those unhappy events and allowing them to mingle in the bloodstream and beat in the silences of his large heart. It was just as their father's church had responded to Leonard when he went in with his atheism and his impatience and his soul tight-shuttered; it had accepted him anyway, regardless, widely and openly.

William gave out peace even as he moved up the stairs or watched television with the boys; he gave it out as he went around the borders of the garden pinning chicken wire to the existing fences and gaps in the hedge, intent on the idea of letting the hens run free during the day. Gone was the aggravated compulsion that had driven him before, and gone too was that short-lived period of fear. Instead there was a sureness and tranquillity as if no part of him doubted any other part of him. Now the hens were oriented and healthy again, he said, they should have their freedom back; they needed more grass, more room to stretch their strengthened legs – so he set to it, and Kathy didn't object.

239

There was no apology in him, nor fear, nor even quite the old inscrutability.

On the Thursday morning the newspapers had gone from the armchair, and Leonard went out into the garden to see his brother tearing their pages into thin strips, which he laid in a pile to his left.

'Good bedding for the hens,' he explained, 'to encourage them to lay.' And he looked up to watch them foraging the new territory of the allotment in a cluster, where they'd dug shallow roosts into the soil.

Leonard sat on the grass next to him to help. For half an hour they ripped the papers into strips and piled them up, and there was nothing but the sound of tearing and the throaty calls of the chickens. It was a job that could have taken ten minutes if they hadn't gone about it with such precise attention; no doubt Leonard wouldn't have done it his brother's way, but there wasn't any harm in it after all. There was a rhythm to it that started to create its own logic, for if you tore the strips to a certain width at a certain slow speed they peeled off with a satisfying uniformity.

For all the world it might have just been the two of them in existence for those thirty minutes; if there'd been planes Leonard didn't hear them, if there'd been traffic noise it hadn't entered that sphere around each of them. The hens' cooing was nothing but the idle sound their thoughts made. The people whose stories they ripped up were from a forgotten dream. Their parents were dead. There wasn't very much in the world that didn't contain for one some vestige of the other. And one of the thoughts Leonard had, that cooed dimly among others, was that his position was impossible – ushering between his brother and the world, and wishing to escape that responsibility, wishing to escape his brother. He watched William gather up the shreds of paper to take to the coop and saw him stop only to squint up for a pause of a few seconds when Kathy moved as a shadow near the bedroom window. A smile that fleeted. Then back to gathering again.

All those shreds of paper that were left on the grass, they'd blow across the garden if he didn't collect them up. So while William made a deep bed of them in the coop, he went to the house to get a bag for what remained. From the kitchen he could see along the hallway and vaguely through the obscured glass pane to the left of the front door, and there seemed to be movement there somewhere in the front garden. It might be the postman, or a delivery of some kind; some children, somebody at the wrong house. It wasn't Kathy because he could hear her vacuuming the landing upstairs. But when the movement persisted he went to the door and opened it. There were three people stationed in the garden taking photographs of the house, faces eclipsed by cameras which clicked rapidly at the opening door. He knew what they were of course from the moment he saw them, with their voracious consuming of all that moved, and their bags at their feet, and the car that was double parked on the street.

'What are you doing?' he said loudly. 'What the hell are you doing?'

For a moment they stopped, and one of the two women asked, 'Mr Deppling?'

'Which newspaper are you from?'

Their only response was to take up their cameras once again like arms, but they didn't shoot. 'He's not here,' he said, taking a step forward. 'Get out of here. Never let me see you again.'

He went inside and closed the door. Through the glass he could see them wait for a few minutes while he sat stiffly on the bottom step. Then they left, to his astonishment. He flexed his hands to expel the heat from them, the outrage he'd thwarted in holding the edge of the stair.

*

As he walked up the front path on his way back from the shops late on Friday morning, a man was just leaving. He didn't speak to him but when he came in through the front door, William was disappearing along the hall.

He asked, 'Who was that?'

William stopped and looked over his shoulder. 'It was Stephen's uncle.'

'Did he want anything special?'

'He came to say that he can offer me a way out of all this. He's prepared to throw his money and influence at my defence.' William let the comment settle, then continued walking away.

Leonard closed the front door behind him and took his shoes off; he followed his brother into the back sitting room and looked at him enquiringly. There was no sign of Kathy.

'You look tired and worried, Leo.' William sat in his usual armchair and, after he'd spoken, seemed to appraise one of his feet, laid so flat and bare on the carpet it looked more like a found object than a human limb. Then he said, 'It doesn't matter what happens to me – but it matters what happens to you, Kathy and the children.'

'It seems to me that it all matters, all of us do – perhaps you ought to care more about what happens to you.'

'I *care*, but that's different to whether it matters.'

'I don't see the difference.'

'I care about whether or not I'm happy, whether I feel well, peaceful – I care about that maybe more than most. But I've trained myself, like an owner trains a dog to follow a scent, to hunt happiness out in myself. What happens to me is becoming less important.' William looked up and his brows were drawn down in avid consideration of what he was saying. 'Finally, after a lifetime of trying, I can say that with honesty. What happens is beginning to matter less and less.'

'Well, maybe others can do the same, William,' he replied quietly. 'Hunt out happiness in ourselves. Why assume we can't?'

'Can you?' William asked with what sounded like true hope. Just a month before, that would have been said with some irony, but not now; and this new, utter earnestness was at once easier and more difficult to cope with, Leonard found. It wasn't cutting – that was good – but it was so rounded there was no way of getting any purchase on it; he was merely slipping about on the surface of his brother's composure, a seeming sphere of it.

'There are moments when I can,' he offered, and it was the truth. His brother was watching him intently. 'In those moments, yes, I suppose I can honestly say that nothing matters. Lying on the sofa at night at the old house, for example, looking at the stars with a strange smile on my face – I used to picture a meteorite sailing towards me, and me dying with that smile on my face. Anything could have happened then and it wouldn't have mattered at all.'

William nodded. 'Yes, I know exactly those moments.'

'But they're only moments. For me, that's all.'

A short, one-sided smile from William, and then he seemed to return to his own world. Leonard stood at the mantelpiece and examined the photograph of the boys; how alike William and Richard were as toddlers – the pictures he'd seen of William at about three years old were strikingly similar, the curled blond hair and heart-shaped face and those cheeks flushed as if with fever.

He began, 'Stephen's uncle—'

William looked up. 'Yes, as I said – he wants to save me. If Stephen and I could put together one coherent defence he thinks it would be easy to get an acquittal for us both – me especially. The evidence is sketchy, he says, it's just that we haven't organised our arguments properly.' He angled his head back slightly into the warm light that came through the window, and a rare rill of

Deppling genes surfaced in the gesture – his mother's catlike gravi-
tation towards warmth and his father's lips poised at the brink of
a word; the old man would never issue a word from that prudent
mouth until his thoughts had thoroughly selected it from the
myriad possibilities and shaped its pronunciation, its tone, its
volume. Such a careful man, and there he was for an instant, his
mouth reincarnated in his oldest son's.

'It seems reasonable in a way, William.'

'Yes, his reasoning is blatant – the more innocent I appear the
more innocent his nephew appears.'

'But if it benefits you too—'

'If I agree to let him take care of my defence and his lawyers
get me acquitted, the proviso is that I stay away from Stephen,
stop running the groups, withdraw, withdraw entirely from it all,
preferably leave London altogether. Switch off, have a quiet life
in the country with my family, he suggested.'

Leonard nodded. In him, too, was a desire for those outcomes,
a desire so great he had to curb the enthusiasm in his speech.
He ventured, 'Have you ever considered that might not be such
a bad thing?'

'For whom?'

'For you.'

'With no offence to the trees and fields, Leo, it's people I love,
and this is my home.'

'With no offence to your ideas about the country, I can confirm
there are people there too.'

The comment might usually have amused William, but his
face became suddenly pinched, almost pained. 'If the trial doesn't
go very well, Mr Malson wonders if we should invoke my – I
quote – *history of mental illness*, and try to get an acquittal on those
grounds. If I could be proven to have, say, a nice neat illness that
would account for the fact that I sometimes get carried away, or

get into a state of mania and stop using reason to curb my thoughts – well then that takes some of the heat out of them, doesn't it, some of the direction. It's just a kind of unhinged raving that all those who know me take with a pinch of salt. The courts should be merciful and clement, shouldn't they? A poor man with a poor mad mind that he'd love to control but can't.'

'William—' Leonard didn't go to his brother as his instinct had first planned. In all their years together they'd never mentioned William's period of so-called mental illness, and now it'd been raised twice, so awkward and so difficult a thing, and probably all the more for having been ignored, but there'd never been a time that justified its mention.

William said, 'If only I could be proven to be a madman who Stephen would never take seriously – who nobody in their right mind would take seriously – maybe I could be free.'

When Leonard didn't answer, William raised his arms. 'I could be released to the countryside, mad and free!'

They fell into quiet and Leonard sat finally, but on the edge of his seat. The idea wasn't a good one, of course it wasn't. He thought of their father in his church, at some point in those few months before he died – Leonard could no longer remember the exact order of things. He'd stood in front of the Victorian reredos that he'd loved, run his eye across the carved panels of the four evangelists, Matthew, Mark, Luke and John, and then turned sharply to Leonard and asked, What has William made of himself? What is it for somebody to make something of himself? Is it for him to be the same, or different?

I don't know, Leonard had said, I don't know – isn't it for him to be happy? And the old man had put his finger to the carved Cross of Christ at the centre of the reredos and nodded, yes – he'd acquiesced at that mention of happiness, as if willing it to be that simple. That nod dawned on Leonard now; it is that simple, you just aim to be happy and the rest follows. Questions of madness and sanity fall away, none of it means anything, one makes it simple by one's own willing.

He said, 'William, I don't have answers, but for what it's worth I think we should look to the future – we should assume the future. As it happens I've been thinking that we should sell the Bellevue. It's never brought us any luck, just trouble – the Bellevue Group, your youth group – why don't we just be rid of it? It's because of those groups that you're in this mess, none of this would be a question if it weren't for that place.'

Slowly William straightened his head once more until it had surfaced from that pool of light. It was a motion thick with thoughts. 'Does luck live in places?' he asked. 'Did you buy it thinking that was one of its features – fully plumbed, sash windows, wicker furniture, luck?'

Leonard hesitated. 'Yes, maybe I did – don't you think we do that sometimes? Have high hopes for a place?'

'I don't think I ever have.' William was pensive, as though trying to remember a time he might have. 'Where, then, does it live, this luck? In the walls? Does it live there like a ghost?'

'Please, forget I said it.'

Leonard leaned forward to prop his elbows on his knees. He cast his gaze down at his feet. When he looked up again his brother was staring at him and waiting for a response.

He said, 'It's become nothing but a noose around our necks, William. And though everything that's happening to you is unfair, and we shouldn't have to walk away from a place we've owned for so long, maybe it's for the best if we do. Maybe things have reached a natural end.'

'The problem is that you've used a lot of ideas in that sentence I can't even begin to understand. The just, the good, the natural—'

In a sudden fury Leonard stood and raised his arms. 'Allow me a sentence free of charge sometimes; *allow* me that, yes?'

'I allow it, Leo.' His brother's voice remained low and steady as always. 'I allow you to speak in Hebrew if you want. But if you want me to be able to understand you we need to use, on the whole, the words I know.'

'Right, and we'll be here until next Christmas defining our terms while the world goes to hell around us.'

'Indeed; and if the terms are so complex that they take until next Christmas to define, they must be worth defining.'

'We *already* agree on them, we already know what they mean for the purposes of a basic conversation.'

William came to his feet; his arms were at his sides and his hands cupped by the outside of his thighs. 'You think I'm being difficult and pig-headed – you think I'm trying to pick fights just for the sheer sport of it. I mean these questions, Leo – they are real questions for me. I *cannot* talk in terms I don't understand, let alone make judgements or take actions based on them – I *will* not. You're asking me to part with a place I love – I will, if there are enough reasons to, I will without regret. But I won't do it without proper thought, just as I won't do anything without proper thought.'

Leonard held gaze with his brother momentarily, then let it drop. What had brought them to this argument? It had been his solemn resolution to stay firmly at his brother's side, even if he was the last person on earth to do so.

'Do you know, at heart, what Mr Malson's fear is?' William walked a pace or two across the room, away from Leonard. 'That I'll drive myself and Stephen into prison with my – manner, my way of doing things. He's frightened I'm a liability with my – what was his phrase? – *logic-chopping*. He said I take a person's logic and hack it up into little pieces and then give it back to them. In my struggle to understand what he means I envisage it a bit like hacking up a man's horse and giving it back to him as dog meat, when what he wanted was a horse. When he doesn't even have a dog.'

The temptation, of course, was to say, You cannot be imprisoned for this. Leonard didn't say it, because on balance, in that moment at least, such practical statements held no consolation for him. One presumably *could* be imprisoned for hacking up another's horse; why not its abstract equivalent? The evisceration of one's thoughts and beliefs was equally violent, more than equally invasive and destructive; he felt it himself. He felt it when William – his own brother – said, I don't understand what you say; I can't even begin to understand you. That statement made him feel like somebody had run at the back of his knees.

'And what did you tell him?' he asked.

'I told him that true logic can't be divided – it's logical because it's indivisible. So whatever I take and hack up, it's almost certainly not logic, more likely it's error, wrong thinking, which doesn't take much hacking, usually it falls apart at the touch.'

William went back to his chair, but he didn't sit. He stood by it and his finger followed the paisley upholstery of its back in an intricate weaving, that thick index finger trailing the curves, the fernlike swoops, as though he were investigating the shapes of a woman's body.

'Mr Malson sat in on my hearing at the magistrate's court. He seemed furious at the way I defended myself, that I chopped logic instead of looking humble – it was for the magistrates to question me, he said, not me them. If I arrogantly chop logic in my trial I'd end up with ten years in prison. If I keep quiet, and if I let his lawyers work their magic, I'll be rewarded with my freedom.' William's look was close to a petition; half of his face was ageless and weightless where the light billowed upon it, the other half mortally sharp and fixed. 'This kind of barter leaves me out of ideas,' he said, 'because to my mind, far from being arrogant, asking questions is the most humble thing a person can do. And my freedom isn't a reward if it's at the expense of reason and honesty. So, what is it that people would have me do and say?'

He flexed his hand and let it rest flat on the chair; the gesture seemed to reiterate his bafflement. What did he see when he regarded Leonard, standing opposite him? Did he see the alarm, the foreboding, did he see the attachment that was severing, or care that it was severing?

'I don't know, William. I don't know what people would have you do and say, you'd have to ask them.'

'Well, something strikes me. If Mr Malson thinks worse of me for wanting to ask questions then that's his business, Leo, not ours – but judging by the way you reacted just then to my questions about the Bellevue, it looks to me that part of you agrees with him.'

That's enough to make a person mad, Leonard thought, to compare him to your enemy when all he's done is remain your ally. He tried to keep his look neutral.

'I don't agree with him.'

William pursed his lips and stared at him, an unrelenting, inescapable gaze. 'I think you should get away. Why don't you? I promise to leave your room here empty for when you come back. This will always be your home. But for now you've got no need to be here, you're just making yourself anxious, look at you. I can't bear to see you like this.'

Leonard sat and smiled into his own lap, an aggrieved smile. He thought of the car with no petrol, and all his idle hopes of family happiness and of breaking away. He muttered, 'Thanks, but I don't need to go anywhere.'

William walked over to him and took his hand. 'But perhaps you could even take Kathy with you if you don't want to go alone, she needs the break too.'

Leonard looked up at him and then away. 'I don't need to go anywhere,' he said, and withdrew his hand from the grasp.

The Salvadorean crosses were really beautiful. Primitive and ingenuous, all yellows and reds. Where William's had a Negro Christ, the Christ on his own had been female; what fragile little statements of brightness and openness they'd made in a dour and skewed world – hanging there by a piece of string to William's hospital bed in a ward of raving and fear. Bright, bright, bright and open, so much so that they'd been the only thing Leonard had been able to look at when he visited his brother, and, other than Aleph, the only thing he really allowed himself to remember from that grey time. The crosses, both of them, on the metal bars of the bedstead, and Aleph balanced on the edge of the mattress with her pale hand on William's like a petal that had fallen there without judgement.

He and William had both received those Salvadorean crosses as teenagers, Leonard in his early teens, William in his latter. The crosses were rainbow-coloured and Leonard liked them for that, and liked them in a no-questions-asked way. He was always set to be the more accepting and the more easily spiritual of the two, and so he showed them off to friends here and there, and then in his mid-teens he shook the vestiges of spirituality from his life naturally enough, as children do shake off the legacies of their parents the moment they can.

William, meanwhile, had been quietly curious as to what the crosses were for. He'd set them up on the bookshelf in his bedroom in contemplation of them, though Leonard had never asked what it was he contemplated. As Leonard lost faith, William gained it. William had put his crosses on his wall by then, along with other articles of faith – or pictures of them – all of which he regarded with that same wildering interest. Bright blue Shiva, mosaic mandala, Islamic wedding garlands, red and white priest's stole – and he began to remark on their colourfulness with slow, collected delight, as though these colours forgave religion its deeper darkness and its basic lack of sense.

So blatantly apparent even at the age of fourteen, so rage-makingly apparent, that religion was dark and senseless! For those crosses were colourful because they were defiant of the truth – their father had been to El Salvador to visit its churches and he'd come back shaken; there was a feeling of perpetual violence and upheaval, he said, even in peacetime the villages sustained the bruising from the times before when their people had risen up and been massacred. Then he'd produced the four crosses from his case with the folk carvings of flowers and lambs and the adobe houses, a Christ so tranquil and appealing in a blue-skied land. Those were some of the first crosses of their kind ever made, their father said. He'd sat himself with the villagers, the campesinos, while they carved and painted them.

Yet William funnelled his gathering intelligence into belief in that Christ, that Lord – be he white, black, male or female – and his mind was never again to change on the subject. In his twenties he moved into childishness and an appreciation of bold colours, and what began as a sceptical enough adolescence devolved into a callow and credulous adulthood. People had begun to think he was a stupid and slow man complicated by flashes of brilliance. Gradually the images of Shiva, mandala, wedding garlands, priest's stole disappeared. Those bright crosses stood central and underpinning in his steady becoming. The trances began. He did nothing to defend the beliefs he'd come to hold deep in his marrow. He heard the voice of the Lord, he said. *The voice of the Lord is upon the waters.* You hear it how, William? I open my ears, he'd say. You open your ears? Yes, listen. There is nothing to hear. There is everything to hear, it's both sonic and subsonic, a song, it's all about.

So it always was; he simply and fiercely believed, and he never felt moved to give that belief up. Years and years that way, year upon year of lengthening trances and emotional disappearances, but years which were punctured also by regular bursts of joy and verve, nights out drinking, roaring laughter, debating, arguing a cause, the Puebla, Rodríguez, the Latin jazz, the ebullient declarations: We are citizens of the world, there is no mine and no yours, just ours!

In truth Leonard wondered often if he should have done more to stand up for his brother; what did he ever say during that family meal when he was in his early twenties, William thirty or thereabouts, the meal to which their parents invited a friend who was a doctor? No, not even a doctor, a surgeon. Not nearly as discreetly as she might have intended, their mother mentioned William's so-called catalepsy in the lapsing conversation between main course and dessert; William has this funny old thing he suffers from, don't you, William? She'd said it with such false levity that Leonard had interjected, Well, I'm sure William's glad you find it so funny. She said, It's just that we worry about it, about him, what with him being in the navy.

While the surgeon and their parents discussed possible causes and cures of an illness William may or may not have had, William himself had arranged the remaining food on his plate into a question mark that he quietly set in the middle of the table and stared at. Unable to bear the strange trajectory the mealtime was taking, Leonard had left and gone upstairs to his room. What had he said in his brother's defence, other than that sarcastic comment to his mother? Really nothing, he'd said nothing at all.

Yet that dinner had turned out to matter, for then the surgeon

kindly offered to refer William to a friend who worked as a
neurologist in a private practice, who would even come to speak
to William at the house if that would be more convenient, with
the family if that would be more comfortable. Once there, and
with them all oddly gathered around a plate of macaroons,
William talked to the man freely and provocatively about the
Lord, the voice in his head, the song, and the growing awareness
of the atomic structure of consciousness that played the spaces
between people as a sound that could be heard by anybody who'd
made the decision to listen; he was no longer content to live at
life's surface, nor to accept again without question anything he
was told; when he went into a trance he was seeking the state of
perfect suspension that existed in the moment between the
erasure of an old belief and the formation of a new one. There,
the song was loud. The doctor listened with deep, understanding,
diagnostic nods and a macaroon held in the impatient pincer of
his thumb and forefinger, and said what William probably needed
at that point was medication.

Probably it was, in all his life, the statement that doctor most
regretted making, for William then subjected him to a delicate
but prolonged and comprehensive interrogation that gathered
around the meaning of the phrase 'a healthy mind', which the
doctor offered forth as a gentle paradigm. William enquired, A
healthy mind? You mean one that isn't sick? Yes, the doctor said,
one that is aligned with the outside world, rather than one that
feels it must escape it through, say, trances. So to be healthy is
to be aligned? Yes, more or less. More, or less? Just yes. What is
it to be aligned? To be in accord with those factors both within
and around you. To be in tune, then, like a musical instrument?
Yes. And just as an instrument is tuned by a professional musician, the human mind is tuned by the professional physician? Yes,
if you will. Does the musician have any objective way of knowing

when an instrument is in tune? He or she will have a – a – tuning fork, I suppose. Of course, a tuning fork with a reference pitch of say, A-440? Yes, if you say so. Does the physician have something of this sort for the mind? Well – he has his expertise, his judgement. Because he's experienced a lot of minds in this way? Yes. I see, and part of his expertise is that he, unlike others, can know when a mind is attuned, in accord, and when it isn't? He has a better chance of knowing, yes.

William pressed on. So his *tuning fork*, as it were, is his expert judgement? Yes. Does his expert judgement exist independently of him, in the world, as a tuning fork does? Well, no, not entirely. Does at least some of it belong to his *own* mind? Of course. Which may or may not be attuned, in accord – in other words healthy? Well, in principle it might not be— If it were possible that a tuning fork, which we believed tuned to A-440, turned out not to be so, would we see it as a reliable way of measuring the tunefulness of an instrument? No— Moreover, if it turned out that every tuning fork uses its own individual sense of what tunefulness is, rather than an objective sense, wouldn't we have to consider that tuning forks aren't the best, or at least final way of establishing tunefulness? Yes— And since a physician uses as a tool his or her own mind to establish the health of another mind, don't we first have to know that the physician's mind is in perfect health? I suppose— Yet how can we know that, when all we have to judge it by is the judgements of yet another mind, which may or may not be in perfect health? Well, I mean— Wouldn't we first have to know and agree on what exactly we meant by healthy, and what exactly we meant by mind, and then what exactly we meant by a *healthy mind*, in the same way that it is agreed what exactly we mean by the reference pitch A-440?

The interrogation had gone on for a long fifteen or twenty minutes. At the point at which William tried to draw him into a universal definition of health, the doctor had stood and left in an inflamed and tender mood, saying he'd let William give the anti-depressants some thought before he made up his mind. The point was that it all might have been nothing more than an intractable meeting one afternoon that was remembered with embarrassment and then forgotten in the fullness of time. But Leonard had never forgotten it, in fact he remembered it more clearly as the years went by, and he remembered it now more than ever.

It was a mortifying matter for their father, not the fact that his son heard the voice of the Lord on the waters, of course not, nor that he sought reprieve from the relentlessness of his thoughts, but that the Lord's voice should speak in the same tone as this querulous, irritating one that had humiliated the doctor, and that the doctor might think less of the Lord for it – for the Lord asks silence of us, and acceptance, and graciousness. He doesn't ask us to humiliate and undermine others. The part of William that did that was in error and did need correcting. Their parents, loving though they really were, took all the way to their deathbeds the barely private wish that was established that day, that their son should be mentally ill so that he could be subsequently cured if only he'd heed the professionals' advice.

Seventeen years later there was the Bellevue Group's involve-ment in the Poll Tax riots; it was only really in retrospect that Leonard could imagine what fears his parents had nurtured over those seventeen years. They were good, broad-minded people, well read, liberal and peaceful; they kept pace with developments in the world, with politics and the arts, with science and tech-nology, with medicine. There were any number of ways a poor human psyche could go wrong under pressure, and God knew the colossal pressure of living in this changing world, battling through the unrest of the nineteen-eighties with one fist thrown this way and the other that, because you might as well fight everything, it was all wrong, Thatcher and the whole godless lot of them. Yes, his parents believed in measurable things and in certainty, and they wanted resolution for their oldest son, restive as he was. An anarchist group! Anarchy, when all they'd ever encouraged in him was peace and a willing, loving mind. All his speaking about democracy and how it didn't work – maybe people weren't prepared to think deeply enough to make informed decisions about important things, William had always said. And yet he was himself the very product of democratic justice – every process he'd been brought up with had been democratic and had invited and honoured his opinion, from what to have for dinner to what religion to believe in – for they'd never been forceful about even that.

Their interventions with respect to the riots – whatever they were – did work, for William wasn't ever questioned then by the police. At the crucial moment he was examined by a psychiatrist for his deepening trances and his withdrawals, auditory hallucinations, elaborate and unconventional beliefs, and he was admitted to a mental ward in the Royal Free Hospital for five weeks with a schizotypal disorder. It was just to ease and realign him, he was assured. He'd hung his two crosses up at the head of the bed, and what with those, and Aleph's red hair and purple velvets, his had been the most colourful ten square feet of the ward. When he came out of hospital the worst of the trouble had faded; the Bellevue Group had disbanded and Aleph and her friends had gone. William could restore his family life, resume his job at the university, take his medication, and find some tranquillity at last in his soul.

All that nonsense, that terrible pretence: make it your task, Leonard, their father had said just before he died – make it your task to find out if William was involved in those riots. It'd been said as though the time in the psychiatric ward had never happened, thus to imply he, their father, had had no part in that interlude. Leonard knew the real nature of the request. It was made by way of really asking, did we do the right thing, your mother and I? Find a way of making certain that we did the compassionate thing, which was the thing we meant to do. Leonard wouldn't have bothered to honour that request if he hadn't seen within it that part of his father that was sorry and was prepared to repent. Neither would he have bothered if he hadn't wanted, in whatever way, to be able to see the compassion in it himself.

Such disdain Leonard had felt towards his parents those last twenty or so years, for their disrespectful anxieties. Catalepsy, perhaps a type of Asperger's, schizophrenia or whatever it might be, why not confer all of them on William's poor open being? This is your son! Your son, my brother; a human being is a complex thing and we are not all the same, we are not all concerned by the same things. The art is to see beyond the person's mouth and brain to his heart and to find there whatever there is to love, and then to love it.

In his impatience with his parents he'd been passive and dismissive; he'd paid little attention to what they said nor truly measured it against William's behaviour to see if it did, indeed, match. I shall love him, I shall just love him, he'd thought. But he'd failed to do that, for there'd been too many moments of late that he hadn't loved him at all, and for precisely those traits their parents had so worried about. That rabid seeking after truth, that hungry, obsessive pursuit that was, he had to concede to himself, a trait of the man who'd lost his grip.

He might have brought his fist down on the windowsill, where he stood holding one of the Salvadorean crosses. I am angry, he wanted to say if only his brother had asked, and the softness in him vitrified. You exempt yourself from mankind; you say that only your view of the world is right, your view that a man can know nothing for sure, and be certain of nothing except his own ignorance

257

– while our view, the common view, is so patently stupid that we fail, and again we fail. I have felt guilty and aggrieved for years about your five weeks on a psychiatric ward; what have you felt aggrieved about on my behalf? What right have you to feel no guilt on any account about any single thing you do?

Leonard breathed deep and calmed himself. Well, if William's right and there is a truth, let it show itself. He looked out of the window, for hadn't William said you had to look, and to open your ears? He looked out of the window, opened his ears and his eyes also, cast them across to the square, flit his gaze between branches, lifted it up skywards, lowered it groundwards, let it rest a moment on the old Austin, let it lose itself for the most fractional of instants on the Austin's backseat, shifted it to the bench where he and his brother had spoken about Christ that hot day in early August, retracted it inwards to the top of the fig tree and then closer, to the crosses on the sill, spun it once more outwards to the horizon which was city-bound and not far enough away, dropped it finally at his hands closed in on one of the crosses, and, in easy defeat, let the cross go.

Here I am, William had written on that brain cross-section on the wall, and it was ironic of course, as if to deride their father for supposing that the enormity of a life – his life, or any – could dwell there between skull and grey matter. Leonard stared at it and then hung his head; it wasn't the enormity of life that overwhelmed him then but the distance of it, which was to say the distance between one life and another, which couldn't be navigated physically or even spiritually, no matter how optimistic one sometimes allowed oneself to be. How could it be that he'd stood through the funerals of both parents without crying when just then, in that moment, he thought he might cry and not be able to stop?

He heard a call: 'Leo, Abe, Richard!' It was his brother's voice and it called from downstairs, deep and lifting. When he responded to it he found William, Kathy and Oli in the kitchen, William at the sideboard peeling a boiled egg. Then Richard came in with an expecting expression, and Abe, with the look of someone greatly inconvenienced.

'Here!' William held up to them the white shivering oval of a thing on his palm. 'The first egg the chickens have graced us with.'

He cut it into six and put the six pieces on a plate in the middle of the table. He opened a bottle of wine and poured three glasses; a bottle of sparkling grape juice, three more glasses. 'I found it in the coop, in the beds we made with those cuttings. A miracle, a phoenix from the ashes.'

They each took their drink and a piece of the egg; a strange ebullience surfaced in that little impromptu space between them, a raising of arm, opening of mouth, and William's eyes were aglow, alive, quite as alive as everybody else's put together. They took egg like communion.

It must have been Kathy's idea for Jonathan to come, for she was at the door almost the moment he knocked. Leonard was waiting in the back living room with his brother, where she'd told them five minutes before to sit, and they were speaking casually about the rugby. Wasps would have no players left, Leonard had been saying, if everyone kept leaving at that rate. A sinking ship, he joked; soon you'll be the only fan.

That was when Jonathan walked in, with Kathy behind him. He said, 'The only fan of what? That God-awful stuff you eat? Piccalilli or whatever it is.'

William gave a gratified smile at his friend's appearance. 'Wasps,' he said.

'I thought you were already the only fan of Wasps.'

Kathy interrupted. 'I'll fetch coffee. I want you all to sit – please. Sit, and I'll be right back.'

They waited for her in a state of quiet obedience. It was just dark but the curtains weren't yet drawn, and there was the aspen again in night-defiant colour as it had been when Tela had come. The room wasn't quite warm enough; Leonard switched on another lamp to try for some extra cheer.

Kathy laid the tray on the table and they each helped themselves to a mug of coffee. Then she drew up the piano stool and sat with legs crossed, looking directly at her husband. Her suspended foot circled fretfully, or so Leonard thought – this way and then that with rigid toes.

'William, I'm asking you to take up Mr Malson's offer of a lawyer.'

She stopped; they'd all expected her to go on, for each of them continued looking at her for several full beats after the final word. When they'd accepted that nothing more would come Leonard looked down at his coffee and then took a sip. He noticed Jonathan look down too, while William gazed broadly at her as if he were observing a sunset or a pushing-pulling tide.

'I cannot, Kathy,' he said.

She sat forward. 'That's just the thing, you can. I wouldn't ask you if you couldn't.'

'We always ask other people to do what they can't, don't you think that's the basic difficulty of human relationships?'

'No, I think the basic difficulty of human relationships is selfishness. Sometimes what we do is others' business as well as our own, and we should remember that. I won't survive if you go to prison, me and the boys won't cope without you.'

Jonathan was intent on his own knee, on which his mug was rested, while his other leg stretched lengthily into the room. With the lamplight behind him the profile of his narrow face was in shadow. He looked awkward on the wooden chair Kathy had brought in from the kitchen, indeed, if he felt as Leonard did, the awkwardness was far more to do with their intrusion on William and Kathy's conversation than with his physical comfort. Yet he'd always been such a placid and private man with buried reactions; if he felt one way or another about Kathy's words, he gave away nothing of what it was.

'I wanted you both here,' she said, turning her head to them suddenly, and her tone was stern. 'To help me talk sense into him. I'm not going to succeed on my own.'

Leonard opened his mouth to speak. He shifted his gaze from her to William and back. He was about to give the weak response: I don't know what to say, I can't help. But there they were at the closing of another day, his brother low-lit and white in the armchair with all the faintness of something that was departing, and the urgency became pressing in that instant.

With a clearing of the throat, and a crushing together of his hands, Leonard asserted, 'Kathy's right, William, this isn't only your decision. You have children to think about, and obviously Kathy herself.' He didn't say, And me. Once he would have, or would at least have been tempted to, but he no longer felt that it was relevant. 'And she's right, about selfishness. There's more for you and your family to gain overall by trying to get yourself out of that court a free man than there is to lose.'

William bit the inside of his top lip; Leonard could see it pull back and thin, and then plump out again. 'That depends on what you think is at stake. I've never been interested in bartering over arbitrary terms, you know that.'

There was a silence, in which Kathy looked across at Jonathan. He acknowledged her but offered nothing.

'There are houses in Cumbria with land and – ponds—' She frowned into an apologetic pause, as if the mention of ponds was

261

at a level so basic and mundane that she'd lost her husband's interest even before she'd gained it. Then her face became harder. 'I've been looking at places we could buy, near to where I grew up. It's where I'd like us all to go when this is over, I see a life there.'

She cast a look out to Leonard when she said the word *all*, and he was moved by it. He'd go with them, he thought; for the first time since Tela had left him he was actually more than merely resigned or accepting about the future; he felt buoyant about that land and that pond, and the prospect she hadn't mentioned, that of mountains and the scraggy pitch of their slopes opposing his efforts as he heaved himself up them one winter noon.

William intervened gently on those thoughts, 'A pond!' He smiled, and it was warm. Kathy turned her head away from him.

'William,' Leonard began. 'I know that nothing's certain, and that even with the help of lawyers you might not be acquitted, but the fact is that you have to at least try, or entertain the possibility of trying.'

Kathy pressed her hands either side of her onto the chair. 'My darling.' Her brow was furrowed into the kind of deep empathy Leonard had never seen in her before. 'I respect your principles and I'm not saying you should give them up. But if we could be free to move – if you could be free to be with us and to live your life, well, it's a question of playing the system, the system that's wronged you. You don't give up your principles, you just play the system for what it is.'

'And the only price I pay is to pretend to agree to be mentally unwell. Then a little stint in a psychiatric ward again, then we pack up the car and we're off.' William prodded at the air with his fist in pretended enthusiasm. 'The system that you speak of, Kathy, plays me. It's played me all my life. I'm not good at games – my only defence is not to play it back but to opt out of the game altogether.'

There was quiet. Jonathan recoiled his outstretched leg and rose. He went to the window and stood there with his back to the room. There was such strictness and sadness about him, and always that sense of disapproval that one could see even in the tense way he held his mug. Those long, skeletal fingers were, for Leonard, immediately reminiscent of Jan's behind, on which he'd used to rest them playfully. Jan and William seemed to be the two things in all the world that had consistently met with Jonathan's approval, in both cases probably for their capacity to be all that he couldn't quite find the courage to be. Well, Leonard understood that feeling well enough. He wished that Jonathan weren't in the room, and he wondered if Kathy now wished the same.

William was watching his friend. He was observing his back and turning his thumbs in a slow, pensive rotation on his lap. Then he transferred his attention to his wife and spoke to her in a quite generous, fatherly tone.

'Land, ponds – mountains and lakes too, I expect. It all sounds so beautiful, Kathy. Your childhood, the way you once described the time you climbed a mountain with your mother and she was up ahead of you, you couldn't see her but you knew she was there. Then you heard her calling your name and saying, I'm here, I'm up here! And you always remembered it, because of the way you felt at the same time safety and freedom. And the den you and your sisters built at the bottom of your land, by the stream, and the sheepskin you had in there. And you used to race your sisters up the hill, sledge on fresh snow, go for treks, all the things you can do when there's space, rather than his egg-box existence we have in the city that makes us sit in our shells and try not to crack.'

Kathy lowered her face and tapped her mug faintly with her nails. She wrapped the unplaited end of her hair around the fingers of her other hand.

William said then, 'That's a form of freedom, but it isn't mine. I don't judge how free I am by how much space there is around my body. I'd rather share elbow room in a prison cell than give away a millimetre of space in my mind.'

Kathy exhaled sharply. 'You'd rather, you'd rather. What about what I'd rather?'

'I solemnly promise, Kathy, that on the terms I'm being offered, you'd rather me distant from you in prison than close to you in Cumbria.'

'I don't accept your solemn promise. You can keep it.'

'I've already given it, whether you accept it or not.'

Jonathan turned away from the window, faced the centre of the room and, as if finding himself exposed, wandered the short way back to the chair.

Kathy said, 'Won't you speak to him, Jonathan?'

With the natural confidence of his height and solemnity, Jonathan replied, 'Only if there's something he wants me to say, Kathy.'

Leonard could see her jaw tighten in disappointment. Perhaps Jonathan had been her greatest hope in that petition to her husband, but those words he'd just spoken were an admonishment and nothing more.

'This pond,' William said. 'This pond you mentioned. Imagine it has a fish in it, and one day after years of swimming, this fish puts its head out of the water and looks around. Imagine what it sees – this world it knew, which it thought was the whole world, has turned out to be one small fragment of a far greater one. If it doesn't die of shock, what will it do?'

'I don't care about the fish.' Kathy crossed her arms around her torso and seemed to shiver.

'What will it do, Leo?'

'I don't know,' he said, and he felt he must answer, but that he didn't want to allow the conversation to go where his brother wanted to take it. Thus he attempted indifference and flippancy. 'Go back under water and forget it ever saw it, probably.'

'Yes, probably. And every time it thinks that the pond is all the world, it'll commit an ignorant error, and it'll go on committing the same error day after day, perhaps all its short and futile life.'

Where Leonard and Kathy had sent their focus to inanimate points in the room, Jonathan had now focused on William with an expression of distant contentment.

William went on. 'But what if it didn't forget, and what if its awareness of the enormity of the outside world never left it? Do you think it would ever be content to pretend it wasn't there? Or do you think it would wonder about it, and in wondering yearn for another glimpse, just to be sure it was real? Imagine it does glimpse it again, and again, and each time it sees a world stretching off in colours it had never known, and it sees flashes of other creatures that move in ways it doesn't, and its sees at its eye-level the surface of a thing it had always thought was endless, and way above that it sees a luminous dome which itself seems to go on forever, but beyond which is probably something else, and then something again.'

William had come to rest at the front of his chair where he could sit a little taller, and from which position he seemed perpetually ready to jump, though in fact he sat without moving at all.

'Once a living creature has seen beyond what it thought were its own limits, it can never be content with its limits again. And why should it be? It will try to find ways to see further, to put its head a little further out of the water for a little longer, and to learn to be able to breathe in that different environment, which will mean using parts of itself it's never used before, and evolving new parts, in other words changing. And along the way it'll want – sometimes more than anything – not to change, and it'll wish it hadn't ever seen above the surface. After all, to stay below is to protect its illusions, and the limits it lives within are at least safe and familiar. The idea of change terrifies it, but gradually, looking around the pond at its blind friends, the idea of no change terrifies it more. Imagine, then, that those others try, in their best and most loving way, to persuade it not to go above surface again, for fear of the consequences. But not only that – to pretend that what it saw it only *thought* it saw, because it was deranged. Once it has made that barter, they say it can simply resume where it left off.'

'William—' Kathy's forehead was dipped, perturbed, towards the support of her hand, and she began massaging the small plateaux above her brows. 'You aren't to ridicule us, William.'

'Would that it could just resume where it left off!' he said. 'But how can it? It's only when it surfaced that it felt it could begin to know itself. And the knowledge it had of itself was that it wasn't born to be afraid, it was born to know ever more, and learn ever more. Now it's glimpsed that truth, and the enormous beauty of that truth, how can it wilfully act out of fear? Even if it can persuade itself to, the reprieve is only temporary, since when it resumes its old surfacing ways it will face the consequences again from those who'd rather stay under. In pretending, all it will do is delay a certain outcome, and in the delaying become more and more afraid of it.'

Kathy uncrossed her arms and legs and stood suddenly. She went from the room. They sat in silence, the three of them, Leonard at first peering reluctantly into the space Kathy had left and wishing for her to come back. Jonathan was running his fingers slowly through his short beard. And William, William drank back the last of his coffee and then beheld the carpet with a fastidious gaze. He seemed to be in a preoccupied state. Leonard leaned forwards onto his knees, and said, more to Jonathan than to his brother, 'We aren't getting anywhere, none of this is getting us anywhere.'

There, again, was Jonathan's look of infinite, reproving patience. Leonard could hear Kathy on the stairs, and her voice giving some curt instruction to one of the boys. When she came into the room she was with all three of the children, and she sat them on the floor in front of William. They'd been taken from bed and were adrift and sleepy in their pyjamas, but it was clear that, now abandoned on the floor, they were rapidly waking.

'Here are your children,' Kathy said. 'Tell them about your fish and about all the beauty the fish sees, which is evidently far better than *their* beauty – tell them how you're choosing against them, your own children, so that you can *know yourself*; explain to them how it will be when you're not there and what they'll have to suffer without a father. Tell them, they're listening, tell them and then that'll be one less mess for me to clear up.'

'Kathy, take the children back up to bed.'

'But I thought you were the one who wanted them to be treated like intelligent beings. Don't belittle them, you say, they each have a brain, you say. Well then, tell them what you told us about how they aren't quite important enough to you to bother to defend yourself in court.'

'Defending myself is exactly what I intend to do – for now I think the boys should be allowed to go back to sleep.'

'They are your *children*. Do you remember? The people you said we should be honest with about everything.'

'Yes, which means not using them as bait for your own catch. Boys, please go back to bed.'

The children were uncertain. Oli stood up but wouldn't take his eyes from his mother in case there was an instruction he was to follow. The other two looked from parent to parent, and Richard's face reddened with the onset of tears. Kathy wouldn't take them; she sat and placed a stoic hand on each thigh, and made it clear she wouldn't capitulate. Then Jonathan stood, and with a stern but forcedly hearty, 'Come on, chaps,' he held out his hands for the boys to hold.

They'd known Jonathan for years, as a kind of uncle whose occasional appearances were never expected but never managed to surprise. So Oli and Richard took his hands, while Abe got to his feet in his own time, and left after them by his own will. The door was left ajar, and the sound of Jonathan's deep and reasonable voice ascended the stairs.

'You will ruin my life,' Kathy said, reeling up onto her feet, sending her arms away from her. 'I've no love for you any more.'

She rushed out. Leonard drew his feet in towards the chair and found that his breath had long since collected and staled in his chest. On that realisation he did exhale, but nothing freed. Will you not go out after her? he asked inwardly of his brother. William was still at the edge of his seat where one single arch of light from the standard lamp above cut a curve across his forehead. One oblique section of his head was fully lit, the colour of flushed and living flesh – and the rest so vastly prosaic in contrast that Leonard couldn't, momentarily, see any great virtue in being human at all. He had a sudden image of the dahlias in the Edinburgh garden on one of the days around their father's death, and how the sunlight had shone through the cyan petals; he'd tried to take a photograph, but their camera couldn't apprehend the thrilling intensity of that light and the almost audible glow. For all human striving, flowers were so much more brilliant than all a man's dreams and hopes combined.

I've left the care of the dahlias to a stranger, he thought in mild panic; the tasks I was set I've failed in. The spoken task to find out the truth about William – no, to somehow settle every family score around William, to exonerate, understand, forgive everybody, to leave everybody happy in life and death. And the unspoken task to take care of the treasured dahlias, the heirlooms. Some stranger is tending them. He might have dug them up and gone with the entire contents of the house; dahlias, Corgi toys, Ealing Comedies, wooden puzzle – gone with four lives' legacy.

In the silence Leonard surveyed his brother's open, trusting face that had, in a way, the rapt and slightly quizzical attention of a baby's. Those tiny theatricalities of expression that often passed it, brows lifting, eyes blinking, mouth twitching, the muscles quivering so very minutely across the flat planes of his cheeks. You can love a person with all your heart, but sometimes don't you wish they would do something to warrant it? By which he meant something unequivocal, that didn't set you at a battle with yourself. He saw this quiet, sweet, upturning face that had appeared at the bottom of the staircase at the Bellevue, and then he saw the man perching upright into his own fate with determined indifference, and he realised something then that was always true – that the very act of even looking at his brother was one of reconciliation between these two opposite views of love and frustration, love and anger, and most often love and incomprehension.

They'd gone just as the first few drops of rain fell, and it was as it had been in his dream. The car went slowly to the end of the street with their bags piled in the boot, and the boys' bikes on a roof rack. It was a large car, a blue people carrier; the bargain was that, since it was such a long journey to Cumbria, the boys could get out at a place Kathy knew part-way up, not far from the motorway – a park with a BMX track that they'd seen before on their way to and from Kathy's parents, but never stopped at. That would be in return for their good behaviour on the backseat, she'd said, and she comforted their main worry – even if they stopped there for an hour they'd probably still beat the removal van – for that race between vehicles had become the boys' foremost preoccupation and eclipsed from view the enormity of what they were leaving behind.

Kathy's father had turned the car right onto the main road and Leonard waved it out of sight. They'd gone, so he walked to the Bellevue. He angled himself up the spiral staircase and came into the room's pale noon light. It was cold enough to turn on the electric heater; he made a pot of coffee. Wasn't it the way of life that in those short months his two boxes, guitar and a bag should have become three boxes, a guitar and violin, and three bags, each of them bigger than the original; wasn't it the fact of life's constant expanding that this should be so? But even still, they took up little room in the corner of the Bellevue, next to the bookcase and its overspill. It was still a minimal haul to show for a life, and he was glad.

There'd be several days now sleeping on the Bellevue sofa until he could move into the house he'd rented. The only items he took from the boxes, aside from those things that served his daily needs – clothes, toothbrush and paste, soap, books – were William's two crosses, which he hung on the wall above the sofa. Don't go off course, my darlings, their mother had used to say; be good, be happy. One's life wasn't pulled from the womb just to be squandered by lawlessness and misdirection, nor by misery, nor by regret. Be good, be happy, lose the Lord should you fail. It isn't that He abandons us in our failures but that He can't go with us into wickedness and unhappiness, for He doesn't know these states, they aren't anywhere in His mind.

Leonard had thought shortly after the conviction that William would kill himself, and that he'd do so with decisive grace. Yet he hadn't. Just before the conviction, when Stephen's own case had gone against him with a resulting sentence of seven years, there'd been talk from William that seemed to lean towards it – it was Leonard's doing really, saying such distressed things as, You won't survive in prison, I can't bear the thought of you being there. A fresh, unconstrained blossoming of media interest after the trial hadn't helped the fear and panic – all that talk of William as this, as that, as madman, philosopher-soldier, corrupter of young minds. William would reply to Leonard's anxiousness by saying that maybe he wouldn't end up in prison anyway, even if convicted. Maybe somewhere between the courtroom and the cell he'd slip through their fingers. So enigmatic, even to the last. My body won't make it there, he'd seemed to say; one way or another I shall not be there. Such a provocative smile at the corners of his mouth that would, for an instant now and then, trick one into thinking everything was going to be perfectly fine.

Thus, on Leonard's first few visits to the prison he went thinking his brother might not still be alive. In the loop of some joined belts there would be his neck, or in his gut some cocktail of cleaning products – a desperate and resolved man could always innovate his own death. And he'd gone with a heart pinched with the anticipation of loss, and a mouth full of the things he felt he must say in case it was the last time they ever saw one another, and then, finding William still alive, would say none of them. After a month the foreboding had passed; now two months, and he'd forgotten what it was he'd wanted to say in such urgency. Now there were four slow years to navigate and nothing to fill them.

He sat on the sofa to drink his coffee; the room was cluttered with things from the house that Kathy hadn't wanted and which he'd agreed to take off her hands. Tomorrow he would sort through it and see what was worth keeping – perhaps the old toaster and sandwich maker, an Afghan rug that had been rolled up against the wall in the playroom those last few years, a vacuum cleaner that was perfectly good, a brand-new bathroom cabinet that had never been put up, a couple of duvets. As for the boxy old television and video recorder that had been in the back living room, they could go, as could some of the bric-a-brac from the shed, and a small fridge that had been in there. But he was reluctant to discard anything that was his brother's, for he'd want it again one day.

At the weekend, when he moved into his new house, he'd go and get the chickens. If he hadn't had to find somewhere that had a garden, and a landlord happy to have a coop and a clutch of hens pecking up the lawn, he'd have been able to move by now

– no squatting at the Bellevue, cleaning his teeth and washing his face in the kitchen sink, using the cranky old spiderwebbed and cracked-seat toilet downstairs which only sometimes flushed. But these were his choices – to have the chickens, to have them at all costs, to keep the Bellevue even when William had, on being convicted, given his blessing for its sale, to keep it because whenever he pictured it in his mind it was with his brother making his ascent of the staircase and his head rising into the sunlight; Up I go. Head of hope, head of optimistic futures.

Then in two or three weeks he'd go and visit Kathy and the boys in their new house, for he'd promised William he'd look out for them all. These promises we make, probably not so much for the other but for ourselves. We do nothing, after all, that doesn't seem to benefit us in some way. There'd been a night shortly after William's trial when Leonard had been restless and tormented. He'd got up to use the bathroom, and Kathy's bedroom lamp was on and the door a few inches ajar. This was unusual, for Kathy always made sure to pull the door closed and it stayed that way until the morning, as much a defence as a way in and out. Through that lit gap he'd seen her asleep on her side with her bare back facing him. A small tattoo of a sailing ship on her right shoulder. White skin, undescriptive, because the light sat flatly on it, her hair hanging over the edge of the bed.

Silently, he'd pulled the door to. A tattoo! There was almost nobody he'd have expected that of less. A tattoo of a ship tossed on the pitch of her shoulderblade where she slept at an awkward angle, and he realised that to think one knew another person was to make an inordinate assumption. Then suddenly, in the realisation of his ignorance about her, he'd wanted to promise that he'd never let her or the boys out of his sight, yes, he'd wanted to sit outside her room all night as a matter of his own safety and sanity, as if to guard his ignorance. There was nothing that made a person more vulnerable than all the things not known by them and not understood.

The room became a little warmer and he could see the ripple of ionised air above the heater. It was a cold March and there'd been snow only a fortnight before which had put paid to one of the hens; he'd have buried it under a fruit tree but the frozen ground deflected a spade, so he and Kathy were agreed that they should wrap it in newspaper, close it up in a plastic bag and put it out with the rubbish without the children seeing. So that was what they did, together, hoping that the joint endeavour of it after dark, with whispered instructions, would make it less callous an act.

He'd told William, and assured him he'd get another hen when he moved house, or maybe another two. William had nodded, though his real concerns at that point seemed outlying and unreachable. That had been just after the first month in prison, and William had sat before him with a bruise to his neck, a healing lip and his arm in a sling. His way and manner had evinced a sharp reaction from the other men. He'd responded by receding from view into what somebody who knew him less might call depression, but what Leonard knew to be otherwise. He'd slipped, as it were, through their fingers. There was no need to worry that he'd be harmed again in prison for he'd stretched away out of reach into a new self-contained immunity that was almost palpable. What Leonard then wanted more than anything was what he'd so long guarded against; I've been thinking about the chickens, he'd say keenly. I've been thinking more about power and fear. Let's talk about morality, let's talk about the stamping foot, the Oneroi, about sin, brotherhood, separation, about how to listen and how to see; I'm sorry that I haven't always been willing, I'm willing now. Yet William wouldn't answer, as though those issues belonged to a world he'd left.

How he missed his brother in those quiet gaps, and couldn't stomach his distance from him, less still the nature of the distance. William wasn't afraid. Almost everybody was afraid, and the fear was the centripetal force that held people separate. Thus when one met a person who didn't have much fear in them, one noticed, one observed, one felt one's own fear reduce. One felt drawn towards the abundance that accrued where the fear wasn't.

He'd watched from the courtroom gallery as William had fought his position: Why do you think I meant to corrupt another person? William had asked. Would I have meant to corrupt him, knowing that a society of corrupt people is more harmful for me than a society of good people? What person who has their self-preservation in mind would knowingly go out of their way to turn others into monsters?

We're all children, he'd proclaimed after hour upon hour of fruitless questioning that had made him spirited and irreverent – and at that point his ailing defence had finally become hopeless indeed. We're all children who do wrong haplessly and ignorantly. How would you punish a child? If I've done wrong, how will you punish me? I suggest that the onus of explanation is on you, not me. You explain to me what I did wrong so I can avoid doing it again, and then, if you must, no dinner for me and early to bed, and I promise all will be well again.

One last flash of folly, of sarcastic energy, of playful and forthright wit, and really that had been the last Leonard had seen of his brother as he'd always known him. William had been silenced, and in that he'd been lost to them. There was no way he'd appeal the ruling, for he said that the decision had been made, that if the courts felt it was right then he respected it, because he respected what was right, that in any case he was at peace. Dear God, Leonard thought, how tyrannical we can be; he hated the very thought of the men who'd beaten his brother, of their vile fists and minds. He went through one of the three bags, which were filled mainly with clothes, found his brother's suit and hung it up by its collar on the corner of the bookcase. He smoothed it out with the back of his hand.

No small creep of light even – no passing of time in the church at all since he'd last watched. The camera resumed its count at 16.54.12 and the late afternoon was deep upon the scene. All was still. Where so much had changed in life since the previous second of that counter, not even a discernible mote had displaced in the church. Light came through the window on the right which showed the Crucifixion, though the camera itself couldn't see that – and where it fell it cast in slants, on the stone recess, what Leonard knew to be colours bled from the stained glass; he remembered that effect from childhood, the dappling of coloured light which fell like a spilt rainbow. Where it descended on the seat of the pews it showed the stippled indentation of the wood that, when aglow, had seemed to him then as shallow water on sand. And here he was almost fifty years later and the light was still behaving in that way on the stone and the wood, so that the great revelation of the security camera wasn't an event at all, but an epic lack of events. It did seem to hunger for action, that camera, suspended a foot or so below the pine pitched roof, keenly soliciting movement. But there was nothing, and there was nothing promised.

Ten minutes and then twenty. Thirty and then forty of vaguely jumping frames. Occasionally a faint shadow would fleet rapidly across the scene, and it took him some time to realise that these were the shadows of birds, possibly kites, of which there were many in that little valley. The light shifted a few inches further across the chancel, across the carved Agnus Dei, or was it some other representation? Leonard couldn't tell from the footage and he couldn't remember. In any case, this was all, this much considered leftwards repositioning of light from Luke to Agnus Dei, or else John to Luke, which flared on the surface of the limestone.

He glanced up to see rain flurrying against the windows of the Bellevue. He thought, Perhaps I am looking into William's soul. If one could go there, truly, it would be like the inside of a church. One enduring faithful structure made of the local rubble of whatever is to hand – whatever questions, whatever can be thrown at an idea to raise it closer to heaven, so that what makes it stand is query, curiosity, an *I think?* that lifts it up beyond itself. And though it was their father's church, Leonard felt that if his father entered it now, it would have to be on William's terms, an act of forgiveness on William's part as though he were allowing this passage of his family through this soul of his that they'd so failed to accept.

It was almost six o'clock by then in the church and the light was beginning to grow sombre. For the first time, Leonard noticed something like a black woollen hat or a pair of gloves on the bench by the door, next to a bookmarked New English Bible. The hat hadn't been there before, he was certain; yet it must have been, for he'd watched every passing moment of that surveillance. And yet it hadn't, and he felt a pricking along his spine. Finally he was forced to rewind the tape by half an hour, and there it was, of course, lying on the bench just the same; he hadn't seen it, that was all.

The camera's long view extended down to the triptych window in the chancel which presented Christ in the Garden of Gethsemane, kneeling with his hands outstretched, Christ in Glory, standing rapturous in white with his arms spread to the skies, and the Road to Calvary, Christ shouldering the cross.

Leonard had learned those by heart when he was a child, in his quest to do something good in his parents' eyes, though in truth they never asked anything of that sort of him. The camera depicted them uncertainly, one could see the window, but the details guttered like flames before the eyes just as focus seemed to be coming.

Gradually the light retreated from the Crucifixion window and thereby retreated westwards away from the church and its girded position there in the crook of the hills. The old oak door opened and that unprecedented movement of anything other than light and shadow made his heart veer forwards suddenly. A child ran into the church, followed by the mother and another child held on reins, and they left the door wide open so that a hefty bar of evening light followed them in and settled across the aisle. Their summer clothes were, Leonard realised, the only real indication there was that it had been hot outside. The mother wandered towards the chancel, looking around her, touching the curved edges of the pews with her fingers. She stood for a few moments at the altar with the smaller child, who knelt to inspect the terracotta floor tiles. The older child ran up and down the aisle, blanching out as he ran through the bar of light, and manifesting again in the shadow, blanching and manifesting like so up and down.

Leonard could see that the mother was speaking to her children, pointing things out to them. And there was the curious thought, which couldn't be shaken, that they weren't real at all but were ghosts drifting through the soul's chambers, holographic, small trails of beauty dissolving back out into the unlikely reality at the other side of the door. Perhaps the image had come from his dream all that time ago of those limbs, those glorious forms which had left him with a hankering for what was beautiful, for the song, as William might have put it. Yes, as though in their soundlessness the mother and children were part of the voice William spoke about. But then in any case they left, the door closed, and the pious dim returned. Three minutes had passed.

Shadows collected in the alcoves and window arches. The only daylight that came directly by then was from the window at the west end, behind the camera, and thus came as though without source. Sinless, sinless place. Give it your sin and it pockets it kindly, stroking your hand in the transaction, and when it inverts the pocket it's empty. Gone the sin, all an illusion. Don't fear. The church opens to you flowerlike, with a sighing of its stone, a soughing through its pews, its exposed rafters held aloft by profound understanding and welcome beyond the usual welcomes of this world.

The sourceless light stretched upwards along the aisle. In the sinking day, the church appeared to him beautiful and merciful in a new way. He could smell the cold stone and hear the airy fall of soles on the floor; he could remember with such vividness the mice carved into the wood under the pews, which as a child he'd often knelt down to and run his finger over.

Seven o'clock came and went. He knew his father had used to come to the church in the evening to see to things that almost certainly didn't need seeing to, as though he felt a parental instinct to put the place to bed. Even in monochrome one could see the hue of the late west light deepen to yolk and begin to shorten. He waited. And when his father did come he knew immediately it was him. The old man – though perhaps he wasn't old exactly back then? – wiped his feet on the hessian mat and stopped long enough to question the black object on the bench; not a wool hat after all, a pair of socks, which he regarded quizzically and laid side by side over the back of a pew. He straightened some of the prayer cushions and wiped, with languid care, some dust or other from the wood with his hand. At the pulpit he displayed the list of Psalms and hymns for his service the following day, a list the camera couldn't even slightly discern. He stood there, at the pulpit, with his head dipped. He stood for some five minutes or so beneath the crucified Christ. Then he went to the chancel and blew out the candles in the hanging lamps, crouched to pick something up from the floor where the child had stood – a hairgrip perhaps, a button? The detail of it was anybody's guess in that poor crumbling light. With that he walked back up the aisle and for the first time his face, though darkly outlined, was fully visible. So like William's face in the deep orbits of the eyes, and in the questions there posed: What? How? Why?

Leonard wanted to put his hand up suddenly to quiet the unheard question; I don't know, Father, I still don't know, don't ask me. Only, tell me it hasn't been our fault. Do we walk with the ignorant and the blind? He raised his voice to the room, against the beating rain, so that his father would hear something and turn his face upwards to the lens. Tell me we've had no part in it and have always done our best. Turn your face up. Look at me.

Acknowledgements

Heartfelt thanks to Anna Webber, Dan Franklin, Tom Avery, Bath Spa University, the Arts and Humanities Research Council and the MacDowell Colony; also to Ian Breckon, Jason Bennet, Karen Jarvis and the other valued members of my writing group; to Jo Fox-Evans, Rick Hewes, Alan and Terri Harvey, Mike Hartley in memory, and my mum, Dana, whose ideas and conversation have enabled this novel to be.